Charm Me

NEW YORK TIMES BEST SELLING AUTHOR

SAMANTHA CHASE

Cover Design: Kari March Designs

Edits: Jillian Rivera

Praise for Samantha Chase

"Utter Rockstar Perfection."

-#1 *New York Time Bestselling Author* **Rachel Van Dyken**

"If you can't get enough of stories that get inside your heart and soul and stay there long after you've read the last page, then Samantha Chase is for you!"

-NY *Times & USA Today Bestselling Author* **Melanie Shawn**

"A fun, flirty, sweet romance filled with romance and character growth and a perfect happily ever after."

-NY *Times & USA Today Bestselling Author* **Carly Phillips**

"Samantha Chase writes my kind of happily ever after!"

-NY *Times & USA Today Bestselling Author* **Erin Nicholas**

"The openness between the lovers is refreshing, and their interactions are a balanced blend of sweet and spice. The planets may not have aligned, but the elements of this winning romance are definitely in sync."

- ***Publishers Weekly, STARRED review***

"A true romantic delight, *A Sky Full of Stars* is one of the top gems of romance this year."

- ***Night Owl Reviews, TOP PICK***

"Great writing, a winsome ensemble, and the perfect blend of heart and sass."
- ***Publishers Weekly***

"Recommend Chase to fans of Susan Elizabeth Phillips. Well-written and uniquely appealing."
- ***Booklist***

Chapter One

Most days, being Jamie Donovan was pretty damn awesome.

But today, it was fan-freaking-tastic.

Walking into his family's pub, he took a moment to simply admire it in a way he never had before. For the next month, he was the one in charge. His parents left early this morning for a trip with their best friends, the Murphys. First, they were driving across the country—something they were dragging out for two weeks—and then they were embarking on a ten-day cruise to Alaska. The plan was for them to drive home afterwards, and when all was said and done, they'd be gone six weeks.

"And now I'm the boss," he said proudly, even though no one was in yet to hear it.

Except...

"Well, boss," Uncle Ronan said as he walked out of the kitchen, "the produce delivery is here early and they're missing a few items."

Jamie was prepared for this and wasn't even bothered

1

about the missing items. He was up for the challenge, and nothing was going to bring him down today.

Famous last words.

Two hours later, he was ready to pull his hair out.

Well…not really. He had really great hair and there was no way he would do anything to harm his appearance.

But he was frustrated.

The missing produce wasn't an issue; he had simply asked his uncle to run to the grocery store to get what they needed. No, it was everything that happened after that—an internet outage in town meant they couldn't process credit card payments and he couldn't finish doing the online banking he was in the middle of. And while all that had been incredibly frustrating, it was the text he was currently reading that was going to push him over the edge.

Jenn: We need to talk Jamie. You've put this off too long and you're going to be sorry

Jenn: You need to call me back today

Jenn: Now, preferably

Groaning, he sat down at the desk in the pub's office. He was the king of the amicable breakup. It was a record he'd kept since he started dating in the seventh grade. Jamie had a rule about always ending things on good terms. That mindset—and his charming personality—had kept him from ever having a bad breakup.

Until this one.

This was the breakup that just wouldn't end.

It had been six months and Jenn Randall kept popping back into his life like a bad penny. It didn't matter how many times he told her it was over or that she deserved someone better or how much he praised her for being too good for him; she had been almost relentless in her pursuit of trying to get back together with him.

Only...

Now that he thought about it, she never said that she wanted to get back together—just that she wanted to see him.

Practically demanded it.

The weird part was how she never said why it was so important and when he told her he couldn't or that he didn't think it was a good idea, she backed off. Today was the first time there was a veiled threat.

Maybe he should have just agreed to meet up with her when she first asked months ago— hindsight and all that. Now it was just awkward and he wished she'd move on.

Still, he stared down at his phone and knew he had to at least say something. But he was afraid that even a simple response would lead to more drama, so he took the coward's way out and put his phone on the desk and went out to see how the lunch crowd was doing.

Within an hour, the internet was back up and running, the produce distributor came back with the missing items, and right now, there was a line of customers out the door waiting for a table.

"Yeah, I got this," he murmured as he walked around helping out wherever he could—bussing tables, delivering food, filling drink orders behind the bar, and flirting with the cute brunette who was waiting for a lunch order that had been called in.

"So...you own this place?" she asked with a coy smile.

"I do," he replied smoothly. Technically, the Donovan family owned the pub and considering he was a Donovan, some would say he wasn't lying. "I don't think I've seen you in here before." She was petite and curvy, with big blue eyes —which were blatantly checking him out right now.

"I'm in town visiting a friend," she told him.

"Lucky friend," he replied smoothly. "I'm Jamie."

Her smile grew a little. "I'm Mandy."

"Nice to meet you, Mandy. How long are you in town for?"

"I'm only going to be here for a few days, but my friend raved about the food here. After all her bragging about it, I knew I needed to try it. So I'm going to surprise her with the burgers."

"You're a very good friend, and I'm sure you're going to love the food." He moved a little closer. "I'll tell you what... I'll throw in dessert on the house. Would you prefer the apple pie or the peanut butter brownies?"

"Ooh...you are speaking my language," she practically purred. "I'm going to go with the brownies. Please."

"You got it," he said, giving her his most sincere smile. With any luck, he'd have her number before she left and perhaps plans to see her later tonight.

Within a matter of minutes, he was handing Mandy her lunch order, and she was handing him a slip of paper with her phone number. "Call me later and I'll stop by when you're done for the night," she said with a sexy grin.

"Well now...I hope your friend won't be too upset with me taking you out when you're here visiting her."

She waved him off. "She'll be fine. She always goes to bed early so it won't be an issue." Then, with a flirty wave, she walked away, and Jamie watched the soft sway of her hips as she went.

A light smack on the back of his head broke him out of his reverie. "*Ow!* What the...?"

"Can you seriously not get through one lunch rush without making a date with one of our customers?" his uncle asked with amusement. "Instead of giving away free desserts, maybe focus on making enough money to prove to your parents that all the improvements you insisted on for the pub were worth it."

"Hey," he said with an easy grin, "don't worry. A couple of free brownies aren't going to hurt anyone. Trust me."

"Jamie..."

"I do this sort of thing when my folks are here too."

"That's not the point," Ronan said with mild disapproval. "Just...try to put your focus on the business and not your bedroom, okay?"

Part of him wanted to be annoyed, but everyone knew he was a shameless flirt and pretty much accepted it. Hell, he enjoyed it! That wasn't going to change because his parents were on vacation. And while he appreciated his uncle's concern, it wasn't necessary.

"Come on...you know most of the time it's just a little harmless flirting..."

"Oh, God. Is he bragging again?"

Jamie turned and saw his brother Patrick standing behind him. "Of course I'm bragging," he said with a laugh. "I mean...I'm awesome. Why wouldn't I brag?"

Rolling his eyes, Patrick stepped around him and shook Ronan's hand. "I'm sorry that you have to deal with him while Mom and Dad are away."

Their uncle let out a hearty laugh. "Patty, I've been

dealing with your little brother on a daily basis for years. I don't think your parents being here makes things any better."

"Hey! What's that supposed to mean?" he demanded.

"It means you're a pain in the ass no matter what," Patrick told him. "And as much as I'd love to sit here and list all the ways that applies, I need to bring lunch back to the office. Can I get a BLT on the hearty whole grain with fries for me and a Greek salad with grilled salmon for Marissa?"

With a nod, Jamie wrote it down and brought it back to the kitchen for their cook to work on. When he walked back out to the bar, his brother still had a stupid grin on his face. "What now?"

"Dude, paranoid much?"

"Please, you're looking at me like I'm some sort of doofus, so..."

"You have to admit, most of the time, that's what you act like," Patrick reasoned. "I just hope you don't burn this place to the ground before Mom and Dad get back."

"Wow. Thanks for the vote of confidence," he murmured.

"Jamie, look...most of the time, you walk around here schmoozing with the customers—particularly the female ones—and you don't seem to take anything seriously. This pub is everything to Mom and Dad. I'm just...concerned. Hell, we're all concerned! You need to buckle down and maybe focus a little less on your social life. I'm sure you can handle maybe dating only three women at a time for the next six weeks." Winking, he reached for a handful of pretzels that were in a basket on the bar.

"So obviously you were talking to Uncle Ronan..."

"Believe me, we all know how you are, but this is the

first time Mom and Dad have taken any time off for themselves. This is a big deal and no one wants them to be freaked out or worrying while they're gone. Just maybe...be a little more conscientious while they're gone."

"I'm totally conscientious, Patrick. I know how to run every aspect of this business and you know Dad went over everything a dozen times with me before he agreed to this trip. Mom was going to go no matter what," he added with a small laugh. "But Dad wouldn't have gone if he didn't think I could handle it. So you all need to just relax and unclench. I've got this."

"We'll see..."

The thing was, Jamie was used to people underestimating him. He was the laid-back Donovan, the happy-go-lucky Donovan, the charming Donovan. He rarely took anything seriously and so to the casual observer, having him run the pub was an accident waiting to happen. But he was going to prove them all wrong. He was not only going to run the pub, but he was going to run it more efficiently than ever. His parents had their way of doing things and that was all fine and well, but Jamie had been waiting for the right time to implement some small changes that were going to yield them some nice profits.

"Order up, Jamie!" Bobby called out and Jamie excused himself to go and serve it.

He worked the room and stopped at a few tables to chat with some of the regulars, and he was in his element. He loved hearing what was going on in people's lives and joking around with them. Both his brothers were far too serious and not exactly people who would be called sociable. Jamie was a people person, and he had a knack for putting people at ease and making sure they left the pub with a smile.

It's also the way he looked at his dating life. He always made sure the women walked away with a smile.

And that had been true until Jenn.

Jenn.

Ugh...

He was going to have to deal with her eventually—especially if her little threat of "you'll be sorry" actually came into play.

What the hell would he have to be sorry for? They broke up six months ago, for Pete's sake!

He remembered that his phone was still in the office, and he really should have it on him in case anyone—other than Jenn—tried to reach him. His family all knew to call the pub but if he was going to play the part of the responsible manager of a successful pub and eating establishment, he should be accessible at all times.

Bobby called out to him again, and this time he knew it was Patrick's order. Walking back to the kitchen, he said a quick thanks and bagged up the food. His brother was still sitting at the bar chatting with their uncle, and there wasn't a doubt in his mind that they were talking about him.

Pfft...let them talk. I've got this.

Handing the bag to Patrick, he was about to make a snarky comment about how qualified he was for this job when Sadie—one of their servers—walked over looking nervous.

"Jamie," she said in a hushed tone. "The people at table four want to know if we can cater a luncheon for them on Thursday."

"Of course!" he replied. It was a no-brainer.

"It's for a hundred people," she explained. "It's short notice and I know your mom usually requires at least two weeks' advanced notice..."

"Hang on. Let me talk to Bobby and see what he thinks we can handle and then I'll go talk to your party, okay?"

She nodded. "Thanks, Jamie."

Smiling smugly at his brother and uncle, he said, "If we can make this work, think of how thrilled Mom and Dad will be. It looks like maybe I *do* know what I'm doing."

And with a confident smile, he went back to the kitchen and talked things through with Bobby. Then he made some calls to see about bringing in extra kitchen staff to help. Once that was all squared away, he walked out to table four with his tablet and worked through all the details. Before he knew it, they were paying him a deposit and making arrangements for the food to be picked up at eleven on Thursday. Feeling confident and more than a little proud of himself for making this work, Jamie thanked them and wished them a great day before heading back toward the office.

He totally had everything under control and it was possibly the best freaking day ever.

"I am the best," he told himself before closing the office door and mentally high-fiving himself.

* * *

"You're fired."

For a moment, Fallon Murphy was certain she was hearing things. "Excuse me?"

"I'm sorry, Fallon, but there have been some complaints and we're terminating your employment effective immediately."

This cannot be happening...

"I'm afraid I don't understand," she began with a nervous laugh. "Complaints?"

Angela Silver, the head of human resources, gave her a slightly sympathetic smile. "You missed several deadlines to apply for those grants we needed, the proposal you submitted last week for a new curriculum wasn't very well researched, and...you're not really connecting with the rest of the team. I'm sorry."

She let out a shaky breath because she was both shocked and...not.

This was the second job she was being let go from in the last four months.

Ugh...I am the worst...

It was pointless to argue because Angela was familiar with the reasons Fallon was released from her previous position. Instead, she forced herself to smile as she stood.

"I'm sorry things didn't work out and I appreciate you taking a chance on me," she said, hating the slight tremble in her voice. Holding out her hand, she added, "I'll just go and clear out my office."

Angela stood and shook her hand. "Fallon, you're a smart and wonderful person. You just need to get better at being part of a team. Reaching out to your co-workers and asking questions isn't a sign of weakness. I think if you can remember that, you'll be more successful with your next endeavor."

"Thanks." With a curt nod, she willed herself not to cry as she left the office.

Walking down the hall, no one made eye contact with her and that told her that pretty much everyone knew she was being let go.

And no one cared.

She might have only been with the regional education service center for six weeks, but Fallon truly believed things were going well. Sure, she'd missed the deadlines for a couple of grants, but...there had been others she was preparing applications for to make up for it. Most people got a bit of a learning curve in their new jobs and somehow she managed to blow hers.

Twice.

It didn't take long for her to clear out her office; she never brought much in to truly make it her own. There were just a couple of framed photos on her desk, along with a wilting plant, her mug, laptop, and daily planner journal.

I'm pathetic...

Making the office a more personalized space had been on her agenda, but everything was fine the way it was, so she never made it a priority.

"Good thing I didn't; otherwise this would be even more depressing than it already is," she mumbled and she put her stuff in her satchel and picked up her plant.

Again, as she walked down the hall toward the exit, no one made eye contact with her.

No one wished her well.

No one cared.

This was starting to become a pattern, and she knew exactly what she needed to snap herself out of this funk before she spiraled.

In her car, she quickly took out her phone, placed it in its cup holder, and dialed her mother's number.

"Fallon! Hey, Sweetie! How are you?" her mother said cheerily.

"Um...not great," she said miserably, her voice catching on the last word as the first tear fell.

"Oh, no! What's going on?"

There were other people talking in the background, and that's when she noticed that it sounded like her mother was in a car. "Mom? Where are you? Are you driving?"

Laughing softly, Caroline Murphy shushed the people around her. "I'm not driving, but I'm in the car with your father and the Donovans. We're on day three of our trip across the country! We had the best time yesterday in Atlanta! So much fun!"

Fallon gently cleared her throat.

"Oh, right. You sound upset," her mother quickly said, changing gears. "What happened?"

"I got fired. Again," she said miserably, and she heard all four of them gasp.

"Oh, no! Oh, Fallon, sweetheart, I'm so sorry! What are you going to do?"

"I honestly don't know. It just happened." Pausing for a moment to compose herself, she knew what she wanted to do, but now that wasn't going to happen either. "I forgot about your trip and I was going to see about coming home to visit. But now..."

"Nonsense," her mother quickly interrupted. "Your father and I might not be there, but I think going home for a little while is the best thing for you."

"Why? No one's there."

"Maybe not at the house, but you still have a lot of friends in Laurel Bay, and your sisters are only an hour or two away. You can always reach out and maybe go stay with one of them if you don't want to be alone."

That didn't sound appealing. Both of her sisters were married and had very successful careers in their fields. Her oldest sister, Margaret, worked in hospitality management, and her middle sister, Shannon, was a dental hygienist. Fallon was the only one who furthered her education and kept chasing after higher degrees because she felt it was important to learn everything she could about early childhood development.

Which was a big fat lie.

As the youngest, she had always felt the need to prove that she was just as smart as her sisters. Now all she had to show for it was a degree and diploma hanging on her wall—or...sitting in a box on her backseat—and no job.

"I don't know..."

"Just know that you are always welcome to stay at the house, Fallon. You know the door is always open for you. Well...it's locked right now and we got a new smart lock for the front door, so I'll have to send you the code..."

"Mom..."

Caroline paused for a moment. "Look at the bright side."

The snort was out before she could stop it. "Bright side? What bright side?"

"You didn't enjoy living in Missouri. You kept saying how much you missed home."

"I know, but..."

"And before that, you didn't really enjoy living in Texas."

"Yeah, but that was only because..."

"You can't keep moving from state to state every other month, Fallon," her mother gently chided. "It's not practical and it's got to be costing you a fortune in moving expenses and fees for breaking your rental agreements on these apartments. Maybe this is a sign that you should move back home and look for positions there."

It wasn't the worst idea, but she hated returning home looking like a loser.

A broke loser at that.

"Hi, Fallon! It's Kate," Mrs. Donovan said, as if Fallon wouldn't be able to tell who was speaking. "I know your sisters aren't there, but you know all of my kids are close by if you need anything. Don't hesitate to reach out to any of them."

She had grown up with the Donovans and all the kids were close in age. Both Arianna and Ryleigh Donovan were good friends, and she always enjoyed seeing them when she went home to visit. On one of her last trips home, she saw Ryleigh's fiancé's new tattoo parlor and it was amazing. But as much as she liked them all—well, most of them—they all had their shit together and currently she most certainly did not.

Still, if she had to sit and wallow in self-pity anywhere, the comfort of her childhood home would be preferable.

"Thanks, Kate. I'll keep that in mind." She paused. "Listen, I should go. I've got a lot to do and think about, but I hope you all have a fabulous trip. Where are you off to today?"

"Today we're going to stop in Birmingham and hopefully make it to Memphis tonight. We're going to spend a day or two there before moving on," her mother said. "But I want you to promise me something."

She had no doubt it was going to be something like promising not to let this get her down or to focus on the positive…something uplifting.

"Sure, Mom."

"If you go to our place, make sure you pay attention to the alarm—setting it and turning it off. Otherwise it will send alerts to our phone and make us nervous."

"Um…"

"I'll text you all the info on the codes if you need it. I hate sending it over a text or email because you never know who's tapping into our personal information." She sighed. "We left the information with Ronan. If you decide to go home, why don't you stop by the pub first and talk to him?

He'll give you everything you'll need and no one will be listening in and stealing our identities."

Good Lord...

"Mom, I don't think..."

"I'm not taking any chances, Fallon. You never know how these things happen, so the less I put those numbers and words out into the universe, the safer I'll feel."

Now it was her turn to sigh. "Um...yeah. Great. I'll swing by the pub. I'm guessing Ronan will be there full-time running the place, huh?"

"It's Kate again, Fallon! Hi!" Kate called out. "Actually, Jamie's running the place for us while we're gone. We're all a little nervous about it, but Shane says it's time to give him a chance. I'm not sure I'm as confident in that, but...here we are."

"O-kay..."

"But you know Ronan's only five minutes away, so if you get to the pub and he's not there, anyone can reach him for you."

"Just make sure he meets you in person," her mother chimed in, "and doesn't just give you the information over the phone! Promise me you'll only get the codes from him if you're face to face!"

"Mom, why are you freaking out so much over this? I'm sure everything is going to be fine and..."

"Fallon? This is your father."

She hung her head and inwardly groaned.

"Hi, Dad..."

"Can you just please do what your mother is asking? Can't you tell how nervous she is about being gone for such a long time? Is it too much to ask that you respect our wishes?"

"It's not, and I solemnly swear that I will only talk to Ronan when no one else is around, okay?"

"Thank you," they all said in unison.

"I'll let you all go. Drive safe and keep in touch, okay?"

"Take care of yourself, sweetheart," her mother said before hanging up.

With nothing left to do, Fallon was about to pull out of her parking spot when Angela came up and knocked on her window.

Rolling it down, Fallon looked up in confusion. Had they changed their mind? Were they giving her another chance?

"Hey, Angela," she began warily. "Is everything okay?"

"I know this is awkward, but...I need your badge back."

So...no second chance.

Ugh.

Reaching into her satchel, she took the badge out and quietly handed it over.

"Thanks, Fallon. And good luck."

She barely managed a small smile before Angela turned and walked away.

This time when she went to pull out of her spot, no one was stopping her, and she forced herself to stay calm until she got home.

Then she was going to scream into her pillow and cry before eating a pint of Rocky Road ice cream. Who cares if it was only 10:30 in the morning? The only one whose opinion mattered right now was her own.

"And I am one hundred percent okay with ice cream for brunch," she murmured.

As she continued to drive, she thought about her options and knew some of the things her mother said were correct. First, she couldn't keep moving from state to state, but...she also didn't want to stay in Missouri. Going back to Laurel Bay made the most sense.

"So I guess now I need to break it to yet another land-lord that I'm leaving."

And then she had to deal with the very real possibility that she was a fraud and knowing that everyone back in Laurel Bay was going to know it too.

Chapter Two

A week into his time managing the pub and Jamie felt like he had blown away everyone's expectations. They had a record week in sales, and because the luncheon they catered last week was such a success, it became a standard monthly order now. He took great pride in the things he was doing, and it felt great.

Granted, all this work had definitely taken a huge chunk out of his social life. His date with Mandy never panned out and the few women he had chatted up led nowhere either.

And oddly, he was okay with it. Work was keeping him busy, and by the time he left at the end of the day, he was practically dead on his feet.

Glancing down at his watch, he saw it was after two and that meant the lunch crowd was just about gone and they had a few hours to prep for the dinner one. It was normally around this time that he and his uncle sat down for their own lunch. Jamie knew he was going to go for today's special—pot roast—but he needed to know what Ronan was in the mood for.

Stepping out of the office, he spotted his uncle standing at the bar talking to a curvy brunette. He knew it wasn't Mandy because this woman was a bit taller, but she was wearing a snug pair of well-worn jeans and the view was spectacular. Straightening, he ran a hand through his hair to give it that mussed up look that he had perfected and then casually strolled toward the bar. His uncle looked up at him with amusement, as if he already knew Jamie was coming over to check out who he was talking to.

Maybe this one will lead to a date tonight...

"Hey," he said lightly. "I was just about to put in our lunch orders, but saw you standing here talking to this lovely lady."

Then the lovely lady turned and...

"Fallon?" he said in horror. "What are you doing here?"

She looked equally annoyed by his presence and he wanted to cringe because he had totally been checking out her ass.

Ew...gross.

Fallon Murphy was his nemesis, had been since they were five years old and she beat him in a bicycle race. Their families had become friends somehow and the Murphys had come over on a Sunday for a barbecue. All the kids had been playing every game possible and Jamie had been holding his own.

Until the bikes.

She hadn't been a graceful winner and he had most definitely been a sore loser and from that point on, it had been non-stop competitions between them.

"It's a pleasure to see you too, Jamie," she said with more than a hint of sarcasm.

"Jamie," his uncle said with a small laugh. "Why don't

you get three plates of the special while Fallon and I get drinks and set up a booth?"

"Um..."

Fallon smiled at him. "That sounds wonderful. Thanks." Then she patted him on the shoulder. "And if you would be so kind as to put in an order of the loaded potato skins, that would be great."

"Yeah, whatever..." he muttered before going to the kitchen. Hell, he'd make the damn potato skins himself and the rest of their order just so he didn't have to go back out there right away. What on earth was she doing here? Last he heard, she was working in Texas and he was thrilled. It was far enough away to guarantee that she wouldn't be coming home too often and yet...here she was.

In the kitchen, Jamie took his time making up the potato skins and while they were baking to melt the cheese, he slowly made three plates of pot roast, mashed potatoes, carrots, and gravy.

Sadie walked over and gave him a strange look. "Um... do you need some help? I didn't see anyone waiting out there, but I don't mind bringing the food out so you and Ronan can eat."

"It's fine. This is for us and uh...a um..."

"Oh, yeah, I saw Fallon out there," she said with a smile. "I wasn't expecting to see her since her parents are traveling with yours."

That makes two of us...

"So...you know Fallon?" he asked as he placed the three plates on a tray.

Nodding, she said, "We went to school together but didn't really hang out in the same circles, you know?"

"Yup."

Fallon had gone to some fancy charter school, so that

spared him from having to go to school with her. He just didn't realize Sadie had gone there too.

"If it's alright with you, I'm going to watch the bar while you guys eat and then I'll start doing the prep work for the dinner crowd."

"That works. Thanks, Sadie."

She walked out of the kitchen as Jamie pulled the potato skins out. "Dammit." It occurred to him that he should have made the skins first and waited until they were done eating them to make the rest of the lunch. With a shrug, he put them on the tray. "Little Miss Fussy will just have to deal with everything being served at once."

Hefting the tray up, he slowly made his way out to the booth where Fallon and his uncle were sitting, and he paused when he saw how intently they seemed to be speaking. Ronan reached over and squeezed her hand and, if Jamie wasn't mistaken, Fallon looked...sad.

"None of my damn business," he murmured before walking to the booth and placing the tray down. He looked at her defiantly. "We don't normally take long lunch breaks, so I just brought everything out at once."

Frowning, she said, "And? What's the big deal?"

And for some reason, that completely flustered him. He was prepared for some snarky comment or for her to at least mention something about how her lunch was going to get cold, but...she didn't.

Ronan was sitting in the middle of his seat, which meant that Jamie was supposed to share Fallon's side of the booth. And by the look on his uncle's face, he did it on purpose.

Again, Fallon didn't make any sort of sarcastic statement or snort at having to share a space with him, and he took that as a win.

"Have you talked to your parents?" she asked him.

"Uh, I spoke to my father yesterday. How come?" He would bet good money she was going to say something about needing to be checked up on so he didn't ruin the family business.

But she didn't.

"They all sound like they're having a great time. They're taking this trip at a bit of a snail's pace, but they're getting to see some fun stuff," she said, looking at him with a smile.

A genuine smile.

And he didn't trust it.

"They're in Amarillo now," she went on, "and I think they're planning on seeing a rodeo!" Laughing softly, she shook her head. "In my entire life, neither of my parents ever mentioned even being curious about a rodeo. But...I guess...when in Rome, right?"

"I guess..."

"Ronan was saying how Ryleigh comes in a couple of times a week to help with the cooking. I wonder if..."

"She did that even before our folks left for vacation," he said hotly. "So if you're thinking that she's coming here to babysit me or because I can't handle running the pub, then you're wrong. Ha!"

Fallon looked at him as if he were crazy. "Um...I was going to ask if today was one of those days when she was going to come in because I'd love to see her."

Across the table, his uncle was laughing behind his napkin.

Traitor.

"Oh. Uh...no, Ryleigh's not supposed to be in today," he murmured and put his focus on his lunch.

"Fallon, you're going to be around for a while, so I'm

sure you'll have plenty of time to catch up with Ryleigh and Arianna," Ronan said.

Going to be around for a while? Seriously?

"Why?" he found himself asking. "I thought you were living and working in Texas?"

Without looking at him, she began pushing food around on her plate. "Things just weren't what I thought they were going to be with the job, so...it didn't work out."

Ha! He knew what that meant.

"So they fired you, huh?"

Now she did look at him and for the first time in all the years they'd known each other, she looked devastated.

Uh-oh...

The look was gone in an instant, and she returned her focus to her lunch. "No, it just wasn't what I was looking for. I rushed to find a position after graduation, so this time I'm going to be a little more thorough in my research. So, as your uncle mentioned, I'll be home for a while."

They all ate in companionable silence for several long minutes and when Bobby called out to him that he needed a hand, Jamie was more than ready to jump up and help.

"I guess I'll be seeing you around," he said with a tight smile and instantly turned and headed for the kitchen.

And stayed there until he knew she was gone.

It was childish and he knew it, but Fallon Murphy was just not someone he wanted to be around. She normally got the best of him in some way or another and she was basically the only person who ever made him doubt himself. Even his siblings—who all loved to tease and poke fun at him—never made him second guess anything.

But she did.

And it bugged the hell out of him.

Fortunately, the rest of the day flew by, but one of his

servers called in sick and he ended up staying until closing to make sure they had enough coverage. He was dead on his feet by the time the last customer left, and all he wanted was to crawl into bed and sleep for a week. Tomorrow was his day off, so he knew he'd at least get to sleep in a little and not have to do anything all day if he didn't want to.

He was walking out to his truck along with Bobby and thanked him for all his hard work today before wishing him a good night. The drive home didn't take long. He was currently renting a small two-bedroom bungalow a couple of blocks from the beach. It was nice having some privacy and not living in a big apartment complex with dozens of other people. Of course, it meant he had to maintain the property, but he found he kind of enjoyed it. Maybe tomorrow he'd go out and mow the lawn or something.

Maybe.

There was an unfamiliar car parked in front of his house, but as soon as he pulled up, it drove away. With a shrug, Jamie wearily climbed from the car and went inside. Tossing his keys on the entryway table, he locked the door and walked right to his bedroom. Next to the bed, he stripped down to his boxers, crawled under the blankets, and promptly fell asleep.

The next time he opened his eyes, sunlight was streaming into the room and someone was banging loudly on the front door.

"What the...?"

Sitting up, he stretched and slowly rolled off the bed. Whoever it was could wait while he put on a fresh pair of boxers and a clean pair of jeans. The banging stopped after a moment, but that didn't stop him from walking shirtless to the door.

When he pulled it open, no one was there, but he noticed a car pulling away.

The same car that was there last night.

Weird.

He was about to shut the door when he heard a noise. A squeaky little sound that seemed oddly out of place. Just as he was about to take a step out onto the porch, he saw it.

A baby carrier.

Not that he was even sure that's what they were called, but enough families came into the pub that he was familiar with the concept. But why was there one...

Oh.

Shit.

Carefully, he stepped around it and crouched down. There was a blue blanket bundled around one very small baby wearing a blue hat. There was a giant duffel bag next to the carrier, and that's where he spotted an envelope with his name on it.

Jamie's hand shook as he reached for it, and that's when he realized how chilly it was outside. Standing, he reached for the carrier with one hand, put the envelope in the other as he reached for the bag and carried it all into the house, kicking the door shut behind him. It wasn't until he was in the living room that he put both the bag and baby down before he sat on the sofa. Tearing open the envelope, he let out a long breath and began to read.

Jamie,

I tried so many times to talk to you over the last several months, but you refused to meet with me and I have to admit, I should have pushed harder. I should have just come to the pub and forced you to talk to me. One look and you would have known exactly why I was there.

This is Asher. Your son. He was born ten days ago and

weighed seven pounds, three ounces, and was nineteen inches long. He's in perfect health. His birth certificate is in the duffel bag, along with enough supplies to get you through at least the next two to three days.

I can't care for him, Jamie. That's why I wanted to talk to you. I knew I couldn't do this alone and I considered a lot of options and ultimately thought I'd put him up for adoption. But even though you were a total ass these last months, I knew I couldn't do that without discussing it with you. I talked to a lot of people and I decided the best way to handle this was for you to take care of Asher for a while. Maybe then we can make some decisions together. I'm not ready to be a mom. I know that and it wouldn't be fair to him. I don't know you well enough to know where you stand, but I have a feeling you're not ready for fatherhood either. Especially with the revolving door of women who seem to constantly be in your life. Still...you deserve the opportunity to decide for yourself.

I'm going away for a while to get some help that I desperately need. You won't be able to reach me for at least three weeks. At that point, I'll be in touch.

Take care of Asher and good luck.

Jenn

For a minute, Jamie was completely stunned.

Then he felt like he was going to be sick.

Then Asher blinked up at him and started to cry and he *knew* he was going to be sick.

"Oh, God..."

He'd never been around babies. None of his siblings or cousins had kids yet, and neither had any of his friends. What the hell was he supposed to do?

Standing, he quickly ran to his bedroom, grabbed his phone, and sent out a text to his siblings. He knew they were all going to come down hard on him for being irresponsible, but once they got over yelling at him, hopefully they'd help him figure out just what exactly he was supposed to do with a baby.

A baby.

His baby.

His son.

Yeah, he was going to be sick.

Meanwhile, Asher started to cry in earnest.

"It's okay, buddy," he said softly as he jogged back into the living room. "Just...give me a minute to send out an SOS and get us both some help. I'm on it."

Jamie: HELP!

Jamie: I'm in serious trouble, guys. I need everyone here at my place ASAP

Jamie: Please.

Liam: Dude, what is going on? It's 8 a.m. on a Sunday.

Jamie: I'm in trouble

Liam: What kind of trouble?

Jamie: There's a baby in my living room

Patrick: You're joking, right?

Jamie: No

Ari: A BABY???

Liam: I'm guessing it's yours

Jamie: According to Jenn

Patrick: Wait, Jenn your ex who's been texting you for months?

Jamie: Yes

Ryleigh: Did she tell you she was pregnant?

Jamie: No, but can you all please come over?

Jamie: The baby is starting to freak out and so am I!

Liam: We'll be there as fast as we can

Patrick: Me too

Ryleigh: Same and I'll pick up coffee and breakfast

Ari: We're on the way! Do you need anything for the baby? Diapers? Formula?

Shit, he hadn't looked in the bag, but Jenn said everything was in there. But just to be sure, he double-checked.

Jamie: It looks like the bag has everything, so

we'll have to figure that all out when you're all here. Hurry!

Tossing the phone aside, he stared down at Asher like he was a ticking time bomb and then realized he couldn't let the little guy keep crying like that. Moving the blanket aside, he unbuckled him and gingerly picked him up.

"Oh, man. Why are you so tiny?" he whispered, but remarkably, the baby stopped crying almost instantly.

They both sort of stared at each other for a moment before Jamie tried to figure out the best way to hold him. There was a pacifier in the seat and he reached for it and offered it to Asher and let out a huge sigh of relief when he took it.

Then, he simply sat there, stiff and uncomfortable, afraid of moving and causing the baby to cry until his family showed up.

* * *

Bored.

Fallon sat down and drank her morning coffee in her parents' kitchen, and realized she had absolutely nothing to do for the rest of the day.

Or tomorrow.

Or the day after that.

She'd packed up her apartment back in Missouri and had most of her things put into storage here in Laurel Bay. She only kept her clothes, her electronics, and a few personal items with her just out of necessity.

Coming home made sense, but she didn't realize just how lost she was until she was sitting alone in complete silence in the house she grew up in. Other than stopping by

Donovan's Pub yesterday, she hadn't reached out to anyone —not her sisters, not her friends...just...no one. Part of it was because she was embarrassed. The other was...well...there was no other reason. She was just mortified that she had been let go from two different jobs in two different states in such a short amount of time.

Her.

The overachiever.

She knew some people were going to have a field day with that information.

Like Jamie Donovan.

Fallon had almost burst into tears when he figured things out yesterday. She wasn't someone who typically lied, but in that moment, there was no way she was going to give him the satisfaction of being right. It was petty and childish, and she just didn't give a damn. Ever since they were kids, they'd had this...animosity toward each other. She knew it was because he was a cocky, arrogant jerk who didn't like to think anyone could beat him at anything.

But she always could.

Well...maybe not always, but definitely more than Jamie was comfortable with.

It was stupid how some childhood games and competitions turned into an all-out war between the two of them, but it was like they couldn't be in the same room or have a simple conversation without trying to outdo each other.

Lately, she had tried to just...have a normal conversation with him—this was back when she was in her last semester of graduate school—and no matter how hard she tried, he just did everything in his power to push all of her buttons.

Hopefully he wouldn't figure out just how fragile she was right now and how much she needed to surround herself with people who could be a little gentle with her.

"Note to self, avoid Donovan's Pub."

Yeah, that was probably the safer way to go. There was no need to go in there to eat and end up with Jamie saying something stupid like he always did and her bursting into tears because she was feeling overly emotional. And there wasn't a doubt in her mind it would happen. Every once in a while, he would say something to her when their families were together that was more hurtful than playful. She never let on, but...her feelings definitely took a hit.

"So what am I supposed to do with myself?"

That was the million-dollar question.

Taking another sip of her coffee, she opened her laptop and began searching for jobs close to Laurel Bay. After all the money she'd spent on multiple moves, it would make the most sense for her to live at home for a while. She was thankful to have the option, but just the thought of the pitying looks her parents and sisters were going to give her was enough to consider taking out a personal loan and finding her own place.

"No, you have to be practical. Until you find a new job, frugality will be my new best friend."

Just the thought was enough to make her groan. How had her life gotten so out of hand? How did the girl who graduated with honors find herself unemployed twice? Was she that unlikable?

And for some reason, that was the thing that pushed her over the edge.

Tears fell, and Fallon didn't even try to stop them.

It was one thing not to be a good fit for a job. It was another when your co-workers just flat-out didn't like you.

Maybe Jamie was on to something all along...

And that just made her cry even harder.

Thank God no one was there to witness this, but she

had a feeling she needed to have this breakdown. It had been coming on for a while—since Houston, if she was being honest—and if this is when she finally could let her guard down long enough to let it out, then so be it.

Time had no meaning and she simply wandered from room to room crying and trying to figure out what to do with her life. Eventually she'd sit back down with her laptop and look at jobs, but she kind of felt like the bigger issue was why she wasn't connecting with employers and co-workers. And how did she even go about figuring that out? An online quiz? Her family doctor? A therapist?

"It probably wouldn't be the worst thing in the world to talk to a therapist..." She groaned. "But with my luck, they probably won't like me either."

And...she was crying hysterically again.

Of course, that's when her phone rang.

Glancing at it, she saw it was Ryleigh Donovan and opted to let it go to voicemail. She was too much of a wreck right now to talk to anyone. Obviously Ronan or Jamie must have mentioned their conversation from yesterday and she was just reaching out to be nice.

"And if you were a normal person, you would have answered the damn phone and asked a friend for a little help or guidance. But no, you have to be stubborn and look where that's gotten you."

Yeah, she was most definitely going to need to research therapists and start making calls Monday morning. The sooner she found someone, the sooner she'd feel confident searching for a job.

Two minutes later, the phone rang again, and it was Ryleigh.

"Well, that's odd..." she murmured, but still didn't answer it.

And her mind instantly wondered if something happened to their parents. Maybe that's why she was calling. But rather than call Ryleigh back, she picked up her phone and called her mother.

"Fallon! Hi! Is everything okay? You know it's early here in Amarillo."

"Everything's fine here. I was just checking on you."

"On me? Why? We just spoke yesterday."

"I know, I know...I guess...I don't know. I just had an overwhelming urge to call, that's all."

"Aww...aren't you sweet," her mother said with a happy sigh. "We're all fine. The rodeo was absolutely fascinating and we had a wonderful time. I'll have to send you some pictures. Your father rode a mechanical bull! Can you believe it?"

The image made her laugh. "I can't, so I hope you took some pictures of that!"

"Oh, I did. Believe me. Shane rode it too, but Kate and I were more than happy to stand back and snap some pictures!"

"I'm glad you guys are having such a great time, Mom. I'm sorry I bothered you. You were just on my mind and... and I just wanted to hear your voice."

Unfortunately, her own voice cracked.

"Fallon, sweetie...are you crying? Wait...hang on a minute. We're eating breakfast in the hotel restaurant. Let me step outside so we can talk."

"No! I mean...no. It's okay. I was feeling a little sorry for myself this morning, but just hearing your voice has helped, so...thanks."

"Are you sure? It's not a big deal for me to go outside and..."

Samantha Chase

"I'm serious, Mom. I'm good. Go back and enjoy your breakfast. I'll talk to you in a few days."

"I'm going to call you tomorrow and make you're okay. I love you, Fallon."

"Love you too, Mom."

No sooner had she hung up than she had a bunch of incoming texts.

Ryleigh: Fallon? Are you home?

Ryleigh: I heard you're in town and we have a situation we need some help with

Ryleigh: Yours specifically

"What in the world could she possibly need me for?" she wondered aloud.

Fallon: Is everything okay?

Ryleigh: Can I call you?

Groaning, Fallon wanted to say that it wasn't a good time, but...now she was curious.

Fallon: Sure

No sooner had she hit send than her phone was ringing.

"Hey," she said when she answered. "What's going on?"

"Hey," Ryleigh said quietly, almost like she didn't want anyone to hear her on the phone. "Listen, um...Uncle Ronan and Jamie both mentioned you being back in town,

34

and considering that your folks are driving across the country with mine, is it safe to say you're currently...uh... what I mean is...you can..."

"I'm not working right now, if that's what you mean," Fallon clarified.

"Okay, yeah. For what it's worth, I'm sorry that you're in this situation, but I'm hoping we can help each other out."

"Really? Do they need help at the pub?" Fallon knew she wasn't particularly coordinated enough to be a waitress, but she could help in other ways, like she had a few times with their computer system.

"No, no. It's not the pub. It's..."

"Is it Ryker's tattoo place? Do you need someone at the front desk? I don't think I really fit the type you'd find doing that kind of thing, but I'm very efficient and good at scheduling."

"Oh, no. It's not Ryker's place either. Look, this is more of a personal thing and the situation is a little...shall we say...delicate."

Delicate? Now she was definitely intrigued.

"Okay, so what's up?"

"I don't want to get into it over the phone. I'm going to text you an address and I'd really appreciate it if you can come over. Are you free now?"

Looking down at herself and her flannel pajama pants and t-shirt, that would be a big fat no.

"I was just about to jump in the shower. But I can be to you within an hour if that will work."

"That would be great. And Fallon? Thanks!"

"No problem. I'll see you soon." Hanging up, Fallon quickly finished her coffee and then walked upstairs to get herself showered and ready. Her mind was spinning with what on earth could be going on that had Ryleigh freaking out like this.

Grabbing a couple of towels and her robe, she walked into the bathroom and turned the hot water on.

"I guess I'm going to find out soon enough."

Chapter Three

Jamie looked around in wonder.

No one had yelled at him or told him how irresponsible he was.

No one was telling him how badly he'd screwed up.

And no one was telling him how he couldn't do this.

But the voice in his own head was saying all those things. Loudly.

Arianna and Will had taken off to go and do some shopping for more formula, diapers, clothes, and other necessities. He still had no idea what all that entailed, but he figured he was going to find out when they got back. Tessa and Ryleigh were organizing his second bedroom—which was really just a giant junk-collecting room—so it could be used for baby stuff. Patrick and Ryker were moving stuff out and putting a bunch of it in the back of Ryker's truck to go into storage. Apparently Patrick had a storage unit that was practically empty and he volunteered to let Jamie use it for whatever he needed.

Or...rather...didn't need.

And as he watched his foosball table go out the door, he figured that was no longer considered something he needed.

With a loud sigh, he raked his hand through his hair and watched as his house was getting a makeover that he hadn't planned on.

"You doing okay?" Liam asked as he cautiously approached.

"Honestly? I have no idea. I think I'm still in shock. Maybe I'm still sleeping and this is all a bad dream."

"Sorry, bro," his brother said as he gave his shoulder a reassuring pat. "This is happening. Have you thought about…"

"I haven't thought about anything," Jamie cut in with a mirthless laugh. "I mean…I woke up to a baby on my doorstep, Liam! A baby I had no idea existed until an hour ago!"

"Yeah, I get that, Jamie." Carefully, Liam led him over to the sofa and gave him a small shove to make him sit. Then, sitting on the coffee table, his big brother got serious. "Look, we all get that you're freaked out and with good reason. But there isn't time for that. A lot of things have to start happening."

Nodding, he replied, "I know that. Ari's out getting supplies, Ryleigh's doing her organization wizardry…"

"Not that stuff," Liam said with annoyance. "The pub. You can't bring a newborn with you to the pub. You're going to need a nanny or something. We all work, but I'm sure we can help out part of the time."

Crap. He hadn't thought of that.

"Then there's Mom and Dad."

"What about them?"

Looking over his shoulder to where everyone was working in the guestroom and then back at Jamie, Liam explained. "Look, I don't think you should tell Mom and Dad about this. You haven't called them yet, have you?"

He shook his head.

"Okay. Good." Pausing, he seemed to search for the right words. "From what the letter said, Jenn's going to be gone for a few weeks and all of this is on you and then...I guess the two of you will decide if there's going to be an adoption, right?"

He nodded even though that didn't sit right with him at all. Now that he'd seen Asher and held him, Jamie knew there was no way he could simply give him up.

"Then it just makes sense to leave Mom and Dad out of this. For starters, they'll end up canceling their cruise and coming home. They've waited far too long to take a vacation just for themselves, so let's not ruin it for them."

"I didn't do this on purpose!"

"I know, I know," Liam said soothingly. "It's just...I wasn't sure what you were thinking."

"Like I said, I haven't had time to really think."

Which was kind of a lie. He thought about getting in his car and chasing after the one that left Asher here. He thought of calling the cops and reporting it so they could find Jenn and wherever it was she was going to get help. But then all he could think about was the baby in his arms and how the hell he was supposed to be a father when he was still acting like a big kid himself.

"Anyway," Liam went on, interrupting his thoughts, "I want you to be a little open-minded to any...suggestions we may have on how to handle the situation."

"Believe me, I am open to anything because I am totally clueless about what to do with a baby! I mean...I can't ever remember being around one since Arianna was a baby!"

"That's what I was trying to explain to Tessa. I mean...

there just aren't any babies in the family yet, so we're not familiar with how to care for one. She's a teacher and studied early childhood stuff in college, but that's not much help with caring for a newborn."

"When does summer vacation start?"

"Eight weeks, so that's no help to you. Plus, she's going to be working with a music camp over the summer, so..."

"Got it. So what do I do? Put an ad up somewhere? If we start calling people we know, word's going to get back to Mom and Dad."

Liam nodded.

"Ryleigh's her own boss, so I'm sure she can either help here a couple of hours a week or maybe at the pub so I can be here." The nervous laugh was out before he could stop it. "I'm not sure which option is better for Asher. Maybe the less time I'm here, the better chance he has of being well cared for."

"Jamie...come on..."

"What? You think I don't know how unqualified I am for this? How no one's willing to say it out loud that I screwed up and how I'm not mature enough to handle being a father? Or...or...how you're all not dying to tease me about how I'll never have a date again?"

At least Liam had the good sense to look embarrassed.

"Okay, fine. We all thought about it, but no one said anything because it's not helpful right now. We're all here to support you and help in any way we can, but we're all just as clueless as you are, so...there's that."

"Yeah, great. What kind of care is that for Asher? He didn't ask for any of this! How could Jenn just dump him with a guy she knows is a screwup?"

"Jamie, other than...this, you're not a screwup. You work hard and yeah, sometimes you're a little self-absorbed and clueless, but you're definitely a good person. We all know that. Hell, everyone in this town knows that about you."

Falling back against the cushions, he let out a long breath. "What the hell was she thinking? I mean...why didn't she come and see me as soon as she found out? And... what if Asher's not mine? I know the timeline adds up, but..."

"Let's just say for the sake of argument that Asher is yours. You can still get a DNA test to put your mind at ease, but do you think Jenn would lie about something like that?"

"That's just it, Liam! I have no idea! We didn't spend a whole lot of time getting to know each other, if you know what I mean. We went out and had fun and it was all very light and casual."

Patrick and Ryker walked through the room carrying more boxes and he didn't even have the will to care about what was in them. He hadn't touched that stuff in the months he'd been living here, so he guessed he didn't need whatever was in them. Surely by now the room had to be organized, didn't it?

As if on cue, Ryleigh and Tessa joined them in the living room. Asher was sound asleep in the carrier. Arianna had fed and changed him before she left and, thankfully, he was a heavy sleeper.

Tessa sat in the oversized chair and Liam got up and squeezed in beside her while Ryleigh came over and sat next to him.

And he knew she was going to take her turn at trying to reassure him about how all of this was going to work out. Soon, Ryker was sitting beside her and Patrick took a chair from the kitchen and joined them.

Okay...now what?

Reaching over, Ryleigh took one of his hands in hers and that's when he got nervous.

"First, relax," she said to him and all Jamie could do was nod. "The room is all cleared out. Patrick and Ryker are going to take the stuff to the storage unit and come back with a bed for the room."

"A bed? Ry, I may not know anything about babies, but even I know Asher's too small to sleep in a real bed."

"Not for Asher, dummy, but for people who come and help you with Asher to sleep on. That room isn't particularly large, but you can fit a full or queen-size bed in there along with a crib and a dresser. It's not ideal, but for now, it will work."

"Oh. I guess that makes sense."

Ryleigh looked around and he noticed that she exchanged looks with both Liam and Patrick, who nodded at her.

And that really made him nervous.

His sister gave him a sweet smile—like she was buttering him up for something.

Now he was borderline terrified.

"As I'm sure you figured out, there isn't really a way that any of us can help you in the babysitting department. We all work and it's important for there to be some...stability for Asher. Babies need a schedule and to feel secure."

"If there were a revolving door of people coming in," Tessa chimed in, "it could be confusing and that would make Asher fussier than he should be. So finding a full-time caregiver along with yourself would be the best thing."

"I'm not disagreeing, but I don't have any idea how to find a full-time caregiver I would trust to have around my son or even in my home! If you know someone, then I'm all ears."

Ryleigh's smile grew. "I was hoping you'd say that."

"You were? Why? Do you know someone?"

She nodded. "Actually, I do, and she's on her way here."

Jamie practically sagged to the floor with relief. "Jeez, Ryleigh, why didn't you say something sooner? I've been sitting here freaking out and you've already found a nanny? You're a genius!" Sitting up, he pulled her in and gave her a huge hug. "You're the freaking best!" When he pulled back, he smiled. "I can't believe how amazing you are!"

"Well, I..."

"No," he cut her off. "It's true. You see a problem, and you fix it! It's like a gift and I'm so thankful for you. For all of you, but mainly for you." He winked at her.

"You weren't saying that a few months ago," she reminded him.

"I know, I know...but it all worked out, and thank you for forgiving me and doing something so unbelievably generous." He stood and looked around anxiously. "When will she be here? Does the house look okay? Should I maybe go and shower or at least brush my teeth?"

"Um...definitely brush your teeth," she said with a laugh. "And I'll send the guys out to do what they need to do."

"But you're staying, right? You and Liam and Tessa?"

"We'll be here," she reassured him.

"But I want to stay and watch," Patrick said with a smirk. "Ryker and I can hang out for a few more minutes. We want to...um...meet the nanny too."

"Shut up," Liam hissed and Jamie got a little suspicious again.

Ryleigh must have noticed his sudden change in demeanor, because she walked over and gave him a playful shove toward his bedroom. "Go and freshen up. Everything's under control and it's all going to be all right. You have my guarantee."

"O-kay..." But he really wasn't feeling as confident as he was a minute ago. Still, he knew he needed to clean himself up before meeting this person so he went to do his thing.

Walking into his en suite, he quickly brushed his teeth, put on deodorant, and ran a brush through his hair. Then he went back into the bedroom and changed his shirt and put on a pair of socks. He considered throwing on his sneakers, but didn't think it was necessary. Off in the distance, he heard the doorbell ring and his heart kicked hard in his chest. With any luck, this person was going to be an angel of mercy and get him through the next three weeks until Jenn was back.

Please let her be the answer I need...

Jamie stayed where he was for a minute while he heard a flurry of voices coming from the next room. Everyone sounded cheery and friendly, and it put his mind at ease.

Okay, if his family liked her, then there wasn't a doubt in his mind that he would. Giving himself a reassuring smile in the mirror, he turned and walked back out to the living room and froze.

Fallon Murphy was standing there in the middle of the room with Asher in her arms.

Shit.

This nightmare of a day just got worse.

* * *

"Oh my goodness, he's so little," Fallon said softly as she snuggled the baby in her arms.

"He is, but he's a fantastic eater," Ryleigh assured her.

"And a good pooper," Tessa added. "That first diaper wasn't pretty."

"I almost threw up," Liam said. "How can one tiny person create that strong of a smell?"

"Oh, hush," Tessa gently scolded. "Their little systems are just learning to work."

Fallon caressed the baby's cheek for a moment before she looked up at everyone. "So, um...I hate to ask the obvious, but...whose baby is he?"

Five pairs of eyes stared back at her, but no one said a word. Until...

"He's mine," Jamie said as he walked into the room.

And then it all made sense—why Ryleigh was so vague on the phone, why they had all lulled her in and immediately put Asher in her arms—it was all a way to get her to soften before finding out which Donovan needed her help.

Clearly now wasn't the time to make a snarky comment —even though there were a dozen of them on the tip of her tongue. Instead, she simply offered Jamie a small smile and waited for someone to explain what was going on.

"Fallon," Liam began, but Jamie instantly cut him off.

"This is my home and my son, so...I think I should be the one to explain to...Fallon what's going on."

She would have almost respected him if he hadn't sneered when he said her name.

Ass.

Jamie made quick work of explaining the situation and even gave her the letter he received this morning so she could read it for herself. A myriad of emotions threatened to overwhelm her. How could someone just walk away from their baby? What kind of help did she need that required three weeks away? Were they really going to just put this sweet baby up for adoption when the three weeks were up?

She felt a little sick to her stomach and slowly turned to sit herself down on the sofa.

All the Donovans—including Ryker and Tessa—remained standing.

"Basically," Ryleigh said after a moment, "Jamie really needs help for Asher. I know the two of you don't have a great history with each other, but I'm hoping you can both put that aside for the sake of the baby."

Fallon glared up at Jamie and saw he was glaring right back.

This definitely won't work...

"You used to babysit a lot when we were younger," Ryleigh went on, "and I know you spent several summers working as a mother's helper. This is basically the same thing. With our parents out of town, Jamie has to run the pub and there's no way he can bring a baby to work with him. That's not a good environment for him."

While Fallon agreed with everything Ryleigh was saying, it wasn't Ryleigh's place to be trying to win her over.

"I understand what you're saying," she began diplomatically, "but considering this is a situation of Jamie's doing, I think he's the one I need to be talking with."

There was a collective groan around the room before everyone started to move away.

Patrick and Ryker announced that they were leaving to take things to storage, Liam and Tessa offered to pick up lunch, which left Fallon, Ryleigh, and Jamie.

And she had a feeling poor Ryleigh had been left to play the moderator.

She sat down on the sofa beside her while Jamie sat in the oversized chair.

"Just so you know," Jamie began, "I had no idea anyone

had called you. So if I seem a little shocked that you're here, that's why."

It was a reasonable excuse, but she held no illusions that he was grateful for her presence.

"And just so you know," she retorted, "I had no idea why I was coming here or even whose house it was so...like you...if I seem a little shocked, that's why."

"Okay, so we're both on the same page. Shocked," he said flatly.

"Exactly," she murmured.

And then it was so quiet you could hear a pin drop.

Ryleigh kept looking back and forth between them for several minutes until she clearly couldn't take it anymore.

"I hate to point out the obvious," she began, "but this ridiculous little standoff isn't helping anything."

Fallon responded first. "You're right and I get it. But I don't think this will work. It's obvious he doesn't want me here, no matter how much he needs the help. And honestly, I'm not sure I want to be the one doing this. I realize I have the free time right now, but...I have some plans in the work."

Liar, liar, liar...

Okay, so maybe she was a little more comfortable lying than she thought she was. It didn't necessarily make her a bad person.

"He'll pay you!" Ryleigh blurted out. "No one expects you to be doing this for free and I know you're probably eager to start job hunting, but...you can still do that while babysitting Asher. Jamie doesn't work all day, every day. He'll be home at night and during the days when you're here, you can do whatever you need to, right, Jamie?"

He shrugged.

"Dude, I am seriously trying here," Ryleigh hissed at him. "Can you maybe take your head out of your butt for a few minutes and see how this is all for your benefit? And maybe thank Fallon for being willing to come here and save your sorry ass?"

"She didn't know it was me she was coming to help!" he argued. "And I'd bet good money if you mentioned that on the phone, she would have had an excuse why she couldn't come over."

He wasn't wrong.

"But the fact is that I'm still here," Fallon challenged. "So either talk to me about how we can make this work, or I'll hand your son to you and leave. The choice is yours."

This would really be a great thing for her right now, but there was no way she was going to let him know that. She wasn't ready to start job hunting and she knew therapy was a serious option, but maybe reading a couple of self-help books would be a step in the right direction. Plus, if he were paying her, she'd at least be getting some form of income so she wouldn't have to dip into her dwindling savings.

Doing her best to keep her expression neutral, Fallon waited him out. Asher was asleep in her arms and he felt so good there that she knew it would be hard to hand him over if Jamie told her to leave.

With a defiant look, he leaned forward in his seat. "You'd have to be here for six to eight hours a day," he said stiffly.

"I'm aware."

"While my folks are away, I'm typically working six days a week. I can be flexible with my hours, but I can't come running home multiple times a day if you're freaking out about something."

"I rarely freak out," she countered.

His snort of disbelief spoke volumes.

"So?" he asked. "Will you do it?"

It would be so much fun to make him squirm, but this wasn't the kind of situation to do that.

"That depends."

"On?"

"How much are you paying?"

His eyes went wide, but he didn't seem to have an answer.

"I think on the weekends your siblings should be able to help out," she said rationally. "And I'm willing to commit to thirty hours a week at $15 an hour."

"Are you crazy?" he snapped. "To sit around and watch an infant sleep? Absolutely not."

"Um..." Ryleigh slowly raised her hand before passing her phone to him. He read whatever was on the screen and his shoulders drooped.

"Thirty-five hours," he countered, "at $15 an hour. Final offer."

She wanted to laugh, but right now, beggars couldn't be choosers. "You'll need to keep food in the house for both me and Asher. I'll give you a list of requests."

"Now I have to feed you too? What the hell, Fallon?"

She shrugged. "I don't think it's a big deal to keep some fresh fruit and produce in the house and maybe some lunch meat. It's not like I'm asking for surf and turf."

"Ugh...if he won't do it, I'll shop for you," Ryleigh said, shooting her brother a dirty look.

"Fine. Give me a list and I'll make sure there's stuff here for you."

"Thank you." Then she paused. "We'll need a car seat and a stroller so I can take him out for walks or if we need to go to the store or if you need me to drop him off at the pub for you."

He nodded. "I think that's what Ari and Will are out shopping for right now."

"Jenn didn't leave any of that stuff?"

"Just the carrier, but I'm not sure if that's part of a car seat or not." He leaned back in the chair and let out a long breath. "I don't think I'd know what a proper car seat was if you paid me. This is all just...it so much."

His eyes closed, and for a moment, Fallon actually felt bad for him. This was a major, life-changing event and he had zero time to prepare. He was lucky that he had such an amazing family.

"Can I ask something?" she said to no one in particular, and they both nodded. "What did your parents have to say about all of this?"

"Oh, um...we're not telling them," Ryleigh said.

Fallon stared at her in disbelief. "Um...what?"

Jamie sat back up. "Considering that things might get messy when Jenn gets back, we didn't want to do or say anything that might ruin their trip. Right now, they're off on the trip of a lifetime and I don't want to be the one to make them miss it. Once things get worked out when Jenn gets home, then I'll figure the rest out."

It was crazy, but Fallon couldn't help but read between the lines.

He didn't want to put Asher up for adoption.

So maybe he wasn't the actual worst person in the world.

Maybe there was hope for him yet.

For the next thirty minutes, they came up with a tentative schedule that would start tomorrow. Today, she was there as part of the family to help get everything set up and just spend time with friends.

Arianna and Will got back first and had a ridiculous

number of packages with them. They had clothes, diapers, formula, toys, bottles, a tiny bathtub, a crib, a changing table, a mobile, a car seat, a stroller...

"How did you fit all of this in your car?" Fallon asked.

"Oh, we took Will's Jeep and Jamie's truck so we could get it all home," Arianna said after hugging Fallon. "Most of the big stuff has to be assembled, and now all the clothes, towels, and bedding need to be washed. Thank God Jamie has a washer and dryer in this tiny house."

Fallon had to agree, and while Ryleigh was holding Asher, she went to work on opening packages and taking tags off of things and sorting it all for the laundry. Once the first load was in, they went to work on all the bottles—making sure to wash and disinfect them. That's when Ryleigh joined them because Asher was asleep again and she knew the kitchen was going to need to be reorganized too.

"You are such a weirdo that you enjoy doing this," Arianna joked.

"And yet you have all reaped the benefits of my weird-ness," Ryleigh said as she began emptying an upper cabinet.

"It's sad but true," Ari said to Fallon. "Watch her work. It's like a thing of beauty."

"Well, I should also watch so I'll know where to find anything tomorrow," she said with a small laugh.

All over the house, people were in motion. When Patrick and Ryker returned with a bed, headboard, and frame, they went right to work putting it all together in the guestroom.

"A second bed?" she asked Ryleigh. "Why?"

"Well, I have a feeling the overnights might become an issue and it's just smart to have a place for anyone helping out to crash rather than making them sleep on the couch."

It made sense, but...

"So then Asher is sharing a room with the guest?"

"It's not ideal, but...as you can see, the house is small. I think it's only like 1,200 square feet. The rooms are all a decent size, and realistically, once Asher's a little bit older, he can use the bed that's in there and anyone coming to visit can stay with any of us. They'd have like...five other house-holds to choose from. This is just a temporary setup."

Again, it made sense. The only reason anyone would be staying over was to help with the baby, so putting the bed in the same room made things easier.

The snarky side of her wondered if Jamie would ask someone to stay over so he could have company of his own in his bedroom without being bothered. Or...so he could stay out all night without having to worry about coming home and taking care of his son.

Don't go there...don't go looking for trouble.

Only time would tell how this was all going to play out and really, it was only her problem for the next three weeks. By that time, this Jenn person would be back and hopefully they'd work out a co-parenting situation and perhaps get Asher into a daycare.

She made a mental note to start researching ones in the area, so maybe she could present it as an option for Jamie down the road. Right now, it was probably the last thing on his mind. Having someone caring for the baby here at home was the smart thing to do right now. But eventually, they were going to need to make alternate plans. Fallon didn't mind helping on a short-term basis, though she had a feeling by the end of three weeks Jamie was going to be happy to see her go.

And there wasn't a doubt in her mind that by that same

time, she would be thrilled not to have to deal with him on a daily basis.

Then she looked down at Asher. Ryleigh had put the carrier close by on the kitchen floor so they could keep an eye on him while they worked.

He was going to be the one she would miss seeing. That was a given. Fallon had always loved babysitting and being around babies. In her mind, she saw herself getting married and having a bunch of kids. This little unemployment detour was messing with her five-year plan, but hopefully she'd get back on track soon.

But for now, hanging out with little Master Asher would give her a baby fix.

And hopefully she wouldn't strangle his father in the process.

Chapter Four

When Jamie's alarm went off on Monday morning, he swore he'd only slept a total of two hours the entire night. No one really prepared him for what it was going to be like since they had no idea how long Asher would sleep once he was in a crib.

And apparently, his son did not approve of his new bed.

At all, judging by how little he slept in it.

Jamie's head was pounding and he was mildly delirious, but for now the house was quiet. If he could just make himself a strong cup of coffee and take a scalding hot shower before Asher woke up, he'd consider it a win.

Shuffling out to the kitchen, he cursed his sister's organizational skills when he couldn't find where his mugs were. On the fifth try, he found them and he fought the urge to hurl it against the wall.

"I'm just tired and cranky," he reminded himself. "No need to get violent at seven in the morning." Putting the pod in the coffeemaker, he hit the button and leaned heavily against the kitchen counter while he waited.

Longest minute of his life.

He added cream and sugar and took that first sip and it didn't matter that it burned his entire mouth and throat. It was worth it.

Carrying the mug to his bathroom, he put it down on the vanity and stared at his reflection and groaned. He looked like he'd aged ten damn years overnight. With a muttered curse, Jamie turned on the shower and stripped.

And realized he forgot to bring the baby monitor in with him.

Obviously today wasn't going to be the day where he got to take a relaxing shower to wake himself up. Nope, this was the day he took a super quick one and prayed Fallon would show up early.

"Ugh...this is how exhausted I am. I'm actually looking forward to seeing Fallon." He shuddered as he soaped up and realized he needed a serious attitude adjustment. If this is how he felt after one night, he really should be a lot more thankful that she was willing to help him out. Of course she was doing it for a cost, but he had a feeling she was going to earn every penny—again, if last night was anything to go by.

Rinsing off, he reached for a towel and got dry before walking into his bedroom and listening to the monitor to see if Asher was awake. He could hear a few little grunts, but figured he had enough time to brush his teeth and get dressed before going into the other room.

In his entire life, Jamie never shied away from hard work or a challenge, and he had a feeling fatherhood was going to be both. If he had known sooner that he was going to be in this position, maybe he wouldn't feel so completely out of his element.

"Well, dumbass, you've got no one to blame but yourself. Jenn kept asking to see you and you thought all your charm would distract her enough to make her go away," he told his reflection with disgust. Yeah, hindsight and all. He was just as much to blame as Jenn was. Neither of them handled this situation the right way, but there was no way he was going to make his son suffer because he got stuck with two parents who sucked at communicating.

Once he was done getting ready, he drank down the rest of his coffee and put the mug in the kitchen sink on his way to Asher's room. His son was wide awake and staring up at him and Jamie felt his heart kick hard in his chest.

"Hey, buddy," he said softly. "You made it a whole two hours in your bed. Good job!" Reaching in, he carefully picked him up before cradling him to his chest.

And instantly cringed.

There must be a secret to securing a diaper better because, clearly, he didn't do it right.

"Okay, let's get you cleaned up and in dry clothes. How does that sound?"

Asher blinked up at him and blew a few spit bubbles.

Adorable...

It took a lot longer than he imagined to get his son cleaned up and changed into something dry, but once he did, that's when Asher really started to cry because he was hungry. With no choice, he had to put him down in the carrier before he could make a bottle. Maybe one day he could handle doing that while holding him, but today was not that day. He spilled the formula, then made it too hot, and by the time everything was just right, the poor baby was almost inconsolable.

"What on earth is going on?" Fallon asked as she walked into the kitchen. Yesterday, Jamie gave her a key so she could come and go when she needed. And right now, he was beyond thankful that she showed up when she did.

"It was a rough night and he was soaked when he got

up, so I had to pretty much wash him off and get him dressed before we could eat," he explained, getting more and more frazzled by the moment. "Then I messed up the formula and...and..."

She was crouched down in front of Asher and gently lifting him from the carrier. When she stood, she took the bottle from his hand and walked over to the sofa while softly talking to the baby.

And then...silence.

Jamie felt like he would never hear it ever again and it almost made him want to cry like his son was not even two minutes ago.

Slowly, he walked into the living room and collapsed on the sofa. Fallon was in the oversized chair and Asher was greedily drinking his breakfast.

"I take it you had a rough night," she said quietly.

"You have no idea."

"What happened? He was calm when we all left last night."

"New surroundings, I guess. He doesn't seem to like the crib. Every time I put him down, he'd cry. Then I'd pick him up and rock him until he fell asleep and then I'd carefully put him down and he'd wake up crying. At one point, I just brought him out here with me and we both fell asleep watching the TV. He was sound asleep on my chest and when I woke up, I startled him and it started all over again. The longest stretch he stayed in the crib was two hours. My alarm went off at seven and I swear I had only finally gotten into the bed at five. I'm exhausted."

She nodded. "I think that's common with most newborns. You obviously have no idea what kind of schedule he had with his mother or what his surroundings were like. I'll try to see what I can do about getting him better acclimated to all his new stuff today." She paused. "I know it doesn't seem possible, but it is going to get better. It was just the first night and I'm sure you were nervous. Babies can sense these things." She paused again. "Um…is there any chance you can take off today?"

"Why? Already regretting your decision to help me?" he snapped and at her startled expression, he immediately apologized. "I'm sorry, Fallon. Really. I'm just…I can't even think straight."

The pinched look on her face said she wasn't overly sympathetic.

"Anyway…you were saying…?" he prompted.

"I thought that maybe having a full day at home with him—with me here with you—the two of you can start to feel more comfortable around each other. Yesterday was loud and chaotic and it was probably a little sensory over-load for him. A quiet day at home where he gets to interact with all his new things and the new people in his life would probably be extremely beneficial."

"I don't know…it's short notice and we didn't tell my uncle what was going on either. I'd hate to leave everyone in a lurch…"

"Okay. I understand that. What about leaving after lunch? Working a half a day. Can you do that?"

Nodding, he knew he would have to. There was no way he could put in his usual ten-to-twelve-hour day feeling the way he did right now. "Yeah. I can definitely do that."

"And what about Ronan? Are you going to tell him?"

Good question.

"I think we can trust him not to say anything to my folks, but…I don't know. I'm not sure you're aware, but Ronan's like the town gossip. Even if he doesn't say anything to my parents, there's a good chance he'll blurt it out to someone else. I feel like it's just one more thing to worry about right now that I don't want to worry about."

"It's your call, but what's going to be your excuse for needing to leave early?"

He shrugged and then laughed a little. "I can just tell him I had a late night with a woman. He always loves hearing about my escapades, so he won't question it. It won't be an issue."

Fallon didn't look even remotely amused.

"I mean, umm..."

"It doesn't matter to me what you tell him," she said primly. "Just know this—I'm not going to give up my time so you can go out and have more...escapades. For the next three weeks, you'll need to keep it in your pants because that's what being a single parent means."

He looked at her with amusement. "Really? That's what being a single parent means? Somehow, I don't quite think that's Webster's definition."

With the eye roll she typically gave him, she shook her head. "You know what I'm saying. Right now, your son is your top priority. He already has a mother who was more than willing to just drop him on your doorstep and walk away. You need to be the parent who steps up and shows him he matters."

Damn, when she put it like that, he felt like a jerk for even trying to make light of the situation.

"Okay, okay...you're right. For the next three weeks, either I'm here with Asher, or I'm at the pub. That's it. You have my word on that."

Her eyes went wide.

"Really? Just like that? You're not going to argue with me or tell me I'm being ridiculous or something?"

"Would it make you feel better if I did?" he teased and couldn't help but smile when he saw her lips twitch.

"I don't know," she said honestly. "I'm just used to you arguing with me just for the sake of arguing."

"Yeah, well...the stakes are different now." Pausing, he studied her for a long moment. It was only eight in the morning and she looked completely put together. Her dark hair was all soft waves, she was dressed in a pair of faded blue jeans with a pastel pink t-shirt, and a pair of tennis shoes. Fallon never wore a lot of makeup, but now that he was studying her, he saw her cheeks had a hint of peach to them that matched the gloss on her lips. She actually looked...pretty.

Say what...?

Yeah, this was how he knew he was delirious—sitting here thinking Fallon Murphy was pretty. Um...no.

Just no.

Definitely not.

It was ridiculous. *He* was ridiculous.

"Are you okay?" she asked. "You've got a really weird look on your face."

Asher was resting his little face on her shoulder while she gently patted his back.

"I'm fine," he said as he quickly got to his feet. "I should...I should go. The earlier I get in and take care of things, the earlier I'll be home. Uh...thanks."

And without looking at her, Jamie practically sprinted for the door and refused to look back.

* * *

The morning was busier than Fallon expected.

Asher stayed awake for a while, and she wanted to fully

interact with him and enjoyed simply sitting and singing silly songs and reading him some stories. She talked in soothing tones to him as she walked back to his new bedroom. Standing next to the crib, she said, "And now we're going to take a nice nap in your new bed and it's going to be wonderful." He was swaddled nice and snug, and she turned on the mobile once she placed him down.

Then she cautiously backed out of the room and stood in the hallway for a solid five minutes to make sure he fell asleep. While he was down for a nap, she took advantage of the time and did a small load of laundry—both for the baby and for Jamie—and then prepped enough bottles for the next twenty-four hours. Maybe if Jamie had one less thing to deal with, the nights wouldn't be so bad.

After that was done, she did some light cleaning. They had straightened up after all the furniture had been assembled yesterday, but there was still a little debris lying around. She didn't hesitate in bringing out the vacuum because she felt that Asher needed to get used to living with Jamie just as much as Jamie needed to get used to living with the baby. There was no way they could live in complete silence, so maybe introducing some basic sounds around the house would be a good thing.

When she was done and Asher was still asleep—and she wasn't sure how much longer that was going to last—she pulled her laptop out of her satchel and did a little research on newborns. It was something she had meant to do last night, but the day had been long and a little mentally exhausting and by the time she'd gone home, she simply put on her jammies and vegged out in front of the TV for a while.

Since it was quiet, she figured she could get in a little research time and when Asher woke up, she'd get him changed and fed and then maybe take him for a walk. Jamie's house wasn't far from the Laurel Bay Community Park and she knew there were some great paved paths she could easily push the stroller on.

It was a full hour before he woke up, and Fallon did everything she planned. When she had him secured in his stroller, she tapped out a quick text to Jamie to let him know where they were going, just in case he got home before they got back.

It was a beautiful day and perfect for getting outside for a walk. It wasn't until she was a couple of blocks from the house that she realized how long it had been since she'd felt so relaxed or had appreciated the simple pleasure of just being outside getting some fresh air.

These next three weeks were going to be like a voyage of self-discovery, and she wasn't sure if it was going to be exciting or horrifying. Asher was going to be an awesome distraction and she hoped his father wasn't going to make her feel bad about herself with his negative comments toward her.

Although...seeing Jamie so vulnerable this morning was very eye-opening. Maybe they were finally done with their rivalry and animosity toward each other. It would be nice if they could at last just be friends.

With a sigh, she crossed the street and headed into the park and went all of ten steps before inwardly groaning.

Friends with Jamie? Um...no. It wasn't possible. They would be civil to each other at best. Basically, she disagreed with everything about his lifestyle. As mean as it sounded, she was actually surprised it had taken this long for someone to show up with a baby. He dated someone new every week, flirted with every woman who came into the pub, and basically relied on his charm to help him get through life.

Well...Fallon could see right through him. And while this morning showed her a side of Jamie that she'd never seen before, she knew he'd get everything worked out in no time and have a line of wannabe nannies a mile long. If word got out that Jamie Donovan had a baby and needed help, there wasn't a doubt in her mind that women would be camped out on his front lawn begging for a chance to help overnight.

"Not me," she murmured as she strolled along the first path she came to. "There is no way I'm pulling overnight duty." She smiled down at Asher. "No matter how cute you are. Your daddy's just going to have to learn to make it work."

According to some of the research she did earlier, this little man most likely won't be sleeping through the night until he's six months old. Granted, some babies start doing it as early as three months, but that's not a guarantee. Fallon believed if they got his schedule stable and she helped Jamie create a bedtime routine, things would definitely get easier. But for now, he was looking at not getting much sleep for a good long while.

They must have walked for an hour and her stomach started to growl so she knew it must be close to lunchtime. They had pretty much walked around the entire park, so she found where they came in and headed in that direction. Asher was sound asleep and she was hoping he'd continue to sleep for a while so she could make herself some lunch and eat it before he was ready to eat again.

Yesterday, Jamie had done an online grocery order, so she already knew there was food at the house for her. Honestly, if he had turned her down on that one point, she would have been fine. Packing a lunch wasn't that big of a deal, but having food already there just seemed easier. Plus, it wasn't like she was asking for that much.

As she strolled up to his house, she saw his truck in the driveway and was impressed that he actually was true to his word and came home early. Maybe they could eat lunch together and sit and have a cordial conversation about how things were going to go moving forward. She knew it was only three weeks, but she still wanted to be sure they were on the same page on everything.

Feeling good about her plan, she opened the front door and carefully pushed the stroller inside. "Jamie?"

No response.

Walking farther in, she got to the living room and had to hide a smile.

He was sound asleep on the sofa.

Snoring and all.

Okay, as much as she wanted to talk with him, she knew he needed some sleep. So with father and son napping, she went about making herself a very quiet lunch. With her turkey sandwich and a bowl of fresh fruit, she sat down at the kitchen table with her laptop and did a little more baby research.

After an hour and not a peep out of either of them, she contemplated moving Asher from the stroller to his crib, but she had just read how some babies prefer the stroller and its close confines because it makes them feel more secure. The only way she could possibly mimic that in his crib was just with good swaddling. She couldn't put anything in there with him because it would be a safety hazard.

Cleaning up her lunch mess, she felt a little at a loss for something to do. She folded the laundry and wiped down the kitchen and was about to sit back down with her laptop when she saw Jamie sit up. He was slightly disoriented and his hair was in wild disarray and for some reason, the first thing that came to mind was, "yum."

Uh-oh...

Fine. There was no denying that Jamie Donovan was extremely attractive. That was part of what annoyed her most about him. He used those looks to get what he wanted, and she found it incredibly aggravating. She didn't know why; she just did.

Then he stood and stretched and, for a moment, she was slightly mesmerized. His t-shirt rode up slightly and exposed just a small band of skin around his middle. She was openly ogling him when he seemed to finally notice she was there.

"Oh, uh...hey," he said before yawning loudly. "Sorry. Did you guys just get back?"

Laughing softly, she shook her head. "We got back almost two hours ago. I figured you needed the sleep so I didn't want to wake you."

He glanced around and spotted the stroller and walked over to it. "And he didn't wake up either?"

"Nope. I think all the fresh air helped with that. Today is kind of all about learning his schedule and the patterns. It will probably take a few days until we can say with any certainty what that looks like, but for now, I'm making notes on all of it."

Raking a hand through his hair, he yawned again. "Oh, okay. Great." Padding into the kitchen, he made himself a sandwich and sat down at the table with her.

"So, how did things go at the pub? Did you have to lie to your uncle?"

"Actually, he took one look at me and told me I looked like hammered shit and should go home," he said with a laugh. "But there were a few things I needed to take care of and then I thanked him and left. I was half asleep on the drive home. It's a miracle I didn't crash."

"That's not good, Jamie. You need to be more careful! You have a son now!"

"Yeah, I'm aware of that, Fallon," he snapped. "It's the only reason you're even here in my house!"

Okay, this was not helping anything, so she was going to be the adult.

Again.

"All I'm saying is that you really need to...you know...be a little more cautious than you're used to. I didn't mean to come off like I was reprimanding you."

Something in her tone must have gotten through to him, because he visibly relaxed. "I realized I should have just called for a ride. Hell, I should have just called you. You have the car seat and could have come and gotten me."

Reaching over, she rested her hand on top of his. "I would have come for you rather than know that you're driving when you're too tired to drive safely. Promise me you'll call me if that ever happens again."

Jamie stared down at their hands for a moment before responding. "I promise," he said gruffly, and Fallon instantly moved her hand away.

"So, um...yeah," she said awkwardly. "I'm sure you can take care of yourself, but if you ever need a ride..."

He nodded. "Got it." He let out a long breath. "So how has Asher been?"

"He's been great. He fell back to sleep fairly quickly this morning and I cleaned and did some laundry. I washed some of your clothes too. They're folded and in the laundry room."

"What? Why?"

"What do you mean?"

"Fallon, you're not here to be my maid. I appreciate your help, but I don't expect you to do anything other than take care of the baby," he said firmly.

She shrugged. "It wasn't a big deal. Anyway, then I took him out for a walk. It was such a nice day out and I figured I'd see if he enjoyed it."

"And did he?"

"Not a peep out of him, so I'm calling it a success."

Nodding again, he glanced over at her. "So...what's next? I'm not sure how much we can possibly plan. Like you said, we need to figure out his schedule first and I know I need to figure out how the hell I'm going to survive on two hours of sleep a night."

"It's not always going to be like that," she promised. "A lot of parenting websites suggest that you sleep when Asher's sleeping. Personally, I don't know how practical that is or how easy it is to do. I know I wouldn't be able to just lie down and fall asleep at eight at night when I normally stay up until eleven."

"I could probably do that today since I'm so tired, but I have to agree with you. I'm not sure if I could do that on a regular basis."

"The only other option is to see if maybe one of your siblings can stay for a couple of nights so you can get some sleep and someone can figure out Asher's schedule."

"Absolutely not. It will never happen. Everyone has jobs of their own and can't stay up all night any more than I can." Elbows on the table, he rested his face in his hands. "I just don't know how to handle all of this. There's just so much to figure out. Most new parents have nine months to prepare. I literally had like...zero minutes."

It would be foolish to point out how if he had only

agreed to meet up with Jenn the first time she asked, none of this would be happening right now.

"I know you didn't have any time, Jamie, but you're going to be fine. There are a ton of parenting books and websites out there, but a lot of being a good parent is on following your instincts. Right now, Asher just needs to be clean and fed and snuggled to make him feel safe and secure."

"Yeah, well...I wouldn't mind feeling a little safe and secure right now too."

He looked up at her and all Fallon could see was utter hopelessness on his face. She was used to seeing him being cocky and arrogant; his confidence was both legendary and often misplaced. But seeing him like this was more than a little unnerving.

"This is all temporary, Jamie. You have to know that. In a few weeks, you'll feel more settled and it will all be alright."

"You don't know that..."

"Yes, I do," she countered. "All new parents—even the ones who had nine months to prepare—are nervous when they first bring their babies home. No one knows what to expect or if their child will sleep or cry a lot...there are no guarantees. You're no different from every other new parent."

"That doesn't make me feel any better. It's just me," he argued, but there wasn't any heat behind his words. "Most new parents are just that—parents. There are two of them and they can take turns. For at least the next three weeks, I'm alone in this."

"No, you're not." Again, she reached out and touched him and somehow they ended up holding each other's hands, fingers linked. "I'm here. I know I'm not Asher's mother, but I'm here to help you. You have your whole family willing to help. Don't feel like you're all alone."

"You don't understand. I know you're here and I can call Ryleigh, Ari, Liam, or Patrick at any time, but the bottom line is you all have lives. You're only here for a certain number of hours a day and they all work. So..."

Sadly, he had a point.

However, this was all part of being a parent. And this wasn't about her being mean or petty or even about their lifelong pattern of trying to poke and annoy each other. This was quite possibly the first thing Jamie was going to have to truly learn to do on his own. He couldn't flirt or persuade or charm his way out of it. He was going to have to be the guy who was up all night and going to work and putting in a full day before coming home and doing it all over again. Fallon knew she would help where she could, but there were boundaries in place, and she needed to stick to them.

No matter how badly she wanted to fix this—and she realistically knew she could by offering to stay over for the next couple of nights—she knew it wouldn't truly be doing him any favors. He and Asher needed to start forming their own routine and creating a bond.

"I still think it's going to be okay," she told him, giving his hand a gentle squeeze. "It's a lot quieter here today than it was yesterday, so you and I can go over things for you to try when he's fussy, and we'll come up with a plan to make the time after I leave at the end of the day easier for the both of you."

He let out a mirthless laugh. "I don't see how that's possible."

Slowly, Fallon took her hand from his and stood. "For starters, I prepped all the bottles for the rest of day and well into tomorrow morning. All the laundry is done so there are plenty of clothes, blankets, burp cloths...everything you might need is ready should you need it."

He nodded, but didn't look like this was good news at all.

"I'm going to show you the best way to keep him swaddled so he'll feel better when he sleeps and...though I'm not sure this is the best solution...he really seems to like the stroller."

"And? What does that mean?"

"It means if the nights are really rough, you put him in the stroller in your room. You keep it next to your bed so he's right there. Hell, we could go to the store and buy a bassinet or something smaller than the crib to put in your room for now and set up a little changing station and get one of those tiny dorm fridges so you never have to leave your room."

Now that seemed to get his attention.

"Seriously? Like...do people really do that?"

"The summer before I left for college, I worked for a family who had five-year-old twins and then just had a baby. The twins were awesome, but the baby had some health issues and needed to be fed every two hours. No one was going to get any sleep like that. So yeah, they put everything in the master bedroom and the parents took turns getting up and feeding him. It wasn't ideal, but it was only for a short amount of time." She smiled at him. "There's no set of hard rules here, Jamie. As long as Asher's needs are being met and he's safe, and you're staying sane, then you're good."

He let out a loud sigh of relief before raking both hands through his hair.

"If you want, I can run to the store and get everything..."

"No!" he said a little too quickly, a panicked look

already on his face.

"O-kay..."

"What if he wakes up? What if I fall asleep? What if...?"

He was spiraling.

"How about this—when Asher wakes up, you and I walk through all the steps of getting him changed and fed and then we all go to the store together? What do you think?"

"Please don't take this the wrong way, but..."

"Oh my God! If you tell me you don't want to be seen in public with me..."

"No! No, that's not it! I swear! Jeez!" Shaking his head, he looked up at her. "I just...I'm not sure I'm ready to risk running into anyone while I'm out with Asher. You know how small-town gossip is and if word got out to my parents..."

Damn. She had forgotten about that.

"Hmm...then I guess we have two options," she began. "First, you go by yourself, but only after Asher wakes up and you help care for him."

"Technically, I'm supposed to be at work and that's why you're here," he said with a nervous laugh and instead of getting pissed at him, she took it in stride because she knew he was freaking out.

"Or...I'll go once Asher's asleep again. This way, the two of you can sleep while I'm gone."

Jamie was studying her hard and for the life of her, she had no idea what was going through his mind.

"Um...Jamie?" she prompted after a minute.

"I have a third potential option," he said slowly.

"Which is...?"

"No one goes to the store and you move in with me."

Chapter Five

It was three a.m. and Asher was wailing.

Again.

Groaning, Jamie reached over and gently rocked the stroller hoping to calm his son and perhaps not having to get out of the bed.

Fallon had completely shot down his request for her to move in, and even though he wanted to be angry, he really couldn't blame her. Hell, he still couldn't believe she was helping him at all.

Well, I am paying her, so it's not really like she's helping...

If anything, I'm helping her while she's unemployed.

He could argue with himself about it to try to feel better, but the bottom line was that she definitely *was* helping him and he was grateful—not as grateful as he'd be if she had accepted his offer to move in, but he genuinely appreciated everything she was doing for him and Asher. She'd been coming to the house for the last three days and while some things were getting better, the nights most definitely were not.

The rocking wasn't helping, so he sat up and came to the conclusion that it was time for another diaper change and a bottle.

Then he got of whiff of something horrific.

"Oh, come on, buddy. In the middle of the night?" But Asher just continued to cry, so Jamie forced himself to get up and do all the things he needed to do.

He had done what Fallon suggested and moved a bunch of stuff into his room—including the changing table, mini fridge, and bottle warmer. He was getting the system pretty much down pat. Bottle went in the warmer before he picked up his son and got him in a fresh diaper and cleaned up. Then he re-swaddled him like a little burrito and by that time, the bottle was the right temperature. Sitting back on the bed, he held Asher close and fed him—still in awe that this little person was his.

"You know...one of these days, you're going to feel secure enough that you'll be okay sleeping in your own room," he said softly as Asher blinked up at him. "But you have to know that I'll always be there for you. I'll never be far away. You and me? We're buddies and I'm not going anywhere. I promise."

Yawning, he got a little more comfortable against the pillows. Within a few minutes, Asher was done eating and let out a loud burp with little effort and Jamie couldn't help but chuckle.

"That's my boy."

He put the bottle and burp cloth on the nightstand, but noticed his son was still fairly wide awake. If he put him back in the stroller, it would be a recipe for disaster for sure.

"Okay, how about this—I give you this awesome pacifier and we sit here and watch a little late-night TV? What do you think?"

More blinking.

Reaching for the pacifier, he offered it to Asher, who greedily accepted it, and then Jamie picked up the remote and put the TV on low. He didn't care what they watched, just so there was a little background noise to keep him awake.

He ended up on ESPN watching some sort of baseball roundup. Sports was always something he followed, but since it was a lot of talking and commentary, it seemed like the perfect mindless solution. Soon he found himself explaining things to Asher just because, and before he knew it, his son was sound asleep.

Carefully, Jamie put the baby back in the stroller, turned off the light and the TV, and promptly fell back to sleep.

The next time he opened his eyes, it was to the feel of a soft, warm hand on his shoulder.

"Jamie?" someone whispered, and he was certain he was still sleeping.

Covering that soft hand with his own, he let out a low hum. It felt like a lifetime since a woman touched him and he wanted to savor this moment. With a slight tug, he felt her fall onto the bed. His back was to her, but that was about to be rectified. Still holding her hand, he rolled over and...

"*Fallon!* What the hell are you doing in my bed?" he cried, practically jumping to put some distance between them and dropping her hand as if she'd burned him.

"I came in to wake you up since you clearly overslept and you pulled me onto the bed, you jerk!"

"I...what?" Looking around frantically, he saw it was eight o'clock. Heedless of wearing only a pair of boxer briefs, he sprang from the bed and instantly looked at Asher who was...sleeping.

Now he knew he had to be dreaming.

If Asher was asleep, that meant...

Fallon was standing beside him and eyeing him like he was crazy. "I've got him," she said, averting her gaze. "Go and get ready for work."

"No...I just need to..." Carefully, he put his hand on his son to make sure he was okay and then nearly sagged to the floor with relief.

"Uh...Jamie?"

He looked up at her and almost cried. "Four hours. He slept for *four* hours! Do you know what this means?"

"Um..."

"It's happening!" he said happily. "He's starting to feel comfortable enough with me to sleep!" Then, without even thinking about it, he hauled her into his arms and hugged her. "Thank you! I didn't think anything was going to work, but I did everything like you said and...and...he slept! You're amazing!"

He moved to kiss her cheek at the same time Fallon turned her head to look at him, and his lips landed on hers. And for a moment, neither moved.

Maybe it was sleep deprivation or maybe he'd simply lost his mind, but Jamie's hands slowly smoothed down her back as he let his lips simply linger on hers before placing a genuine, soft kiss there. When he pulled back, her eyes were still closed and she was completely still.

And he had no idea how to explain himself. Obviously, he hadn't meant to kiss her. That would just be insane. Fallon wasn't someone he ever wanted to kiss or even thought about kissing, so...

Okay, then why did I kiss her?

He watched in fascination as her eyes opened and she slowly licked her lips. Their gazes locked and held, and he waited for her to either mock him or tell him off.

"Like I said," she began, "I've got Asher. I'll take the stroller out to the living room so you can get ready for work." And then she did just that, closing the bedroom door behind her.

"Denial works," he murmured and finally realized that not only had he kissed her, but he'd done it in his underwear and was currently sporting a hard on.

Groaning, he did his best not to think about that and quickly gathered some clean clothes and got ready for work.

He preferred getting to the pub before anyone else, but he had a feeling his uncle was going to be there before him again. For the last several days, he'd simply let Ronan believe he was exhausted because he had spent the night with a woman, but he felt guilty lying to him. His parents were already on their cruise, so it wasn't like anyone could call them, so maybe...

No, definitely. Today he would *definitely* tell him what was going on.

Decision made, he got dressed and walked out to the kitchen where he found Fallon cleaning up his dinner dishes from last night. "You know you don't have to do that," he reminded her as he walked over to pick up his sneakers.

"It's not a big deal." Her back was to him as she continued to put dishes in the dishwasher and scrub the sink. "So what time did you put Asher down last night the first time?"

"Oh, um...it was around eight, but then he was up at 9:30 and was really fussy until eleven." He tied his sneakers. "Then he went down for two hours and I gave him a bottle but he didn't seem to want it and we hung out in the living room for a while until I couldn't keep my eyes open. Then we went into my room and I tried to feed him the rest of the bottle he wouldn't finish, but he wasn't having any of it."

Now she did turn and look at him. "Did you read to him before you put him down at eight?"

"No, but..."

"Did you dim the lights like we talked about?"

"No, but..."

"Did you rock him while he had his pacifier?"

"I couldn't find it at that point, but..."

"Jamie!" she cried. "You have got to start taking his routine seriously. You're torturing both of you out of sheer stubbornness!"

"Yeah, but...that last feeding when he went down, he slept for four hours! And I did all the stuff you said!"

"Exactly! And it worked! Imagine if you listened to all the other stuff I suggested!"

Getting to his feet, he gave her a lopsided grin. "I promise I'll try it tonight. I've just been so tired and it's hard to remember all the instructions. Cut me some slack."

Rolling her eyes, she went back to wiping down the counters. Asher let out a small cry and Jamie walked over and lifted him out of the stroller.

"Hey, buddy," he said softly, cradling him to his chest. "I've got to go to work, but Aunt Fallon's here to take care of you today. Make sure she sticks to her schedule and if she doesn't, I want you to tell me, okay?"

He caught her second eye roll and smiled.

"You're ridiculous," she told him, taking Asher from his arms. "Go. We'll see you later."

He leaned in to kiss Asher and he saw Fallon flinch

away. "Relax," he told her. "I'm just kissing him goodbye. Like I always do."

"Yeah, well..."

There was no way he wanted to get into that whole thing now. "I'll see you later," he said and quickly made his way out the door.

Fifteen minutes later, his uncle was giving him a knowing smirk.

"You know you can't keep lighting the candle at both ends, Jamie. Maybe save your...um...extracurricular activities for the weekend, huh?"

This was his opening...

"Is anyone else in yet?" he asked.

"Nah. Bobby won't get for another hour. How come?"

Motioning to one of the booths, he walked over and sat. Ronan joined him cautiously.

"Everything okay?"

Letting out a long breath, he clasped his hands on the table and just blurted out everything that had been going on. When he was done, he finally found the courage to look up. Ronan was like a second father to him and he feared seeing the disappointment there.

"So...all this week, you've been dragging your ass in here after not sleeping all night? Because of the baby?"

He nodded.

"And...and...Fallon's staying with him all day?"

Another nod.

Leaning back in his seat, Ronan swiped a hand through his graying hair and let out a loud sigh of his own. "Jeez, Jamie...why didn't you say anything? We could have covered for you so you could take a few days. My God... every new parent needs some time to sort of settle in. And a single parent definitely needs that."

"I didn't want to say anything because of...well... because of what I think Jenn's planning."

"You're not going to allow her to put that baby up for adoption, are you? Jamie, think about it!"

"I won't allow that to happen. I don't care if I only get two hours of sleep a night for the next ten years; I'm keeping my son," he said fiercely. "I just...everyone's gonna look at me like I'm irresponsible. If I took time off—especially now when Mom and Dad are away—it was gonna look bad. The timing just sucked."

"Now you listen to me," his uncle said sternly. "Even married couples find themselves pregnant when they weren't planning on it. These things happen. The important thing here is that you're doing the right thing by your son. And that means taking care of yourself too. Have you talked to your siblings? Maybe one of them can sleep over and you can take turns getting up with the little guy."

He shook his head. "They were all there on Sunday and helped me so much that I didn't want to impose. They all have jobs and lives of their own. Asher is my responsibility. As it is, I'm paying Fallon what feels like a small fortune to be there during the day. I had no idea childcare was so expensive."

"Are you sure she wasn't just needling you a bit and asking for more money that she should have?" he asked with a laugh. "Because with the way the two of you are with each other..."

His mind instantly flashed to kissing her this morning and how he wanted to know what would have happened if she had kissed him back.

"Jamie?"

"Um...no. She was right on the nose with it. Ryleigh looked it up online to prove it to me."

"Speaking of Ryleigh, she's coming in today to help in the kitchen. I think you should ask her if maybe she can help out for a night or two. Her schedule's the most flexible and I'd trust her before I'd ask Patrick. His schedule's fairly flexible too, but I can't imagine him caring for a newborn."

"That makes two of us," he agreed.

"Do your parents know?"

He shook his head. "Like I said, with what Jenn was proposing and them being on their first real vacation ever, I didn't want to ruin it. I've been kind of paranoid about anyone finding out and telling them."

With a nod, Ronan hauled himself out of the booth. "I have to agree with you on that one. Let them have their vacation and then break it to them gently when they get back. If anything, your schedule will ease up at that point."

"Maybe. I had hoped they'd both start cutting back their hours because I was doing such a great job running the place. Now that's not going to happen and it's all my fault."

Reaching out, Ronan put a reassuring hand on his shoulder. "No one's going to blame you for anything. Your father isn't going to let this place go yet. He's too young. The two of you are going to have to work out a way to run it together and so you both have the time away that you need. You know if he was home right now, he would tell you to go home and be with your son."

That made him chuckle. "I don't agree with that. I think he'd tell me my hours could be flexible, but that I needed to honor my commitment to both my job and my son."

"Yeah. That does sound a little more like him."

"And Mom would either insist that I bring Asher in to work with me or she'd go over and babysit."

Laughing, Ronan said, "And she'd do it for free, so...you

have something to look forward to. You'd cut your childcare expenses almost 100%."

It was true and Jamie already considered that option, but he wasn't nearly as excited about it as he thought he'd be.

And he absolutely refused to think about why that was.

* * *

It was a little after three when there was a knock at the door. Asher was in her arms, and when she answered the door, Ryleigh was standing there. Her entire face lit up when she saw her nephew.

"Oh my goodness! I'm so glad I timed it right and he's awake!"

Fallon stepped aside and laughed as Ryleigh scooped the baby right out of her arms. "Hey! I didn't know you were stopping by today."

"It wasn't originally on my agenda. We're all trying to give my brother a little space and let him settle in, but after working at the pub today, I knew I needed to come over and talk to you."

"Uh-oh. Why? What's wrong?"

Sitting on the sofa, Ryleigh took a few minutes to coo at Asher. When she looked up at Fallon, she looked completely serene. "Can you get my phone out of my bag? I want to show you something."

"Sure." Taking the phone out, she handed it to Ryleigh, who swiped the screen a couple of times and then handed the phone back. "Um...what am I looking at?"

"You're looking at proof of how exhausted my brother is. He face-planted in the potato salad," she said with a smirk. "So naturally I took a picture and then helped him up. It's obvious that he's completely worn out. Clearly, he needs help with the overnight stuff until Asher starts sleeping a little easier."

"He would sleep easier and longer by now if your brother didn't disregard the schedule I gave him. Every time I talk to him about it, he simply rolls his eyes and tells me he knows how to handle his son. There isn't a doubt in my mind that if he had his way, poor Asher would be eating pizza crusts and french fries rather than formula."

Ryleigh didn't even try to argue or defend him.

"Okay, I get what you're saying and...you're right. But I think he's seeing the error of his ways, so...maybe you can crash here a couple of nights a week?"

"Ryleigh..." she whined.

"I know it's a bit of an imposition, but...look at this sweet baby's face," she said, pointing to Asher, who was watching them both intently. "Doesn't he deserve to feel loved and cared for?"

"Of course he does. But shouldn't that guilt trip be laid on Jamie? I do all of that for Asher all day long and then your brother comes home and drops the ball."

Although he had started to see she was right this morning.

Before the kiss.

Ugh...the kiss.

Why? *Why* would he have kissed her?

And why didn't you kiss him back?

Yeah, that had been something she'd been asking herself all day. The obvious answer was because it was Jamie. She didn't kiss Jamie. Ever. Had never even considered it. But now that he had kissed her? It was all she could think about.

Dammit.

"I hate saying it, but we all know my brother is stubborn and arrogant and clueless. He knows you're doing all the right things. He even admitted it to me after the whole potato salad incident."

"I'm already spending a lot of time here, Ryleigh. If I started spending the nights, it would be like we were living together and that's just weird."

Move in with me...

It was exactly what he'd asked of her just a few days ago and she was against it then, just like she was against it now.

But...

"It wouldn't really be like moving in and it would be a short-term thing. If you get Asher's schedule firmly in place and he starts sleeping better..."

"It will all go away once I leave and Jamie doesn't follow it. Trust me, I've thought about all of this and it wouldn't be helping either of them."

They sat in companionable silence for a minute. Ryleigh was playing with Asher's feet and talking softly to him, and that left Fallon with time to...think.

How bad would a couple of nights really be? Now that he saw her suggestions actually worked, he should be a little more willing to listen to her. Was she being spiteful just for the sake of being spiteful?

"I can practically hear you thinking from here," Ryleigh teased.

"It's hard to think about all of this and spending more time with Jamie. We've never gotten along and I fear that me being here all the time will be...tense. And that's not good for Asher either."

"Okay, how about this—I stay here with Asher for a

little while so you can go home and pack a bag. Just a small one. Enough stuff for, let's say...two nights. You can go home when he gets home from work or just leave for a couple of hours and come back later on when you know the baby's asleep. No need for the two of you to go all domestic and eat dinner and watch TV together." She shuddered dramatically. "Now that would be weird."

"You're telling me," she mumbled.

"And if things are genuinely awful, I'll get everyone together and we'll work out a schedule, so we all take a night here to give Jamie a break and so we're all not losing sleep. What do you think?"

I think I never should have answered my phone on Sunday...

"Ryleigh..." she whined, but she knew she was losing the battle with saying no. She already knew Jamie wouldn't mind since he was the one who initially asked her days ago.

"I'll bring dinner over every night so no one has to cook! And...and...I'll make sure there's always ice cream or cookies or brownies in the house for dessert! Whatever you want or need, we'll make it happen, Fallon. Please. I hate to think of this precious boy being neglected in any way. It's bad enough his mother abandoned him..."

"She said she's coming back. We need to give her the benefit of the doubt."

"Um, no. I don't. She let Jamie off the hook by not telling him what was going on and then she just comes by and leaves Asher on the porch? I mean...who does that?"

"Okay, I know it looks bad, but we don't know this girl or what her history is like. For all we know, she struggles with depression or some other mental illness. She said she was going away for a few weeks, maybe it's a rehab sort of thing."

"Oh my God! What if it's rehab for drugs? Has Jamie made any appointments with a pediatrician? Shouldn't that be something he needs to do immediately?"

Fallon gasped because Ryleigh was right. No one had thought of that.

"You're right. That is something we should have done first thing. When Jamie gets home, I'll talk to him about it. In the meantime, I'll see where the closest one is. Obviously it's been a long time since I've been to one."

"Yeah, me too."

Unable to sit still, Fallon got up and grabbed her laptop and immediately began searching.

"And where did we land on you sleeping here for a few nights?" Ryleigh asked.

"Ugh...you are relentless. You know that, right?"

"Part of my charm," her friend said with a small laugh. Standing, she snuggled Asher a little closer. "I think he definitely needs a fresh diaper so I'll go take care of that and then, when he's all clean, you can give me your answer."

Yeah, she was relentless, but Fallon was too busy researching local pediatricians and seeing who was accepting new patients. Of course, she'd need to find out what kind of insurance Jamie had and if he'd added Asher to it.

"Why is there so much to do with a new baby?"

Behind her, she heard the front door open and turned to see Jamie walking in.

"Hey, you're home early," she said before returning to her search.

"I see that my sister is here," he began cautiously. "And by now, I'm sure she told you about what happened."

Grinning, she looked at him. "That was a terrible waste of perfectly good potato salad."

"Yeah, yeah, yeah...I know. Bobby just about skinned me alive about it. I had to sit and peel five pounds of potatoes before I felt okay about leaving."

"Well, that was nice of you."

Nodding, he collapsed in one of the chairs. "Where's Ryleigh?"

"Changing Asher."

"And what are you doing?"

"Researching pediatricians."

He jumped up. "Why? Is something wrong with Asher? Is he sick? Did he get hurt?" He began frantically looking around. "Do we need to go to the ER?"

"For crying out loud, relax," she told him. "Ryleigh and I were talking and realized that was something you should have done right away. Just because Jenn said he was healthy doesn't mean you should take her word for it. Were there any medical records in the bag she left?"

"Um...no."

"Then it just makes sense to get him to a doctor to be seen. What insurance do you have? Did you add him to it?"

Muttering a curse, he sat back down. "Fallon, I haven't had time to do any of that. It didn't even cross my mind. Right now, my main goal is to sleep so I don't face plant in the deep fryer next time." He yawned loudly and that's when she knew for sure she was going to be moving in.

Temporarily.

"Well, then tonight's going to be your lucky night."

He eyed her warily. "Why?"

"Because I'm going to go home and pack a bag and... stay," she said, almost forcing the words out. "Just for a couple of nights and..."

She never got to finish. Jamie was on his feet and hugging her for the second time that day.

"Thank you," he said softly. "Seriously, thank you."

Unable to help it, she hugged him back. "You're welcome."

Now she just had to hope she wasn't making an awkward situation even worse.

Chapter Six

He couldn't sleep.

How was that for bizarre?

After face-planting in a bin of potato salad and nearly falling asleep in his plate of beef stew for dinner, Fallon had told him to just go to bed. He'd helped her clean up after dinner and then she had rested her hands on his shoulders and gently turned him before her hands were on his back again to give him a playful shove toward his room.

However...

Her touch felt like it lingered.

And he was really hoping that was the case.

So this is what sleep deprivation does to you...

Honestly, it was the only thing that made sense right now. He and Fallon had grown up together and they'd obviously touched each other a hundred times—normally in the form of poking or shoving to annoy each other—and never once did Jamie ever give those touches a second thought.

Now they were all he could think about.

Turning his head, he looked at the clock and saw it was only a little after ten. He'd been in here for over two hours

88

and still hadn't fallen asleep. Knowing he was just going to frustrate himself, he kicked the blankets off and pulled on a pair of sweatpants. The rest of the house was quiet, but that didn't mean anything. If Asher was awake, he wanted to see him.

When he stepped out of his bedroom, he saw that there was only one small lamp on in the living room; the rest of the house was dark. However, down the hall, he saw a sliver of light coming from Asher's room. Slowly, he made his way there and paused outside the door when he heard Fallon's soft voice.

"And then, the itty-bitty puppy and the teeny-tiny kitten became best friends. The end." She paused. "Maybe someday, when you're a little older, you and your daddy can adopt a puppy or a kitten. Wouldn't that be fun, Asher?"

She hummed and was whispering something to him that Jamie couldn't hear, but he desperately wanted to.

"Okay, sweet boy. Let's get all snuggly in your bed...and watch the little sheep float around on your mobile."

He could hear the music coming from the mobile and then Fallon humming softly along with it.

"Sweet dreams, Asher," she whispered, and he held his breath because normally when he put his son down in his crib, he never went peacefully. That's why he ended up with the stroller in his bedroom. But there didn't seem to be a peep coming.

It was completely peaceful until...

"*Gah!* Holy crap, Jamie!" she hissed as she stepped out of the bedroom. "What the heck are you doing? I thought you were asleep!" With the baby monitor in her hands, she shushed him before he could respond and headed to the living room. Then she rounded on him. "Why are you still awake?"

"Because I haven't gone to bed at 8:00 since I was ten years old. It felt weird."

"So? You should have turned on the TV or something instead of sneaking around trying to scare me."

"It wasn't like I purposely tried to do that," he argued. "I really just thought I'd say goodnight to Asher again, that's all."

"Oh...well...sorry. He was pretty much asleep before the sheep made their first go-round."

"Really?"

She nodded. "He was yawning while we were reading and sucking away on the pacifier, but by the end of the book, it was just about to fall out of his little mouth. He's so darn cute."

"That's because he looks like me." The words were out before he even realized it, and she groaned.

"Wow, way to ruin a moment." Walking to the kitchen, she said, "I'm going to make a cup of tea. Do you want one?"

"Tea? Do I even have tea in the house?"

"I brought it with me. It helps me unwind at the end of the day. Would you like one or not?"

There was that snap in her voice that he was so familiar with, but he didn't feel like snapping back. "Yeah, sure. Why not? Maybe it will help."

"Go and sit on the couch or something and I'll make them," she told him and began pulling mugs down and putting water in the teakettle.

"You know you can just use the Keurig, right? It's a lot faster."

"It is, but sometimes you still get the taste of the coffee and it ruins it. This is fine. Go and relax. I've got this."

The thing was, Jamie wasn't used to someone waiting on

him like this. He lived alone and did everything for himself. Even when they went to his parents' place for Sunday dinners, everyone helped. His mother didn't believe in being forced into being the only one working in the kitchen. He'd been living on his own since he was eighteen and it just felt weird to have someone in his home doing stuff for him.

In the last week, Fallon had washed his clothes, cleaned the house, and taken care of his son. And what had he done for her? Given her grief and forced her to work longer hours than she originally agreed to.

I'm the worst...

Five minutes later, she was handing him a cup of tea and sitting on the opposite end of the sofa. The room was dimly lit and it felt oddly intimate.

Well, that and the fact that he was wearing nothing but a pair of sweatpants, and she was wearing some sort of cotton dress or gown with thin little straps. Her feet were bare, her hair was loose, and she looked incredibly soft and feminine.

Two words he'd never associated with her until right this moment.

"So, you never told me how things went with Ronan today. Did you tell him about Asher?"

Nodding, he said, "I did, and he was incredibly understanding. He wants me to take a little more time off, but...I don't know. It doesn't feel right, but at the same time, I feel like it's what I'm supposed to do. I swear I'm not normally this confused."

"To be fair, it's been a wildly unusual week," she reasoned before taking a sip of her tea.

That was putting it mildly, he thought. Between suddenly becoming a father and then finding himself attracted to Fallon, Jamie felt like he'd stepped into some kind of parallel universe.

Or the Twilight Zone.

They sat in companionable silence for several minutes before Jamie remembered something from earlier. "Did you say you had found a pediatrician?"

Nodding, she cradled her mug in her hands as she tucked her feet up under her. "I did. They're both accepting new patients, but I wanted you to check them out before I called and made an appointment."

"You don't have to be the one to call. Asher's my responsibility and I'm going to have to figure out how to do all this stuff eventually."

She studied him. "You keep telling me I don't have to do stuff, but I know you need the help. I'm happy to do it."

All he could do was nod.

"Can I ask you something?"

He nodded again.

"What are you going to do when Jenn comes back? I mean...I'm hoping you're not even considering adoption..."

"I'm not."

She seemed to visibly relax. "So then...what? Are you going to co-parent with her? Or maybe...like...get back together with her?"

"Definitely not getting back together," he said firmly. "Jenn and I...we weren't a good fit and only dated for a like a month."

"That's a record for you, right?"

Frowning, Jamie fought the urge to say something sarcastic, but...she was right. Instead, he shrugged. "It's about the average. But...I knew after the first few dates that we were all wrong for each other. She's the first person I ever dated, though, that simply wouldn't let me break up with her. So really, that's on me. Maybe if I had been the kind of guy who didn't care about hurting someone's feelings..."

"You wouldn't have Asher," she said quietly.

And that's when it hit him.

He wouldn't have Asher, and just the thought of that caused his heart to squeeze hard in his chest.

"It's been less than a week and I already can't imagine life without him," he told her with a small laugh. "Crazy, right?"

"Not really. I think that's what it's like to be a parent. Or what it should be like. There's a connection there that's incredibly strong." She paused. "Could you imagine giving him up? Even temporarily?"

He wasn't an idiot. He knew what she was implying and shook his head. "I couldn't. Even when I was terrified when I first found him on the porch...no, wait. That's a lie. For a minute, I wanted to chase the car down that dropped him off and make them take him back. But that was before I held him, before he wrapped his little fingers around one of mine. I swear, Fallon, he looked me in the eye, and I just...I knew. That whole day was so chaotic and I probably let my sisters do far more for him than I should have, but...each day I just feel like I love him so damn much."

Her smile was beautifully serene and he saw tears in her eyes.

"What?" he asked quietly. "Why are you crying?"

"Because you're amazing," she admitted. "I was so nervous when I showed up here on Sunday and found out the baby was yours. But sitting here and listening to you... I'm blown away by you, Jamie. Seriously, seriously impressed."

Her honesty humbled him and, putting his mug down

on the coffee table, he moved a little closer. "I feel like I should say something profound here, but...I can't. It all just happened organically and even now, knowing he's in the next room, I want to go and see him and touch him and... and...make sure he's okay."

Fallon mimicked his move and put her own mug down, inching closer until they were both in the center of the couch. She took one of his hands in both of hers. "That is exactly what you're supposed to want to do. I know it's been rough because you're so tired, but the fact that you're thinking of him and worrying about him tells me you're going to be okay. You're going to be a terrific father." She smiled again and he felt it almost as strongly as he did just thinking about his son. "But you really need to remember to take care of yourself. And that means getting a good night's sleep." Squeezing his hands, she added, "Take the tea inside with you, crawl into bed, turn on the TV, and just relax. You'll feel a million times better tomorrow, I promise."

That all sounded good, but...there was something he wanted that would make him feel a million times better right now.

And if she got pissed at him, he'd simply blame it on lack of sleep.

But he seriously hoped she didn't get pissed.

"There's something else I need first," he whispered, moving just a tiny bit closer.

Her eyes seemed to fixate on his mouth and he took that as a good sign.

Slowly, he pulled his hand from hers and reached up to gently caress her throat before wrapping around her nape and drawing her closer.

And then, he kissed her.

* * *

Fallon swore if Jamie tried to kiss her again that she wouldn't freeze up. She'd give in and kiss him back and just go with it.

She just hadn't expected him to try again so soon.

Not that she was sorry, but...she felt a little vulnerable sitting with him in the dimly lit room when both of them weren't wearing much clothes. It felt a little scandalous but...incredible. Not that she was a prude, but to think that someone like Jamie wanted to kiss her was slightly thrilling.

That was something she'd examine at a later date. For now, she wanted to memorize how soft his lips were, how warm his hand was, and how good he smelled. Reaching up, she cupped his jaw and loved how scratchy it felt. They both inched even closer, and soft, teasing kisses turned a little more urgent.

Fallon felt his tongue gently touch hers, and that was all it took to angle her head and let him take the kiss as deep as he wanted. It had been so long since she'd been kissed and she knew no man had ever been as masterful at it as Jamie was. It was like he knew exactly what to do and how to tease and torment in the most delicious ways. She crowded even closer as her hands moved from his jaw, down over his shoulders and then to his chest. He was so warm and hard, and she wanted to run her hands over every inch of him.

That would be wrong, wouldn't it?

In that moment, she didn't care how right or wrong it was; it was what she wanted.

Jamie must have felt the same way because his hands lowered to her waist and maneuvered her until she was straddling his lap.

And boy oh boy, did that feel incredible.

Her breasts pressed against his chest, his hands were gently kneading her bottom, and the kiss just kept going on and on and on.

In her mind, he was going to lift her up and carry her to bed. No man had ever done such a thing with her, but right now she could envision it so clearly in her mind that she was practically willing it to happen. She felt bold—brazen—as she moved against him, and when they broke apart, he trailed kisses along her jaw and throat.

"Yes...that feels amazing...so good..." she whispered breathlessly.

Her hands smoothed back up his body and raked through his hair. She'd always thought Jamie had the greatest hair she'd ever seen on a guy and to be able to touch it felt a little decadent.

Whispering his name—panting it, really—Fallon hoped he could read her mind. His movements slowed a little and she took it to mean he was savoring what he was doing, but then...he stopped.

What the...?

And that's when she heard it.

A snore.

Pulling back, she stared down and noticed his head was thrown back against the cushions, his eyes were closed, and he was most definitely asleep.

Right then and there, it was hard to say which emotion was stronger—rage or mortification.

Mortification, she thought, as she carefully climbed off of him.

There was no way she could move him to his room, so she took a solid minute to compose herself—glaring at him the entire time—and then picked up their mugs and put

Charm Me

them in the dishwasher. Walking back over to him, she tried to wake him, but he was out cold.

The only thing she could do was awkwardly guide him into a better position on the sofa and cover him with a blanket.

And pray that she didn't have to face him in the morning.

* * *

Luck was on her side the next morning and she was just coming out of the room with Asher as Jamie was putting his shoes on to leave.

"Hey," he said, looking a little guarded. "How did he do last night?"

"Great. He slept for a little over four hours the first time. When he woke up around three, I kept the room dim and spoke softly to him so he would know it wasn't time to really be awake. I changed him and had his bottle ready and he was back to sleep by 3:30 and then just woke up a few minutes ago. So hopefully he'll stay on this four-to-four-and-a-half-hour schedule for a bit and then move on to a five-hour stretch."

The entire time she spoke, she was in motion—putting Asher in his bouncy seat, grabbing a bottle from the fridge, and putting a coffee pod in the Keurig for herself. She didn't want to look directly at him because she was incredibly embarrassed that she wasn't appealing enough to keep a guy awake while they were making out.

Ugh...making out. Do adults still call it that?

When she had no choice but to turn around, he was talking to Asher and being a little silly and that helped her not want to strangle him and tell him off for still crushing her self-esteem without using his words.

"Aren't you going to be late?" she asked, hoping to nudge him out the door, and that was her downfall. He knew what she was doing and now he was going to want to talk about it.

And Fallon knew she couldn't let that happen.

"I'm sorry about last night," he finally said.

She looked at him oddly. "What do you mean?" Because, yeah, there was no way she wanted to discuss this, so she was just going to pretend it never happened.

"What do you mean, what do I mean? Last night? On the couch? We were...you know...kissing and I fell asleep?"

Frowning, she turned and walked over to the fridge to get some cream for her coffee. "Jamie, I think you must have been dreaming. We sat on the couch and talked for a little while, and you fell asleep mid-sentence." Looking at him, she shrugged. "It wasn't a big deal. I'm just sorry you had to sleep on the couch all night. I couldn't get you to wake up, so I grabbed a blanket for you and went to bed."

His dark eyes narrowed. "Wait...no. No, we talked, but then we kissed. I distinctly remember that. We were in the middle of the couch and I pulled you into my lap and..."

"Sorry, dude. That never happened. I think you were just overtired and maybe imagining things." She finished fixing her coffee and heating Asher's bottle. She moved both to the coffee table in the living room before picking Asher back up and taking him over to the sofa. "Hey, sweet boy. Who's ready for breakfast?"

Out of the corner of her eye, she saw Jamie still standing in the kitchen, looking thoroughly confused. Part of her felt bad for lying to him, but there was no way she could handle the embarrassment of talking about how unappealing she was.

I literally put men to sleep. Awesome.

"I guess I'm gonna go then," he said, scrubbing a hand along the back of his neck. "You're staying tonight, right?"

"Mm-hmm...but I have plans to meet up with some friends for dinner, so..." She shifted Asher slightly in her arms. "I'll be back by ten to put him to sleep so you don't have to worry."

"I wasn't worried," he countered. "I just, uh...I didn't know you had plans tonight."

"Well, I didn't realize I was going to be staying here when I made them. It will be fine. No worries. Have a good day."

Luckily he took the hint and finally left.

The day was fairly uneventful and when Jamie walked in the door at five, Fallon had everything set out for him that he should need. Asher had bottles ready, she had laid out pajamas for the baby, and even set up his bath supplies in the bathroom for them.

"I'll be back by ten, but if you see that he's getting sleepy, take him into his room and make sure the lights are dim and talk to him softly and read him a story. The rocking chair is super comfy and he seems to like when we sit in it. But most importantly, don't tense up when you put him in the crib. He can sense that."

All Jamie did was nod.

"Okay, then. I'll see you later!" With a wave, she walked out the door and made her way to her car.

And drove directly to her parents' house because she had nowhere to go.

She'd made a few calls during the day, but no one was available to hang out and it seemed like too much of an effort to keep trying. Now she was going to call for some Chinese takeout, watch a little TV and enjoy the alone time, and possibly do a little job hunting. That had been put on the back-burner this last week, but it was something she couldn't keep putting off. In two weeks, Jamie wasn't going to need her anymore and she wanted to at least try to look like a responsible adult by the time her parents got home from their trip. There were two packages waiting for her on the front porch and she knew they were a couple of the self-help books she ordered online.

"Yippee..." she murmured, as she opened them up and then promptly tossed them aside. "So not in the mood to read these right now."

So...she ate some dumplings and egg drop soup, watched a couple of episodes of *Gilmore Girls*, and then applied for two positions that sort of fit her field. The first was an education consultant and the other was for a part-time position as an early childhood education coach. Neither one thrilled her, but she knew she needed to start somewhere.

By 9:30, she had everything cleaned up and put away and had taken the trash out. Getting back in her car felt like she was driving herself to her own execution. The last thing she wanted was another late-night encounter with Jamie. With any luck, he would still be tired and looking forward to going to sleep.

She could only hope.

The drive back was short, and most of the lights in the house were out when she pulled up. Relaxing, she grabbed her purse and quietly let herself in. She didn't see Jamie in the living room, and when she walked to Asher's room, she found the two of them sitting in the rocking chair reading a story. The sight was so damn sweet that she felt herself tearing up again. Jamie gave her a small smile but never stopped reading. So rather than intrude and risk startling the baby, Fallon went out to the kitchen and made herself a cup of tea.

Everything was clean and wiped down. She checked the refrigerator and saw that Jamie had made a few more bottles of formula, and then checked the laundry room and saw that he had done a small load of Asher's clothes.

Okay, maybe I won't have to stay overnight beyond tonight...

Honestly, it looked like he was getting the hang of things on his own and that he was finally taking her advice. With any luck, they could finish out the next two weeks with their original schedule.

Back out in the kitchen, she took her steaming mug and sat down at the table with a sigh.

"Rough night?" Jamie asked as he walked into the room.

"What?"

"You sighed. I thought maybe something happened tonight."

"Oh, uh...no. Nothing exciting. I guess I'm just tired. I'm not used to getting up during the night either."

"Damn," he murmured, pulling out the chair beside her and sitting. "I guess I hadn't thought about that."

"It's okay. I'll sleep at home tomorrow night and get caught up on it. And I think you and Asher should be fine going into next week so we can go back to our original plan."

"You think?"

"Jamie...you got him to sleep in his crib, right?"

He nodded.

"And we'll see how long he stays asleep tonight, but I don't see any reason he won't stick to the four-hour schedule. You'll be able to handle that fine without me here."

He didn't look convinced, but he also looked like he had something to say.

Something she wasn't willing to take a chance on listening to because she had a feeling it had to do with last night again.

"So, um...I'm going to go to sleep," she said. "You know, all the books say to sleep when the baby does."

"Before you go," he began, and Fallon wanted to curse. "Everyone's coming over tomorrow night for dinner and I thought you'd like to join us." Pausing, he stood when she did. "I mean, you don't have to, but since your folks are out of town, we thought we'd all try to hang out again. Only this time no one will have to be doing baby shopping or organizing my house." He gave her that boyish grin of his. "We're going to barbecue so it's nothing fancy, but...I hope you'll join us."

After her pitiful night, she definitely wouldn't mind hanging out with friends. And with so many Donovans, she knew she would have plenty of distractions and other people to talk to.

"You know what? Sure. That sounds like fun. Is there anything I should make?"

He shook his head. "Nope. We've got it all under control."

"I kind of feel like I need to contribute something."

"You're going to be here taking care of Asher before everyone gets here. I've got to go into the pub in the morning, but I'll be back by two and everyone's coming around three."

She nodded and then forced herself to yawn. "Sounds good." Taking a step back and then another, she said, "Welp...goodnight."

"Hey, uh...Fallon?" He took one step toward her and then hesitated.

"Hmm?"

"Look, I feel like I need to apologize again."

"What for?"

"I know that we didn't kiss—at least according to you—but it was rude of me to fall asleep while we were in the middle of talking last night. You were probably telling me something important and I couldn't even stay awake to hear it. So...I'm sorry."

Just take the apology and go to bed...

"It's fine, Jamie. Really. No big deal. I'll see you in the morning."

"Goodnight, Fallon."

With a small smile, she turned and walked to Asher's room and grabbed her things and went into the bathroom to get ready for bed. And by the time she crawled under the blankets, she was confident she had convinced Jamie that he had imagined the whole kissing thing.

Plus, she had gotten an apology and that went a long way in making her feel better about the whole thing. So basically, she was counting it all as a win and managed to sleep like a baby.

Well...for four hours until Asher woke up.

Chapter Seven

Everyone was talking and laughing and having a great time, and Jamie felt like Asher finally made him look like an equal in his siblings' eyes. This was the first time he had offered to host anything, and it turned out that it was kind of nice to have everyone over when there wasn't some sort of crisis.

Liam was manning the grill while talking to Will and Patrick, Arianna and Tessa were playing with Asher and chatting with Fallon, and he was in the kitchen with Ryleigh.

"So? How's everything going?" she asked as she tossed a pasta salad.

"I don't think I'd call it calm around here yet, but things are definitely improving."

"I'm sure having Fallon here overnight helped."

"You have no idea," he said as he pulled some potato salad and coleslaw out of the fridge. "I really thought she was crazy with some of her suggestions, but every single one of them worked and I think I'm feeling more confident as a parent because of it."

She nodded. "Yeah, Fallon is awesome. I knew she'd be the right person to help you out."

"Go figure, right?" he said with amusement. "If anyone would have told me that my nemesis would turn into my savior, I would have said they were crazy."

"Jamie, nemesis? Really? Isn't that a bit dramatic?"

"What? It's the truth! That's how we always treated each other."

Shrugging, Ryleigh walked over and washed her hands before tackling the fruit salad. "I still think it sounds ridiculous, but if the two of you have called a truce, then I'm happy."

"We've definitely called a truce." He paused and looked out to the deck where Fallon was sitting with Asher in her lap, and he couldn't help but smile. She was a natural with his son, and that made him like her even more.

"Any word from Jenn?"

"What? Oh, um...no. But I haven't tried calling her either. I'm trying to respect her wishes from the letter. Plus, I don't know that I'm going to be able to stay calm when I talk to her. After all, she's turned our lives upside down. And what kind of person just dumps a baby like that?"

"Again, dramatic," she said with a sigh. "She didn't dump him on the side of the road. She left him here with his father."

"She left him on my porch."

Shrugging, Ryleigh picked up the melon baller and went to work on a cantaloupe. "You have every right to be pissed, but she's Asher's mom and she's going to be in your life, no matter what."

He sighed loudly. "Yeah. I know. And I hate that he's getting stuck with a mom who didn't want him."

"Okay, whew!"

Frowning, he looked at his sister like she were crazy. "Whew? Whew, what?"

"That tells me you're not going to get back together with her and do something stupid like marry her. I mean...I get that all kids benefit from having two parents, but I'd hate to think of you getting back together with this girl. You deserve to be happy."

"It's crazy, and...I know it's only been a week, but I can't imagine bringing a girl home here anymore. I don't want to have some...you know...*fling* hanging out here with him."

"Maybe you should just stop having *flings* and find someone to settle down with," she said firmly. "Seriously, Jamie, you have a son now. Playtime is over. I know you'd be fine as a single dad, but...after having Fallon here with you, don't you think it would be better to have something like that?"

"So...what...now you want me to *marry* Fallon?" he asked incredulously.

Much to his surprise, his sister burst out laughing. "Oh my God! That's not what I said at all! But I kind of love how your mind went there right away! That's awesome!" Dropping the melon baller, she doubled over with laughter.

"It wasn't that funny..."

"What wasn't so funny?" Fallon asked as she walked into the kitchen.

"Where's Asher?" he asked.

"Arianna's got him in the stroller in the shade. He was starting to doze. I just wanted to come in and get something to drink." She looked over at Ryleigh who was starting to compose herself. "So? What are the two of you joking around about?"

There was no way he wanted Fallon to know that, and fortunately, Ryleigh figured that out.

"Jamie's just being his usual juvenile self," she said, waving her off. "No big deal."

"Oh." She walked over to the kitchen island and saw all the salads. "Ooh...is that tortellini salad?"

"Yup," Ryleigh said proudly. "I do it with a lemon pesto vinaigrette. Here, try it." She grabbed a fork and put some on it before handing it to Fallon.

Jamie watched as she tasted it and was almost fascinated as she licked her lips.

What is wrong with me?

"Mmm...Ryleigh! Oh my goodness, that is *amazing*! It's so good!" Then she grabbed herself a bottle of water and walked back out to the yard.

But Jamie was frozen in his spot. It was like an overwhelming sense of déjà vu. He'd heard her say something like that just recently, hadn't he? When was that?

Yes...that feels amazing...so good...

He could hear it clear as day in his head. Her voice was a little breathless and...when would she have said something like that to him?

Yes...that feels amazing...so good...

And then it hit him.

Holy.

Shit.

It wasn't a dream or his imagination. They *did* kiss the other night on the couch! He knew it! It was far too vivid to just be a dream, so...why would she lie to him about it?

And that's when the rest of it hit.

He'd fallen asleep in the middle of it.

Not in the middle of a conversation, but in the middle of a really sexy encounter on his damn sofa. No wonder she lied to him. She must think he's the worst human being on the planet.

God, maybe I really am the worst...

Suddenly, he wished everyone would leave because he needed to talk to Fallon alone. Needed to apologize again and make her see that he really wasn't such a bad guy and tell her how much he'd like a second chance to...

To what?

There was no way he could have a fling with Fallon.

Could he?

"Dude, what's wrong with you?" Ryleigh said, snapping him out of his thoughts.

"What?"

"Your face is all scrunchy and you haven't moved or blinked for a solid minute. You're freaking me out."

That makes two of us...

"Sorry," he mumbled. "My mind just wandered for a moment."

"Wandered or shut down?" she teased. "So...what were we talking about? Oh, yeah. You settling down with someone now that you have a baby."

"Ry, come on. It's been a week. Do I have to have the rest of my life planned out? My main focus right now is on Asher and taking care of him."

"And I get that, but you've only got two weeks before Jenn comes back and you lose Fallon."

"I'm not *losing* Fallon," he denied hotly. "She was never mine! You can't lose someone you never had!"

By the look on his sister's face, he knew he screwed up. Carefully, she walked around the island until she was standing in front of him.

"Okay, now we're getting somewhere," she said, glancing over his shoulder toward the deck. "Look, the food's all going to be done cooking and everyone's going to be coming inside any minute, so talk and talk fast."

He'd rather have a root canal with no anesthesia, but he knew Ryleigh would just dog him all freaking day long if he didn't tell her what was going on.

So he did.

All of it.

The kissing and the falling asleep.

"Oh, Jamie..." she groaned before smacking him upside the head. "What is wrong with you? Why would you do something like that?"

"I don't know! Everything's weird right now!" he said defensively, raking his hand through his hair. "This is the longest we've ever gone without...you know...fighting, and once that was off the table, I just sort of...saw her differently. It's not a big deal."

She didn't respond right away, but she was studying him with a small smile.

"What? Why are you looking at me like that?"

"As much as I'd love to torture you a bit and drag this out, the truth is...I think you've always been a little into her."

"What?! You're crazy..."

"Do you remember the day of the opening? You know, Ryker's grand opening celebration for the tattoo parlor?"

He nodded.

"When Fallon was leaving, she kissed you on the cheek —presumably to annoy you—and you totally blushed. It was kind of adorable."

"I don't blush," he countered. "And everything I do, women find adorable, so...you're just...you're wrong."

She shrugged. "Ask Ari. She'll tell you she saw it too. We all did and I can guarantee you if we put it out there to the group, it probably wasn't the first time someone caught you reacting like that to her."

"Who's reacting to who?" Patrick asked as he came in and grabbed a beer.

Great...more witnesses...

Ryleigh gave him a smug smile before looking at Patrick. "Okay, so with no context, what are your thoughts on Fallon being here to help Jamie?"

He took a pull of his beer and then shrugged. "It makes sense, but I was a little concerned about how our resident Romeo was going to handle having the girl he's been secretly pining for living under his roof."

"I knew it!" Ryleigh cried triumphantly.

"What?!" Jamie snapped again. "What are you talking about? No one's pining for anyone!"

"Jamie, please! Everyone sees it! You go out of your way to poke at her—no pun intended—and you watch her all the damn time when she's around." Another shrug. "It's been fun to watch."

"You're both wrong," he huffed. "There's no pining, no watching, no nothing."

"Interesting," Patrick commented. "You're defensive and protesting just a little too much..." Then he laughed. "Besides, what's the big deal? Fallon's an attractive woman." Pausing, he frowned, and Jamie knew whatever came out of his brother's mouth next wasn't going to be complimentary. "Although...maybe this wasn't a good thing."

Groaning, Jamie didn't even ask why.

"Because he's going to hit on her and make things awkward forever, right?" Ryleigh asked and naturally, Patrick agreed.

"To be fair, he's been making things awkward with the Murphys since he was five, so that's not anything new. But if he sleeps with her..."

"Like you know he's dying to..."

"And then breaks things off after she took such good care of Asher..."

"He's going to look like an even bigger jerk. Damn, this does not end well." Ryleigh gave him the side-eye. "Why can't you just be a normal guy like Patrick and Liam? They know how to behave themselves."

He was just about to explode on them when Liam walked in with a platter of food. "Dinner is served!" he called out, and soon everyone was following him in.

Except Fallon.

She was still out in the yard with Asher, but he could tell she was trying to decide whether or not she should bring him inside.

Without even looking at any of his siblings, he walked out to the yard and over to her. "Hey," said casually. "Is he asleep?"

"He is," she replied. "I know we're all going to be scattered around between eating inside and out here, but I'm not sure if I should let him be right here in the shade or move the stroller into the house."

She had placed one of those mesh covers over the stroller to keep bugs away and the yard was completely fenced, so it wasn't like anyone was going to get back here that shouldn't be. "Why don't you go and get something to eat and I'll stay here with him?"

Fallon glanced toward the house. "Are you sure? I don't mind waiting while you get your food first. Or...you can go and make plates for both of us while I stay here?"

"Are you sure? I can..."

"Jamie," she interrupted with a soft laugh. "I'd love a burger and some of the tortellini salad. Oh! And some of the fruit salad please."

"You got it." And damn if he didn't almost lean in and kiss her. Clearing his throat, he said, "I'll be right back."

When he stepped back into the house, everyone was watching him with knowing looks.

"I'm screwed, aren't I?"

And, as expected, they all nodded.

* * *

Liam and Tessa were the last ones to leave, and it was after nine when that happened. The entire day was so much fun and Fallon couldn't remember the last time she'd laughed so much or felt so relaxed. She'd always loved the time her family spent with the Donovans, and it was nice that it was still like that even when their parents weren't there to orchestrate the get-together.

Everything was mostly cleaned and put away, but she couldn't help but walk around putting everything back in its place. Then she prepared bottles since tomorrow was her day off. It was important for Jamie to have a day at home alone with Asher, but Fallon still wanted to help make things easier for him.

Or am I just lingering because I don't want to go?

Yeah, there was that.

Today had been...pleasant, and there were several times when it felt like she and Jamie were a couple and Asher was their baby.

Which was just crazy.

Only...she was quickly beginning to wrap herself in that little fantasy with little to no prompting.

Which was even crazier.

She was practical, a planner, an overthinker. She didn't

do anything spontaneous, and she certainly was never prone to envision her life with any kind of whimsy.

Maybe her sudden fascination with Jamie was more about how much she was falling in love with Asher. That little boy had stolen her heart from the first moment she held him. And spending so much time with him and learning his little quirks and likes and dislikes had her bonding faster with him than she thought possible. Almost all of her thoughts were focused on him.

Liar...

Okay, fine. They were focused on the baby *and* his father.

So where did that leave her?

She was standing in the middle of the kitchen lost in her own thoughts, when Jamie came up behind her. He rested his hands briefly on her hips, which made her jump.

"Sorry," he said. "I just wanted to get by and grab a bottle. He's starting to get fussy, so I figured it was best to get prepared."

Nodding, Fallon quickly stepped aside. "Um...it looks like everything is done, so if you're good with putting him down, I'm gonna get going."

"You're leaving? I thought tonight was still...I mean...I just..."

Fallon knew what he was getting at. "Originally, I thought I'd stay and then go home tomorrow morning, but it looks like you've got it all under control and since you're off tomorrow too, it's not like you need me here."

Her heart was racing, and it felt like the room was suddenly too warm.

"It's late," he said softly, and was it her imagination or had he moved closer?

The nervous laugh was out before she could stop it. "It's not even 9:30..."

"Long day," he countered, and yes, he was definitely moving closer.

When they were practically toe to toe, she looked up at his face—his ridiculously handsome face—and swallowed hard. "I really should go..."

But he shook his head. "You really should stay."

"Jamie..." It was the weakest protest in the history of the world.

He didn't say a word, he simply took her hand and kept it in his as he warmed Asher's bottle and then walked back to the living room. Tugging her gently down on the sofa beside him, he gave her a warm smile. "Thank you."

"For what?"

"For not arguing with me. I feel like we have some things to talk about and..."

"I'd really rather not," she said nervously because—again—she knew where this was going.

At first, he didn't say anything. He picked Asher up and gave him his bottle. But as soon as the baby was settled, he looked at her. "We kissed, Fallon. Twice. And I am beyond embarrassed that I fell asleep like I did."

Sighing loudly, she forced herself to focus on Asher. "I told you, it's not a big deal."

"No, you said it wasn't a big deal that I fell asleep while we were talking," he corrected. "We both know that wasn't the case, and you have every right to be ticked off at me."

"Fine. Yes. I'm ticked off. Can I go now?"

She knew she was sounding incredibly bitchy—and a little childish—but...that was who they were. She was simply reverting to what was comfortable between them because this conversation was making her very uncomfortable.

"Come on, Fallon. I'm trying to apologize here. I really am sorry, and...I'd really like another chance."

Her eyes went wide and she was fairly certain her jaw was on the floor. "Excuse me?"

"I think we were both really into what was happening the other night and I'd like another chance to kiss you," he admitted quietly, and he looked a little like he was blushing. "My falling asleep...it had nothing to do with you. You're a beautiful, sexy woman, and you need to know that. What happened wasn't...it wasn't for any other reason except that I wanted you. I still want you. Please tell me I didn't completely blow this."

For a minute, all Fallon could do was stare.

Jamie Donovan wanted her?

He thought she was beautiful and sexy?

She was about to pinch herself to see if she was truly awake, but didn't. "Jamie...I...I don't know what to say."

"Say you'll stay." He looked down at Asher, who was almost asleep. "In about fifteen minutes, this little guy will be sound asleep and then we'll...talk."

The smile he gave her was downright lethal. No wonder the women in this town threw themselves at him.

And I'm about to be one of them.

That alone should have had her jumping up and leaving, but...she didn't.

When he said they were both really into what happened the other night, he wasn't lying. It had been playing on a constant loop in her head, no matter how much she tried to forget about it. But was this something they should do? Jamie had a reputation, one that she had always hated and disapproved of. Staying here tonight and even if all they did was kiss, it would make her a hypocrite.

It would make you human...

While she was lost in her own thoughts, he stood and took Asher to his room.

"What am I doing?" she whispered. "This isn't who I am."

True, but being who she was had done nothing for her but cost her two jobs in the last few months, so maybe she needed to stop being that person and try embracing a more laid-back version of herself.

One that meant some sexy time with an attractive man who could have his pick of any woman in town right now and yet wanted her.

It was a bit heady to think of it like that.

She just wasn't sure she was brave enough to follow through with it and have it be enough. But when she looked up and saw Jamie walking toward her, she knew she was about to find out.

"Is he asleep?" she asked.

"Went down without a peep. I think he stayed awake a lot longer today because everyone was here and didn't get to nap as long. With any luck, he'll sleep a bit longer tonight."

Fallon wasn't sure she agreed with him; right now, she kind of wished Asher was fussy so there'd be a distraction. Now that Jamie was back on the sofa with her, she knew what was coming.

And it both terrified and turned her on.

Ugh...I'm a mess.

"So," he began.

"So..."

He took her hand in his again. "Did you have a good time today?"

Nodding, she said, "Uh-huh. I always enjoy hanging out with your family."

For several minutes, they made small talk and it was so normal and yet...not.

Was he having second thoughts? Did he decide it would be a bad idea for them to kiss again?

Oh God...maybe I really am boring enough to make men fall asleep.

"Fallon?"

"Hmm?"

"Breathe."

She looked at him oddly. "What?"

"You look like you're ready to have a panic attack." He gently caressed her wrist. "If you're really this against being here, I'm not going to force you to stay. I just thought..."

"Kiss me."

She didn't have to ask twice.

Strong hands cupped her face as he dove in to a kiss that started at an eight on a scale of one to ten. He didn't have to coax anything from her. She was completely on board with skipping the slow build. In an instant, he had them back in the same position they'd ended in the other night—with Fallon straddling his lap and her hands in his hair. It was wildly passionate and she felt completely out of control, and once his hands gripped her bottom, she was more than ready to simply rub every inch of her body against his.

I shouldn't be this needy, but who knew it could feel this good?

Yeah, she sure as hell didn't.

Never had a man made her want to be reckless and so erotically bold. Maybe it was because they had known each other their whole lives that made them this comfortable, but she would have sworn it should have made things awkward.

As his tongue brazenly dueled with hers, she knew there was nothing awkward about this. She knew Jamie and he knew her and maybe all these years had been like some weird form of foreplay.

And if that were the case...yay!

He held her close and then maneuvered them again so his hands could leave her ass and move up to cup her breasts.

Tearing his mouth from hers, he gave her a wicked smile. "You are so damn sexy, Fallon." He teased her nipples and she arched against him, silently begging for more. His hands were magic, his gaze was hypnotic, and the erection she was currently grinding against was incredibly impressive.

Her eyes scanned his face in wonder. "How did this happen? How did we get here?" she murmured before leaning in and kissing him again.

She cursed her clothes and the fact that she couldn't just whip her shirt off.

Wait...why can't I?

And...deciding to embrace that laid-back version of herself, she broke the kiss and did just that. Jamie's eyes went wide at the sight of the purple lace bra she was wearing.

"If I'd known this is what you had on under here, I would have thrown everyone out of here hours ago." Then his mouth replaced his hands and she cried out at how good it felt. Even through the lace, it felt so incredibly decadent and made her feel a little naughty.

Which was a completely new sensation for her.

On and on it went until Jamie mimicked her move and took his shirt off. As soon as her hands smoothed over his chest, she knew there was no turning back. If he fell asleep right now, she'd slap his face as hard as she could to wake him up and make him keep touching her.

There was so much more that she wanted with him, and, as if reading her mind, he looked up at her. His breath was ragged as he said, "Let's move this inside."

She knew exactly what he meant and...

"Jamie, wait," she said and hoped she wasn't about to make a huge mistake. He reached up and caressed her cheek as he waited for her to explain. "This is...this is all happening a little fast."

Fallon saw him swallow hard, but he didn't argue with her.

That's when an idea came to her.

Rising, she held out a hand to him and pulled him to his feet. When they were outside Asher's room—which was also currently her room—he looked at her like she was crazy.

"Hear me out," she said softly. "I'd like nothing more than to stretch out on the bed with you and keep doing what we were doing, but I'm not sure I'm ready for more. I'm not sure that's a line we should cross."

"O-kay..."

"If we're in here, I know we're not going to go too far." It sounded ridiculous even to her own ears, but there was a sliver of truth there too. "I'm not ready for the night to end, but I'm also not ready to..."

Placing a finger over her lips, Jamie leaned in, resting his forehead against hers. "I know what you're saying, and it's totally fine." He eyed the bedroom door warily.

"No, it's weird," she said. "Totally weird. I just thought..."

Taking her hand, he led her back through the living room and right into his bedroom before facing her. "You can set the pace, Fallon. Whatever you want, that's what we'll do."

Biting her lip, she nodded. "Just...give me a minute." Walking back out to the living room, she grabbed the baby monitor and turned back to his room.

"Is it wrong that I found that incredibly sexy?" he said, waggling his eyebrows, and it was the perfect way to ease some of the tension. Fallon still couldn't believe she was just walking around his house in her jeans and a bra and nothing else, so his light comment was a great distraction.

Putting the monitor down on the bedside table, she turned to find Jamie standing right there. In the blink of an eye, they both moved and were instantly wrapped around each other, kissing. They stood like that—just kissing and touching for several minutes—before Jamie carefully maneuvered them onto his bed.

"Oh, that's so much better," she said as he moved over her and gently settled between her thighs. "And now it's perfect."

"I have to agree." His gaze was hot and intense and he dove back in for another kiss.

And true to his word, he let her set the pace, and for tonight, this was it.

Chapter Eight

The week that followed was unlike anything Jamie had ever experienced in his life.

Between the pub, Asher, and Fallon, Jamie never had a moment to himself, and it didn't bother him one bit.

Things were running smoothly at work; he implemented a new accounting program to work with their POS system, and Ryleigh made sure everything was synced up and working as it should. It made closing down at night and counting receipts much easier.

Fallon had called a pediatrician on Monday morning and they lucked out with an appointment the following day. Asher was in perfect health and was growing like he should. The doctor had told them not to be concerned by any new fussiness, as that was normal for 3-week-olds. Unfortunately, neither of them was prepared for just how fussy Asher had gotten seemingly overnight. Now they were dealing with colic, which was exhausting, but Fallon seemed to handle it better than he was.

Actually, Fallon seemed to handle a lot of things better than he was.

She had essentially moved in full-time and every night there was a lot of hot and heavy kissing and fooling around, but they hadn't gone any further than that. They were always in his bed until Asher woke up for that first bottle and then she went to sleep in the baby's room.

Meanwhile, Jamie would lie awake frustrated as hell and yet not wanting to do anything to push her for more.

Having a conscience really sucked.

But what didn't suck was how all this normal and sometimes boring lifestyle was all actually very...comforting.

He enjoyed coming home and finding Fallon and Asher there waiting for him. Sometimes he'd find them on the floor while Fallon gave his son tummy time, or they'd be in the kitchen with Fallon cooking and Asher sitting in the swing they bought a few days ago.

Either way, it was all very domesticated, and he was happier than he thought he could be.

It was Friday night, and when he walked in the door, everything was quiet. A quick look around showed that the house was immaculate, but as he stepped into the living room, he saw Fallon sitting in the oversized chair, crying.

"Hey," he said, walking over and crouching down in front of her. "What's going on? Are you okay?" Then he glanced around and saw his son dozing in his infant seat.

"I got another rejection today," she said through the tears.

Another? He didn't know she had been applying for any jobs. "Oh, man. I'm sorry." He took both her hands in his and kissed them. "What can I do?"

Shaking her head, she pulled her hands back and wiped away her tears. "There's nothing you can do. I'm clearly unlikable and no one wants to hire me." Then she looked at him. "I'm sure you're not surprised by any of that."

Pulling back, he frowned. "Why would you even say that?"

"Because we both know you thought I was a pretentious snob for going for such a high degree, and even teased me that I was spending so much time in school because I couldn't get a job." She sniffed and then pushed him aside so she could stand. "Well, you were right. I can't get a job."

"Fallon, come on. You said you weren't the right fit for the Texas job and wanted to live closer to home. You'll find something." Jamie awkwardly got to his feet and followed her into the kitchen.

"You don't get it," she said with exasperation before facing him again. "I got fired from the Texas job *and* the one in Missouri! I'm only back in Laurel Bay because no one will hire me! I'm a failure! The only thing I'm apparently qualified for is being a nanny!" Then she collapsed in one of the kitchen chairs and began crying in earnest again.

And then Asher joined in.

Jamie felt torn, but went to pick up his son to calm him first. Once he rocked him a bit and gave him his pacifier, he seemed to relax. Then he sat down next to Fallon and pushed the basket of napkins toward her.

"Okay, so those jobs weren't right for you. It's not a big deal," he reasoned. "And I realize we've kind of been dominating your time, but..."

She groaned as she snatched up a napkin. "I have plenty of time to apply for jobs, Jamie. Everything is done online and interviews can be done over the phone or via Zoom before they decide to bring you in for an in-person meeting. And so far, I've been rejected five times! Five!" she repeated for emphasis. "And they all say the same thing—I'm not a good fit! How can they know that, you ask? Well, it's because that's why I got fired from my other two positions.

123

I'm unlikable, and when they do a reference check, that's what they're told. So...basically, I'll never work anywhere because I suck."

"You don't suck, Fallon. You've just spent a lot of time in the classroom and you haven't relaxed enough yet in the workforce. You have to know that. You've got plenty of friends and people who like you..."

"You didn't," she reminded him. "You never liked me. You always used to tell me that and you have no idea how much that messed with me."

Wait...so this was all his fault?

He was about to argue that, but knew it was pointless.

Standing, he walked back over and got Asher's seat. Placing it on the floor, he put his son down and took a moment to find the right words.

"Fallon, we were kids. And before you point out how I was still saying stupid shit six months ago, who cares what I have to say? Look at my life! I work for my parents, I've never left Laurel Bay, and now I'm a single dad who has no idea where his baby's mother is! Believe me, I'm not someone you should listen to!"

And damn, did he hate to admit all of that.

Mainly because it was true.

"This persona you see," he went on, "actually hides a lot. When you're one of five kids, you need to appear confident, otherwise you get picked on."

"They all always pick on you..."

He chuckled. "That's because they're just jealous of how awesome I am." With a wink, he squeezed her hand. "I know things seem bad right now, but they're going to get better. I swear. And as for being a nanny, you're a freaking rock star at it! Think of where Asher and I would be without you! You're amazing and kind and loving and...in case I haven't mentioned it today...sexy as hell."

Rolling her eyes, she sighed his name.

"It's true. And for as much as I'm a doofus and kind of a mess, I'm not a liar. So if I say you're sexy, then it's the truth."

Standing, he looked around the kitchen. "How about I go and pick up a pizza or some Chinese food for us tonight? We'll eat in front of the TV and just relax."

"We kind of do that every night. It's not like we're doing hard labor around here," she teased.

Leaning over her until they were practically nose to nose, he said, "Sweetheart, every night that I don't get you naked in my bed is like hard labor. Or maybe it just keeps me hard."

Her mouth formed a perfect little "o" and he kissed her before straightening.

"So? Pizza or Chinese?"

Clearing her throat, Fallon wiped away the rest of her tears and stood too. "Actually, I had a fantastic dinner planned for us tonight."

"Really?"

She wouldn't look directly at him as she spoke. "I went shopping today and was going to make us some chicken marsala, mashed potatoes, and a salad. I picked up a bottle of wine and thought we could sort of have a date night."

Damn.

He wanted to kick himself for not thinking of that first. They'd been getting closer and closer, but he hadn't even thought of doing something romantic, like getting her flowers or picking up a bottle of wine for them on his way home.

This was all new to him and he'd never really had to try before, but now he was seeing how it was important.

Stepping in close, he wrapped his arms around her. "I'm sorry."

"For what?"

"You've been doing so much and I have done nothing for you." Then he kissed her, slow and sweet. "But I promise to do whatever you want later on." Another kiss. "As many times as you want."

Okay, he was practically begging for them to take things to the next level and hopefully that's what tonight's romantic dinner was supposed to lead up to.

She hummed appreciatively. "I'm going to hold you to that."

Thank God!

"Good. I want you to," he told her before kissing her again a bit more thoroughly. Behind them, Asher started to fuss again. "I've got him. You do what you need to do."

And with the divide-and-conquer approach, they broke apart. Fallon started making dinner, and Jamie fed Asher and gave him his bath. By the time he had the baby in his pajamas and placed him in his swing, Fallon was putting dinner on the table.

The table had a tablecloth on it and was set like something you'd see in a fancy restaurant, including candles.

"I felt a little silly turning off the lights," she began, "but I still wanted to use the candles."

Rather than say anything, he walked around and shut off several of the overhead lights, but left one table lamp on in the living room. The main part of the house was one big open space, so between the lamp and the candles, it was perfect.

Then, walking over to her, he kissed her softly before holding out her chair.

"You don't have to do that..."

Leaning in, he whispered, "Just say thank you. We're on a date."

Even in the candlelight, he could see her blush. "Thank you."

Moving over, he took his seat and looked at everything she had done. "It smells fantastic. Thank you for making this."

"I enjoy cooking, but it's not as much fun cooking for one person."

"You know, I help in the kitchen at the pub, and I can make a few things, but I can't say that I enjoy it. It's just something I do."

"I get that. I'm sure it becomes a chore when it's part of your job."

"Exactly." He took a bite and moaned with pleasure. "Damn, Fallon, this is delicious."

"I honestly wasn't sure what I should make, all I knew was that I didn't want it to be messy or too heavy on the garlic."

Yup, they were finally going to take things to the next level tonight.

Carefully, he glanced at his watch and saw it would be several hours before Asher went down for at least the first part of the night, and he wasn't sure how he was going to survive the wait.

So they talked about current events and little milestones she was noticing with Asher and it was like they never ran out of things to say. Could it have been like this all along if he hadn't been such a jerk all these years?

There was no way he was going to examine that too closely, because he already knew the answer.

After dinner, they cleaned up together and then watched a little TV while Asher had his bottle. By that time, Jamie was more than ready to head to bed himself, but he knew the importance of this nighttime routine.

"How about I read him his story and put him down and...you go inside and get comfortable?" he said gruffly before kissing her soundly.

Nibbling her lip, Fallon nodded before kissing Asher's cheek. Her big brown eyes looked almost sultry when she looked up at him and said, "I'll meet you in the bedroom."

"Soon."

As soon as she was out of the room, he forced himself to relax while reading about a tiny pug and his adventures with his lamb friend.

"Least sexy thing in the world," he murmured, but knew it would all be worth it in a few minutes.

* * *

Meanwhile, Fallon felt like she was dealing with her own least sexy thing in the world.

"I think I'm going to throw up."

Well, not really, but she was nervous enough that it felt a little like it.

In Jamie's en suite, she got undressed and changed into the sexy purple silk nightie she'd bought especially for tonight. It barely covered her, and she felt a little self-conscious wearing it, but she knew he was going to love it.

She'd waited a week before telling herself it was okay to sleep with him. He never rushed her or made her feel bad about going and sleeping in her own bed every night, but more than that, she found that she genuinely liked and respected him.

Which was strange after doing nothing but bickering with him for almost twenty years.

Still, she wanted this—wanted him. And from the way he touched and kissed her, she knew he wanted this too. There was no going back after tonight and she could only hope that when things ended between them—because she knew Jamie had zero interest in settling down—that they could at least hold on to the friendship they finally cultivated.

Checking her reflection one last time, she added a touch of gloss to her lips and fluffed her hair. "That's as good as you're going to get," she murmured. Turning out the light, she stepped out into the bedroom and froze.

Jamie was standing next to the bed and looked like he was ready to pounce.

"Damn, Fallon...you look so fucking sexy."

She kind of loved that he saw her that way, even if she didn't quite believe that about herself.

Slowly, she walked toward him and braced herself for what was to come.

Knowing Jamie's reputation, there wasn't a doubt in her mind that she was in over her head and she could only hope he wouldn't be disappointed.

"Hey," he said softly, his warm hands gently grasping her arms. "You're freaking out. If this isn't what you want..."

"It is," she quickly interrupted. "I'm just..."

Ugh...just say it!

"I'm afraid you're going to...you know...be disappointed," she mumbled.

"Are you freaking serious right now?" he demanded,

and if she wasn't mistaken, he sounded just a wee bit offended.

"Jamie, come on…"

This time, he wasn't gentle as he tugged her toward him. "Why would you even think such a thing? You've had me tangled up in knots for weeks, Fallon! And if you want to know the truth, probably longer than that."

"What…?"

"You intimidate the hell out of me," he admitted. "You're beautiful and sexy and so freaking smart and I'm just some loser who wasn't smart enough to get into any big colleges. I took classes at the community college because it was the only one that accepted me. So if anyone's feeling inferior here, it's me."

She fought the urge to roll her eyes. "This isn't about academics, Jamie. It's about sex! You've been with a lot of women. Everyone knows that! Meanwhile, I didn't exactly have guys knocking down my door trying to get me into bed."

"Then they were fools," he said roughly. "Once I got my head out of my ass and really looked at you, I realized how much time I wasted. We argued and teased each other for years because I was…intimidated. But as soon as we started spending time alone, I wanted you. Hell, Fallon, I think I've always wanted you."

There was a fluttering in her belly—but the good kind. Pressing herself closer to him, she let her hand move up around the back of his neck. "How about this," she began, her voice taking on a huskiness she almost didn't recognize. "Why don't we both forget about what we knew about each other before—or how we felt about each other and ourselves before—and focus on how we feel right now?"

Her breasts were aching for his touch and she was done talking.

"Because right now, I want to know more about this man standing in front of me. The one who's been kissing me and touching me and making me ache every night."

"Sweetheart, you've left me aching too."

Smiling up at him, Fallon took one step back and then another until the back of her legs hit the edge of his bed. "Then let's do something about that." Sitting down, she crooked a finger at him.

She was still a little nervous, but anticipation was the stronger feeling. Jamie whipped his shirt off and tossed it aside and she felt like she couldn't sit still—wanted to be doing something with her hands and mouth and...

"Don't you worry," he said, his voice low and rumbly, "we're about to get to the good stuff. Finally."

Then he covered her body with his, and Fallon knew this moment was worth the wait.

* * *

It was official.

She'd clearly been having sex wrong for like...ever.

What they'd just done—twice—was like sensory overload.

Obviously Jamie only had two hands, but it always felt like he was touching her everywhere at once. His hands, his mouth, his...well...everything. She was breathless and bone-less and exhausted in the best possible way.

And beside her, Jamie was still panting.

Yeah...I did that to him, she thought with a satisfied grin.

"Go ahead and gloat," he said breathlessly. "And if you need the words, you destroyed me."

Turning her head, her smile grew. "I did need to hear that."

Laughing, they rolled toward each other and quickly became a tangle of limbs as they got comfortable.

"Holy shit, Fallon, that was..."

"Everything," she told him. "That was literally everything. I never knew sex could be like that. I never knew it was so all-consuming and wild and fun and..."

"What kind of guys were you sleeping with? Sex should be all those things all the time," he explained. "Of course, it's different every time because not everyone likes the same things, but...I don't know...it should always leave you feeling good."

"It was always...you know...fine," she said lamely. "But I never had...you know...a...a, um..."

"An orgasm?"

All she could do was nod.

Hugging her tighter, she didn't even have to see his face to know he was looking smug.

"And I think I lost count," he went on. "How many did you have?"

"Shut up." He had her in too tight of a hold to smack him playfully, and he knew it.

"At last count, I thought it was four. But you know...I'm not the educated one..."

Fallon burst out laughing, and she found this was also something that made this experience so much more. They were laughing. There wasn't that awkward rolling over and going to sleep because there wasn't much to say. This was so much more than she ever let herself imagine.

"Who cares about being educated?" she said to him after a moment. "You more than make up for it in so many other ways." Snuggling closer, she kissed his chest. "And I believe you taught me several things tonight."

"Oh, yeah? Like what?" he teased.

"Like how many erogenous zones there really are."

"I love how sensitive you are," he replied as his hands started to roam again.

"And how sexy some good dirty talk can be."

"You shocked me a time or two." Loosening his hold, Jamie moved down and began kissing her breasts.

"But more than anything," she said as her breath grew ragged, "you taught me how much I love having your mouth on me."

"That's good, because you're fucking delicious, Fallon. I could kiss and lick and taste you all damn day and not get enough."

"Prove it," she begged.

And he did.

* * *

As predicted, Asher woke a little after two and they were both still awake. Jamie went to make a bottle while Fallon got Asher changed and was rocking him in the rocking chair when Jamie came in.

He sat on the bed and simply watched her as she fed the baby and got him back to sleep. This feeding never took long, and they both watched him for a minute to make sure he was truly asleep.

Taking her by the hand, Jamie led her out of the room and back to his. "You're not sleeping in there tonight. You're staying in my bed."

It was a little possessive and she liked it.

Honestly, she hadn't been sure what was going to

happen next or if he'd even want her to come back to his room, but she was wildly relieved that he did. After everything they'd shared tonight, she wasn't ready for it to end.

But she was ready to sleep.

"Jamie, it's late and..."

"Oh, we're definitely going to sleep," he told her. "But I wanted you here with me. I wanted to hold you."

Her heart melted at his admission.

Together, they crawled back into his bed and turned out the lights. Fallon couldn't help but smile when he reached for her and pulled her in close. They shifted around and finally settled into a comfortable position. Sharing a bed for the entire night with someone wasn't a new experience, but sharing it with someone who liked to snuggle was.

And she found that Jamie was definitely a snuggler.

And a toucher.

The more she thought about the last few weeks, she realized he did that sort of thing a lot. Maybe it brought him comfort to simply be touching another person, and it obviously didn't always have to mean something sexual. It was the little hand squeeze, or touching her arm, or even the way he held Asher. Physical contact was clearly a big thing for him and while Fallon had never been one to give it too much thought, she was suddenly seeing the appeal.

Everything about Jamie was suddenly having an appeal and it made her a little nervous.

He wasn't someone to get serious with and he wasn't someone to be thinking about a future with. They were living in a bubble right now that had very little to do with reality; she knew that.

She just wished things were different.

Ugh...when did I start romanticizing thing?

Oh, that's right, the moment she held Asher in her arms and discovered how much she wished he were hers.

"Fallon?" he whispered.

"Hmm?"

"Can I ask you something?"

"Of course."

"Did you ever think we'd be here like this?"

That sounded like the type of question that was really a trap.

"Jamie..."

"Because I never did," he said, and his voice sounded sad. "I was blind for so long because of my ego and...I don't know...I hate the way things were between us. I like this. I like what we have now."

That's just the orgasms talking...

Okay, there was no way she was going to say that, but she had a feeling he was possibly over-romanticizing things too. After all, this was temporary. In another week, she more than likely wouldn't be needed as a nanny—especially if Asher's mother came back. Things would get seriously awkward, and she didn't want to cause any issues for Jamie that would affect how things moved forward with his son.

"I do too," she finally said. "I definitely like this new turn in our relationship. And not just what happened here tonight. I've genuinely enjoyed getting to know you."

She felt him relax before he placed a soft kiss on top of her head.

"Let's get some sleep," he said quietly, and she could tell he was almost there already.

Snuggling closer, she kissed his chest. "Goodnight, Jamie."

"Night..."

Chapter Nine

"Mmm...Jamie...your alarm..."

Rolling over, he slapped the damn clock to get it to shut up.

He was thoroughly exhausted, but for all the best reasons, and as he rolled back over and pulled Fallon into his arms, he seriously considered calling in sick today. She was all warm and soft and sleepy and this was just the best way to wake up in the morning.

Glancing at the clock, he knew he had about an hour before he had to leave, but Asher would be getting up soon.

Then take advantage of this moment, he told himself.

Carefully, he rolled Fallon beneath him and began kissing his way down her curvy body. Honestly, he had no idea she had all these curves, and he was loving every second he got to explore them.

She hummed softly. "Mmm...not that I'm not loving this, but...shouldn't you be getting up?"

Chuckling against the smooth skin of her belly, he said, "Believe me, I'm up."

"Only you could make such an immature comment sound sexy."

"Again, part of my charm," he replied as he kissed his way lower.

All her movements were slow and languid and made her completely pliable under his touch.

"Asher's going to be awake soon..."

"Then we better make this fast," he said as he made his way back up her body and kissed her soundly.

And then it wasn't quite as fast and frantic as he imagined, but it was infinitely better. The feel of her legs wrapping around him, the sound of her soft sighs...it made him want to savor every moment. They moved together as if they'd been making love for years instead of hours, and he swore sex had never felt like this.

Because there's a connection there...

And there was—one that was growing stronger every day, and instead of freaking him out, he was really finding the appeal in it.

In her.

Fallon Murphy was becoming something vital to him, and he hoped he hadn't screwed things up so much in the past that she couldn't see a future with him.

Okay, take the sex goggles off, dude. A future? Really? Don't you have enough on your plate?

Pushing those thoughts aside, he finished loving her and making sure she started her day knowing how amazing she was.

Breathlessly, Jamie rolled off of her and did his best to catch his breath just as they heard Asher fussing through the baby monitor.

"Wow...what timing, huh?" she teased before rolling off the bed and stretching.

She was gloriously naked and even though he'd just been enjoying every inch of her body, he watched with pure appreciation as she moved around and picked her nightie up off the floor and slid it on. Then she walked over and gave him a rather chaste kiss.

"Go and take your shower and I'll take care of Asher."

When she was out of the room, Jamie simply stayed where he was, staring up at the ceiling. His mind instantly went back to what he was thinking about minutes ago.

It wasn't that he was looking at this situation through sex goggles—although the sex was so freaking good that he knew he'd be sporting a hard on all day—he was finally looking at his life a little more seriously.

Asher's arrival on his doorstep did that.

It was finally time for him to grow up and stop goofing around, time to start thinking about his future. He had a son to consider, and if he were brutally honest, it had been a long time since meaningless hookups and no-strings-attached relationships were fulfilling. To the rest of the town he might be a shameless flirt, but what most of them never knew was that most of the time, things never went beyond that. He hadn't really dated anyone in months.

Since Jenn.

And it wasn't because there were any lingering feelings there—because there weren't. It was more because it was the first time a breakup didn't go the way he wanted. They didn't part as friends and it wasn't smooth and it left him feeling uneasy.

More with himself than anything else.

What would have happened if he had found out sooner that she was pregnant?

He'd like to think that other than knowing about

Asher's arrival, not much else would have changed. He never would have asked Jenn to marry him, but he supposed it would have been nice to have a little more advance notice about becoming a father.

The bedroom door opened and Fallon walked in with the baby. She'd put her robe on to cover her sexy attire and all he could think was how that was a damn shame.

"Is everything okay?" he asked, sitting up.

"Just making sure you didn't fall back to sleep," she said with a knowing smile. "I know neither of us got much sleep last night."

"And it was well worth it." Kicking the blankets off, he walked over and kissed the top of his son's head before giving Fallon a kiss that was borderline dirty, and he groaned. "You have no idea how much I want to say screw it and stay home all day. You and I could take advantage of Asher's naptime."

"As tempting as that sounds, you know it's not the right thing to do. Not on short notice. Maybe see about arranging for a day off another day so we can plan something and play another day."

He pouted. "But I want to play now."

She playfully patted his cheek. "Aww...poor baby." And with a sassy wink, she walked out of the room.

With no other choice because she was right, he turned and went to take a shower.

It was going to be a long day.

* * *

The lunch crowd was thinning out when Patrick walked in, looking about as tired as Jamie felt.

His brother never looked tired.

Ever.

Something must be up for him to be out in public looking less than put together, he thought.

"Rough night?" he asked with amusement when Patrick pulled up a stool at the bar.

"I need coffee and a bowl of chowder," Patrick murmured before resting his head on the bar.

"Dude, what is going on with you? Are you sick? Because if you are, take your ass out to your car and I'll bring the food out to you."

Lifting his head, his brother glared at him. "I'm not sick. I never get sick. You know that."

Sadly, it was true.

"Then what the hell is going on with you? You look like hell."

"I was up all night."

Me too, but I sure as hell look better than this, he thought to himself.

"And?

"And what? That's it. End of story."

"Most guys who say they were up all night tend to sound braggy, not bitchy," he commented, pouring the mug of coffee and sliding it over. "I'm guessing maybe this story doesn't have a happy ending?" And that just made him crack up. "Get it? Happy ending?"

Patrick took the mug and gave him a hard glare.

"O-kay...c'mon, Pat. Just spit it out because you know I'm gonna hound the shit out of you until you do."

"It's none of your damn business, Jamie. Just drop it."

"No," he countered, feeling more than a little annoyed. "You never drop anything when you want answers, so deal with it." And, crossing his arms over his chest, he waited.

Taking a sip of his coffee, Patrick looked defiant. But it didn't take long for him to open up.

"Marissa's got a shitty family situation going on. Her mother's an alcoholic, her father's out of the picture, and I'm pretty sure her brother is abusive."

"Holy crap..."

"Exactly. She showed up at the office last night after hours and I guess she didn't think I'd still be there. We kind of surprised each other." He shook his head. "It was obvious that she'd been crying and I think she was planning on crashing there."

"She still lives at home?"

He nodded. "Yeah. She claims she does it because she worries about her mom; something about keeping her drinking under control and making sure her brother doesn't come in and steal everything." He muttered a curse under his breath. "I asked why she didn't go to her boyfriend's place if she needed a place to go and she just sort of waved that off without giving me a direct answer."

"Pat, that's messed up. What did you do?"

"I brought her back to my house and ordered us some takeout and tried to get her to let me help her. But...you know Marissa; she's stubborn."

Actually, Jamie didn't know that about her. Any time he'd ever been around Patrick's assistant, she'd been bubbly and cheerful and possibly one of the friendliest people he'd ever met. On top of that, she was crazy organized. On some levels, she reminded him a lot of Ryleigh, but even more efficient.

And that was saying a lot.

"So what happens now?"

Sitting up a little straighter, he stretched. "I stayed up all damn night trying to think of a solution—some damn way to either fix this problem or to get her the help she needs and I came up with nothing. I can easily help get her mom into rehab, but it doesn't sound like she's willing to go."

"That's not unusual, but maybe if the two of you sat down with her mom…"

Patrick shook his head. "Not gonna happen. Marissa made it abundantly clear that she doesn't want me interfering or trying to talk to her family."

"Damn."

"I know."

"So, again, what happens now?"

He shrugged. "My hands are tied. I'm not going to behind her back and talk to her mother. The brother, however…" He paused and took another sip of his coffee. "I'd pound that little shit into the pavement if I ever find out he laid a hand on Marissa. He's nothing but a punk. I've only met him a handful of times and you can just tell he's worthless."

"You know, there are times we've all griped about one another or about Mom and Dad and then you hear something like this and realize just how lucky we are."

Nodding, Patrick gave him a weak smile. "I totally agree. I'd much rather just think of you guys being mildly annoying than have to actually live in fear of you doing something that would hurt me."

With a nod, Jamie took a moment to study his brother. "So, um…was it weird having Marissa stay the night?"

Patrick glared at him. "She stayed in the guest room and there was nothing weird about it. She's a friend who needed help. I'd do the same thing for anyone."

"Yeah, but…" Pausing, he chuckled softly. "I mean… come on. You can't tell me you're not even a little bit attracted to her. It's not possible." Then something occurred to him. "Is that why you don't date much? Do you have a thing for Marissa?"

If the death stare Patrick was giving him was any indication, Jamie would say he was definitely on to something. However...

"I date plenty."

"Really? Because I haven't seen you with anyone in..."

"Unlike the rest of this family, I enjoy my privacy. And I don't date local."

That was...an odd statement.

"You mean you don't bring your dates anywhere in Laurel Bay or you don't date anyone who lives in Laurel Bay?"

Groaning, Patrick rubbed a hand over his face. "Dude, can you please just let this go?"

He could, but...

"Just tell me how you're meeting these women and I'll stop."

Reaching for his phone, his brother held it up. "It's a dating app. There. Are you satisfied?"

Frowning, Jamie shook his head. "Wow. That was a little anticlimactic. Meet anyone interesting?"

"I thought so, but..." After a moment, he shuddered. "Anyway, enough about me. How are things going with you? How's Asher? Have you heard from Jenn?"

Doing his best to keep his expression neutral and not comment on the fact that Patrick really didn't answer his question, he shared how things were going. "So basically, he's sleeping better, but it will be a few months before he sleeps through the night."

"Maybe Fallon should stay over more often then. You know, to give you a couple of nights where you can sleep."

"Uh, yeah. Um...maybe..."

"Oh, no..."

"What?"

His brother gave him a look that said, "Really?"

"Why are you looking at me like that?" And yeah, he knew playing dumb certainly wasn't helping.

"You slept with Fallon."

"How do you do that?" he asked incredulously. "I mean, seriously. How could you even know that?"

"First, you blushed. Then you stuttered. It's a dead give-away every time." Then he groaned. "Don't you have enough on your plate without messing with a family friend? And I thought you didn't even like her?"

He shrugged. "Turns out I was wrong. She's awesome. We've been spending a lot of time together and believe me, it wasn't all one-sided."

"Yeah, okay. Great. So what happens next week when Jenn comes back?"

"What does that have to do with anything?"

"For starters, this girl seems like she has issues. I mean, she jerked you around and never told you she was pregnant, she dumped Asher on your porch, and then disappeared. You think when she comes home and sees that you're sleeping with the nanny that it's not going to trigger anything? C'mon, Jamie. Even you're smarter than that."

Actually, he wasn't, because that aspect never even occurred to him.

Shit.

"Just...be careful," Patrick said after a moment. "And seriously, I need some of the chowder. Please. I'm starving."

"Yeah, sure. I'll be right back."

Most of the time he ignored any advice his siblings gave

him because he thought he knew better. But this time, he seriously hoped that was the case.

* * *

"Dear Ms. Murphy, thank you for your application, but at this time...blah, blah, blah..."

Fallon deleted the email without giving it much thought. She felt too good for anything to get her down.

It was amazing what good sex and personal happiness could do to someone's perspective.

While it had only been four days since the turn in her relationship with Jamie, she felt lighter and happier than she had in possibly her entire life. Having this kind of time away from her normal life was exactly what she needed to start figuring out what came next for her.

Moving forward, Fallon decided that she wasn't going to look for any more executive positions. She was going to start small and work her way up and hopefully people would see another side to her if given the chance. Maybe starting with a small charter school or even a private school or nursery school. There was a good chance her advanced degree would be a red flag to potential employers, but she had a feeling that now that she had unclenched a bit and wasn't so stressed out, she'd make a better first impression.

Lying on the living room floor with Asher while he had some tummy time, she smiled as she watched his little arms and legs moving around. He was holding his head up for a little longer each day and she loved seeing all these milestones. Sometimes she'd take out her phone and catch something cute on video that she'd either send to Jamie or show him when he got home.

But most of the time when he got home, if Asher was asleep, his attention was fully on her.

And she loved every second of it.

In fact, she was loving *him*.

The analytical part of her brain was all like, "This is too soon. You don't know what you're doing." But her heart said otherwise. They'd known each other for over twenty years. They weren't strangers or just mere acquaintances. They had a strong foundation, even if a lot of it was built on animosity.

She was falling in love with Jamie and there wasn't anything she could do to stop or change it.

Since the night they first made love, he'd become more attentive. He brought home flowers or desserts that he knew she loved. He texted her during the day just to see how she was. Over dinner, he encouraged her to follow her dreams and not sell herself short while searching for a job. But mostly, he spent every night making love to her like it was his absolute mission in life to bring her pleasure.

Some nights, she swore she would die from it because it felt like it was too much.

Jamie just took that as a challenge.

One that she was more than willing to allow.

They slept in each other's arms, they got up in the night with Asher together, and it felt...right. It felt like they had formed this perfect little family and it was one that she desperately wanted to be a part of.

Neither spoke about the future, but she knew he had to be wondering when he was going to hear from Asher's mom and what kind of drama that was going to bring. And not that she'd ever say anything to him about it, but she was thinking a lot about that herself.

As far as their personal relationship went, Fallon felt

that they were good—solid. But would she still be here in a nanny capacity a week from now, or would they decide to send Asher to daycare? Or would Jenn want to take custody back? Would Jamie allow that? There were so many questions that she was afraid to ask because she didn't want to rock the boat. Things were so good that she hated the thought of introducing a topic that would make things...less good.

"Or maybe I'm just a coward," she murmured, reaching out and letting Asher hold her finger.

Most of her life, Fallon thrived on having a plan and a schedule. She hated surprises or being caught off guard. But right now, it felt like that was how she was almost being forced to live because she didn't want to know what was coming. Sort of like ignorance being bliss and all that.

"Ugh...I barely know who I am anymore."

Asher blew a spit bubble and it made her smile.

"Okay, I know that I am a woman who is just in love with you, you sweet little boy," she told him. "You make me smile and make my heart happy just looking at you." Nothing else had ever given her that feeling and she had to remind herself that he wasn't hers and maybe she shouldn't get too attached.

Nonsense, even if things don't work out with Jamie and we return to being friends, it's totally fine to still adore his son...

Wasn't it?

For a highly educated woman, she found herself knowing less and less lately. Second-guessing her feelings was now the norm because it was all so new to her, and she wished she had someone to talk to about it. Of course, she could call one of her sisters, but she didn't want to share what was going on with Jamie—the part about Asher, specifically—because it wasn't her place. Plus, she didn't want them sharing anything with their parents.

"Okay, so...no sisters."

At least...not *her* sisters.

Glancing at the clock, she saw it was almost lunchtime and wondered if maybe Ryleigh was free to talk. Before she could second-guess herself again, she picked up her phone and tapped out a quick text.

Fallon: Hey! Are you busy?

Ryleigh: Nope! Was just getting ready to make some lunch. What's up?

Fallon: Any chance you can come over?

Ryleigh: Is everything okay? Do you need someone to watch Asher?

Fallon: Actually, I just needed someone to talk to

Ryleigh: Uh-oh…

Ryleigh: Give me 30 minutes and I'll be there with lunch

Fallon: Thanks!

Twenty-seven minutes later, Ryleigh was at the door with a cooler bag in her hand.

"Hey! I hope you don't mind, but I made a quiche this

morning and some pasta salad and just brought that with me," she said as she walked in.

"Are you kidding? That sounds fantastic. You didn't have to bring anything, though. I could have made something here."

"Nonsense. You have your hands full with Asher." Pausing, she looked around. "Is he sleeping?"

Fallon nodded. "I just put him down, so we have time to talk."

"Okay, whew!" Putting all the food out on the kitchen table while Fallon got plates and silverware and drinks, she asked, "Since we might have limited time, tell me what's going on."

It seemed like a good idea when she texted Ryleigh, but now she wondered if talking to Jamie's sister about their personal relationship was the smart thing to do.

As if sensing her hesitation, Ryleigh looked over at her and smiled. "If this is about you and my brother, let me just say that we all know he's into you. So, if your relationship has turned...uh...romantic...no one's going to be surprised."

"Oh. Really?"

"Yeah. We all saw it the day of the barbecue, so you can relax." She sat down and began serving the food. "Is that what this is about? Are things good? Bad? Do you want out and don't know how to leave and break things off? Is it weird for the two of you?"

Laughing, she held up a hand to stop her. "That is a lot of questions!"

"Well...like I said, we're on a time crunch and I'm just trying to get things rolling."

"Okay, so fast and to the point. Got it." Pausing for a moment, Fallon tried to think of a way to delicately talk about this, but what ended up coming out was, "Jamie and I are sleeping together and I think I'm really falling for him and I don't know what's going to happen when Asher's mom gets back and I'm freaking out because I don't want to chase after some big career anymore!" She let out a long breath as she slouched in her chair. "Oh my God, did it feel good to get that out!"

Meanwhile, Ryleigh's fork was perched halfway to her mouth as she stared at her with wide eyes. "Wow. Um... okay. That was...a lot of information."

"You said you wanted to roll things along..."

"You're right. My bad."

"I'm sorry," she blurted out. "This is weird, right?"

"No, no...it's not that. Like I said, you and Jamie? I think that's great. I kind of suspected it for a while, but never wanted to say anything. The part about Jenn? Believe me, we're all worried about that. And the job thing? I'm a firm believer that there's nothing wrong with changing your mind. I think you had this vision for what you wanted and you were academically motivated to go after it. Unfortunately, things aren't always what we think once we're out in the workforce. Why do you think I ended up working for myself? I had this dream of working for a big creative company and having these fun meetings with my co-workers and how awesome it would be. It was the furthest thing from reality ever."

"Really?"

"Oh, yeah. Lots of petty jealousy and backstabbing over really crappy projects that weren't creative in the least. It was awful. Now, I get to work one-on-one with clients and I've had the opportunity to do a lot of amazing stuff. Now I'm working on projects with Ryker and it's incredibly challenging but fulfilling too. So if the things you've tried so far weren't doing it for you, then there's nothing wrong with re-evaluating and taking another approach."

"It just feels wrong. Like I'm letting my parents down because I went to school for so damn long and now it's like I'm taking a step backwards."

"Fallon, you know your parents only want you to be happy, right?"

All she could do was shrug.

"Okay, as your friend, I think I can share this with you," Ryleigh began. "All that time you were in college? Your parents worried about you."

"They did?"

She nodded. "They were afraid that you were so focused on your degrees and studying that you were missing out on life." Pausing for a moment, she took a bite of her quiche. "There's nothing wrong with being smart and wanting to advance your education, but...you have to admit you kind of had tunnel vision with it. Did you date much while you were in school?"

"Not really. I mean, I did. I had two boyfriends, but neither were particularly serious. They were academically oriented like I was, so I think it was a little more about sex and stress relief."

There was no way she was going to go into how fantastic the sex with Jamie was and how much better it was than she ever imagined.

Nope. Keep that to yourself...

"I look at it like your life was a little in a holding pattern and now that you're finally living a little, you're seeing that maybe your plan wasn't quite right for you. And again, there's nothing wrong with that. So don't let your fear over what your parents or anyone else are going to think stop you from going after what makes you happy. You're an awesome person, Fallon, and you deserve to be happy."

She nodded and took a bite of her own lunch.

"As for this situation with Jenn...I wish I knew what to say. I honestly believe that—contrary to popular belief—my brother isn't stupid. He's not going to fall for anything she has to say when she gets back. Has he talked to a lawyer or anyone?"

"No. I think he's a little too trusting and wants to hear what Jenn has to say when she gets back. But I don't know that for sure because we don't talk about it. Like ever."

"That first week he had Asher, I know how freaked out he was. I think he needed to just put all his attention on making sure his son was taken care of."

"But...?"

"How do you know there's a but?"

"Ryleigh, please. There's always a but."

"Okay, fine. He might not have wanted to talk to a lawyer, but the rest of us did."

"Oh, no..."

"It's not all bad, but it also has the potential to be complicated. For all we know, Jenn will give up her rights and everything will be awesome."

"Yeah, somehow I don't think it's going to be that easy."

"Yeah, me neither. Considering that he obviously doesn't want to give Asher up, and we don't know if Jenn will either, they'll most likely have to come up with a custody agreement and figure out how to co-parent together. It's not ideal and I hate it for Asher because it means a lot of going back and forth from one house to another, but as long as he's being cared for properly in each house, it can work. I just would love a little more stability for him."

"Well, to be fair…even if Jenn doesn't want to co-parent and Jamie becomes the primary caregiver-slash-parent, things aren't going to be perfectly stable. It leaves him as a single parent who has to juggle a baby and his job. There's going to be daycare and babysitters or another nanny…it's a revolving door of people in Asher's life, and that's not always great either."

"There's no perfect solution here," Ryleigh argued lightly. "Even if you and Jamie fell madly in love and got married, you're going to go to work too, so it's not like having two parents living together in the same home is the answer."

"No, I guess it's not," she said sadly.

"Hey," Ryleigh said as she reached over and gently squeezed her hand. "I didn't say that to upset you. I'm just… I'm a realist. And having two working parents isn't a bad thing. Obviously, it's the way most families have to be these days. All I'm trying to say is that I want my nephew to be loved and taken care of. And if that's with just Jamie and doing the daycare thing, that's great. If it's him and Jenn co-parenting, great. If it's the two of you?" She smiled broadly. "Well, that one would be my vote."

Mine too…

With a small smile of her own, she took another bite of her lunch and tried to change the subject. "This is all delicious. I've never made a quiche before."

"They're super easy and I kind of love how versatile they are. Ryker's not a huge fan, so I make ones I like and then know I can have it for breakfast or lunch."

"You'll have to give me a recipe to try because this is so good."

"Jamie likes them too."

Oh, good grief…

Carefully, she put her fork down and leveled Ryleigh

153

with one look. "Can you honestly see your carefree, consummate flirt brother settling for someone as boring as me? Or do you think this is just him killing time because I'm here and convenient?"

Ryleigh's eyes went wide. "Wow. You kind of went right for the jugular there."

"Because I know you can handle it and won't lie to me," she said firmly. "We can sit here and do the girl talk thing and pretend that Jamie and I aren't just playing house, but the reality is, I know who I am, and I know who your brother is. I know that I may end up getting hurt and I went and did it anyway."

"Well, now I feel guilty because I'm the one who pulled you in."

"At the end of the day, I'm not going to have any regrets."

I hope.

After letting out a long breath, Ryleigh picked up her fork again. "I think Jamie's stepped up where Asher is concerned and with taking on more responsibility. He's running the pub and it's doing great and he's doing it while his entire life was turned upside down. I think the irresponsible playboy is a thing of the past."

"O-kay..."

"However...you might have to be a little patient since this situation is a little...you know...wonky."

"Wonky?"

"It's a word. Trust me."

"If you say so..."

"Fallon, if you really have feelings for my brother, then you have to decide if he's worth the wait and dealing with the mess that's bound to happen in the coming weeks. I can't speak for Jamie, but I'd like to think he's serious about you. He wouldn't mess around with you like this if he wasn't."

Fallon wanted to believe her, but unfortunately, only time would tell.

"So...what's Jamie's favorite kind of quiche?"

Chapter Ten

"If you're trying to kill me, just know that I'll die a happy man."

The sun hadn't even come up yet, and Fallon was kissing her way down his body and stopping at all his favorite spots. His hand was fisted in her hair, and he swore he was seeing stars.

"You're a freaking goddess, Fallon," he panted. "So good. So sexy. So damn perfect..."

She hummed softly and it felt wildly erotic against his skin.

One week.

They'd been sleeping together for one week and he swore each damn day was better than the one before. But the best part of this morning was that he had the day off. So they could do this as often as they wanted without him having to get up and leave.

He murmured words of encouragement, as well as praising her touch, and when she came back up and kissed his lips and straddled his lap, Jamie knew he'd never seen anything so beautiful. Reaching up, he cupped her face and said those words to her.

"Jamie..."

"I'm serious. You are so beautiful...I could lie here and look at you all day."

Her smile was shy and a little impish. "That's because I'm naked..."

"Well...I am a little partial to that because your body is mouthwatering, but it's this face," he said solemnly, caressing her cheek. "It's your face that just fascinates me." He paused and shifted a little under her. "I think about you all the time, Fallon. All day, every day. I can't believe you're here with me and you're mine."

Ducking her head, she ran her hands over his chest. "It's the same for me too. Sometimes I forget that I'm supposed to be looking for a job because I love being here with you and Asher. I get caught up in this being everything that I want, and..."

He never let her finish. Tugging her down, he kissed her with everything he had, everything he felt. More than anything, he found that this was what he wanted—Fallon and Asher and the life they were creating here, just the three of them. And while he knew it wasn't going to be easy, that's what he was going to fight for.

When they broke apart with ragged breaths, he still kept her close. "I want all of that too, Fallon. All of it. This isn't just a temporary thing. I know we originally planned on you being here for three weeks, but...I want you to stay. I know you have plans and you're going to keep applying for jobs, and whatever you want to do is more than fine with me. We'll make it all work somehow."

She pulled back slightly. "What are you saying?"

Oh, God...what was he saying?

And was he really prepared to say it all right now?

Yes.

"I'm saying I'm falling in love with you," he said earnestly. "I don't want you here just as Asher's nanny or as a family friend; I want you here because of how I feel about you, because I want you and need you. I want you to be here because maybe you feel the same about me. And I know how much you love Asher and watching you care for him has been...you've been..."

God, I'm rambling like an idiot!

She mimicked his move and caressed his cheek. "I have loved every minute of it. These have been some of the best weeks of my life. You have to know that."

"Mine too." Then he let out a small laugh. "The day I found Asher on my porch, I didn't think I'd be able to do this. But then you showed up and made everything better. I can never thank you enough for that."

"You don't need to thank me, Jamie."

Carefully, he maneuvered them so she was lying down beside him. "I do need to thank you, or, at the very least, show my appreciation," he said silkily, and Fallon caught on immediately.

"Ooh...I'm listening..."

Slowly, he moved over her. "Let me show you, Fallon. Let me love you."

"Yes..."

So he did.

And it was the best Sunday ever.

* * *

"I don't feel good about this..."

"Nonsense. It's going to be fine."

"But what if something goes wrong?"

"Then they'll call us."

"What if we can't get back here in time?"

Chuckling, Jamie grasped her by the shoulders and gave her a playful shake. "You need to relax. Arianna and Will are going to stay with Asher so you and I can go out for a little while. It's not a big deal. Everything's going to be fine. Besides, I thought you'd be more excited about getting out on an actual date!"

She looked around nervously. "I know I'm being silly. Asher's got a solid schedule and your sister knows exactly what to do, but...it feels weird to be out." Then she laughed softly. "Wow...he's not even my baby and I feel like a part of me is missing without him being with us. Sorry!"

"For what? Acting like a real mom?" With a small snort, he said, "Fallon, this is exactly the sort of thing that makes you so amazing. You're upset about leaving him for a couple of hours. Jenn left him for weeks. Who do you think the better mom is?"

Her eyes closed as she shook her head. "I don't want to even go there. Let's go and have something to eat and enjoy ourselves."

"That's my girl!"

He had made reservations at a seafood place up in Beaufort and was excited about them being able to do this. When he mentioned it to his uncle, his first response was that he should totally do it. Then he had to decide which sibling to call to babysit. Ari and Will were making wedding plans and talking about how much they couldn't wait to start a family, so he figured they'd be the first ones to ask. Fortunately, his sister jumped at the chance—right after she nearly caused him to go deaf when she screeched with pure joy into the phone.

Needless to say, he now knew exactly who to call if they ever needed a backup babysitter.

They walked into the restaurant and were seated immediately. The atmosphere was casual but romantic and when he looked across the table, he couldn't help but smile.

"You look gorgeous tonight," he told her, and, as expected, she blushed.

"And you look very handsome yourself."

They discussed the menu and ordered their dinners and, for the first time in weeks, he wasn't sure what to talk about. He didn't do this sort of thing—the romantic dinner date—and wasn't sure what rules applied. Were certain topics off-limits? Was it okay to joke around? He seriously had no idea.

"I heard from my mom today," she said.

"Really? Is the cruise over already?"

"It is! She texted me a bunch of pictures and it looked beautiful. I've always wanted to go to Alaska, but I'm not sure about the cruise part. That doesn't thrill me."

"How come? They seem like they could be fun."

She shrugged. "I don't know. Something about not being on land for that many days is just beyond unappealing to me. And then you see those pictures online where it's so crowded and that is totally not my thing."

"I guess in the right circumstances it could be fun, but I don't think I'd pick a cruise for my vacation either."

"How come?"

Leaning forward, he rested his arms on the table. "It's always been my dream to see The Grand Canyon and to go hiking through Zion National Park. I'm more of an outdoorsy person and that sort of thing appeals to me."

"I think seeing both those places in person would be

amazing. I've never gone hiking and I think we both know I'm not overly athletic..."

"Nuh-uh...you're totally athletic. Our whole rivalry started because you beat me in a bike race," he reminded her, making her laugh.

"Oh my goodness! I forgot about that!" Laughing harder, she shook her head. "We were like five or six years old. Trust me, that may have been the peak of my athleticism!"

"Again, I disagree. All the times our families hung out together, you know we always ran around playing some sort of game or doing all kinds of crazy challenges. Remember the year we competed to see who could climb the highest in that tree in Laurel Bay Park?"

"I believe Liam beat us all."

"Yeah, but that's just because he was the oldest and the tallest," Jamie reasoned. "But you still came in third. You beat me by a foot."

"If you say so..."

"Or how about the Fourth of July when we were at that big community picnic and they had the three-legged race? You beat me in that too!"

"I was paired up with my sister Shannon and she was a lot taller than me! Still is! Anyway, she's the only reason we won. She practically carried me the entire time! I had nothing to do with it."

He shook his head. "Trust me, you're more athletic than you think."

"Then how come I always had to do extra credit work to avoid failing PE in school?"

"Seriously?"

"Oh, yeah. Believe it or not, the only reason I was able to do any of that physical stuff was because I was trying to prove myself—to you and my sisters. Even now, the most physical thing I do is either yoga or walking. And I haven't taken a yoga class in almost two months. Tummy time with Asher is the only time I get down on the floor and stretch."

"Okay, but that's kind of adorable."

"I can't wait until he's a little more mobile. We're going to have so much fun doing baby yoga."

"That's a thing?"

She nodded. "You can start them at around six weeks old. I do some little stretches with him now to help with the colic, but there are classes you can even take."

He knew his eyes went wide. "Like...at a gym?"

"Not the kind you're thinking of, but there are places that specifically cater to just moms and babies. It's supposed to be a great bonding thing."

Shaking his head, he let out a long breath. "There is just so much to know. How is anyone supposed to know all these things?"

Reaching across the table, she gave his hand a gentle squeeze. "Jamie, no one knows everything about parenting. And if you never did yoga with Asher, everything would be fine. It's not something you have to know or do." She shrugged. "I just happened to go to school for early childhood development, so I'm a little more aware of stuff like this."

He felt himself relax. "And that's why Asher and I are so lucky to have you. You've done so much for us."

"And as I've said probably a million times already, I've loved every minute of it."

Their server came over to take their orders, and after that, he noticed how Fallon was finally relaxing. They talked about Asher and more baby programs they could get involved in. She talked about milestones they should be noticing soon, and he just genuinely enjoyed hearing her talk. She was passionate about children—particularly his son—and he knew she'd be a great benefit to any company that hired her.

She was different than she was even a few weeks ago. Even though Jamie knew he was all tense and defensive the day she'd shown up at his house, he could say with great certainty that there was a change in her too.

And it had nothing to do with their new relationship.

It was as if she had tapped into a part of herself that she never had before. She was softer but more confident. The superior attitude she normally presented wasn't there and in its place was someone who seemed more at ease in their own skin.

It looked good on her.

He knew it was only a matter of time before she found a job. It wasn't like she was going to stay working as Asher's nanny forever.

He just hoped he'd be ready when she told him she needed to move on—because he knew it wouldn't just be about the job; she'd more than likely be ready to move on from him too.

* * *

Date night was a total success. Will and Arianna had loved coming over to watch Asher and said they'd be willing to do it once a week—and even take him for an overnight—should Jamie and Fallon want that.

And she kind of did.

Although she was getting used to getting up with the baby, it would be nice to have a night all to themselves with no disruptions. So that was on the agenda for next week and she already couldn't wait.

It was nearing the end of the week, and Fallon felt uneasy. She kept waiting for someone to show up at the door or for the phone to ring or...

Hell, who was she kidding? She was waiting for Asher's mom to return. But so far, there'd been nothing. The only thing that was going on was that Ryleigh had apparently convinced Jamie to meet with the lawyer she and their siblings had talked to before.

That's where Jamie was now and she was anxiously awaiting what he was going to find out.

When her phone rang, Fallon nearly jumped out of her skin. Seeing her mother's face on the screen, however, made her smile.

"Hey, Mom! How's today's adventure going?"

"Oh, we are loving it! We took a bit of a detour because none of us had ever been to Colorado, so...that's going to add a couple of days to the trip."

"Wow! But that sounds like fun! What's in Colorado that you want to see?"

Laughing, her mother replied, "Everything!"

"O-kay..."

"Obviously that's not going to happen, but we decided to go up to the Rio Grande National Forest and do a little exploring."

That made her think of the conversation she and Jamie had at dinner the other night. "I'm sure it's going to be beautiful."

"Oh, Fallon, I can't tell you how much we've enjoyed ourselves. It's nice not having a rigid schedule." Then she laughed softly. "Although, I don't think I'll get in a car any time soon after we get home. This sort of thing gets old fast.

But just knowing we're going to see some amazing sights makes it all worth it."

"I'll bet."

"So? How's the job search going? Any leads?"

"Um...no. I'm kind of re-thinking some things."

"Really? Like what?"

"Like...not going after the big positions," she said hesitantly. "I know it's what I went to school for and why I insisted on staying in school and getting the advanced degree, but..."

"But you want to work your way up to it," her mother finished for her. "I think that's very smart."

"You do?"

"Fallon, you always wanted to be at the top of everything—your class, your field, even any hobbies you had. Most people start slow and work their way up. No one is the CEO after graduation. So yes, I think what you're doing is wonderful and I'm proud of you for figuring it out."

Wow.

"Thanks, Mom."

"See? This time alone has been a good thing. I knew going home and being around familiar things was going to be helpful." She laughed again. "I might not have a fancy college degree, but sometimes I'm pretty smart."

"Yes, you are and I love you."

"Love you too, sweetheart."

"Now go and have another adventure and be sure to send pictures!"

"Always! Love you too and we'll talk soon!"

They hung up and even though she felt better because her mother was fine with her change of career plans, she hadn't been completely truthful with her about the things going on in her life. They had a few more weeks before they'd all be back in town, so that meant she couldn't mention anything about Asher or Jamie.

Which, really, was for the best considering so many things were still in limbo.

Right now Asher was napping and she had no idea when Jamie would call, so rather than simply sitting around doing nothing, she took out her laptop and went about doing another round of job hunting.

There seemed to be a ton of positions available in preschools as both teacher and director, and there were a few positions open for a childcare center director.

None of them were in Laurel Bay or even the surrounding towns.

This had the potential to be a huge stumbling block in her personal life.

Of course, there was the possibility of staying on as Asher's nanny for a while longer, but it felt weird for Jamie to be paying her while they were sleeping together. There was a total ick-factor that was going to have to be addressed. Unfortunately, she desperately needed the money she'd get from an actual job.

Groaning, she shut the laptop. "This is getting me nowhere."

It wasn't like she was surprised by the results. Obviously, there weren't a lot of options in a small town. It was one of the reasons she had opened herself up to living anywhere in the country. But now that she was back—and with Jamie—the thought of moving far away was beyond unappealing.

"So now what do I do?"

The decision was made for her when Jamie walked through the door. She tried to get a read on how he was feeling, but his expression was just as it always was—pleasantly neutral. Normally that was great, but right now, she just wanted a hint of what was to come.

Standing, she was about to ask him, but he took her in his arms and kissed her until she was weak and breathless. When he released her, all she could do was murmur a breathless, "Wow."

"How's your day going, beautiful?"

"Um...okay. How's yours?"

Shrugging, he walked into the kitchen and grabbed himself a bottle of water. "Would you like one?"

"No, but thanks." She was jittery and her stomach was in knots, and she was on the verge of demanding answers, but he beat her to it.

"Okay, so I spoke with the attorney," he began as he sat down at the kitchen table. "And, technically, Jenn abandoned Asher."

"Technically?"

"Abandonment normally applies to situations when the child is left either unattended, with strangers, or dropped off at a firehouse or police station, or with a social worker."

Nodding, she sat down beside him. "But because she left him with his father..."

"Yeah. It's not quite so black and white. The fact that she left him the way she did will count against her if we had to go to court to argue over custody."

"Do you think it's going to come to that?"

He shrugged. "That's just it, I don't know. Will she even want to share custody? Does she want to co-parent?"

"What about you? What do you want?" she asked carefully.

"I know I should say we should co-parent, but considering she hid her pregnancy from me and then took off? I'm going to sue for full custody and termination of her parental rights."

"What?" she cried. "Jamie...that's a little extreme, don't you think?"

"Not at all. Think about it, Fallon. If she was detached enough to just leave Asher on my porch and walk away, what kind of mother would she be to him? I'd be worrying all the damn time about whether or not he was safe with her or if she was leaving him alone. That's not a chance I'm willing to take."

"Okay, okay, I get it, but...from her letter, it sounded like she was going to get help for something. Maybe she's dealing with depression and knew she needed to leave Asher with you for his own safety. She should be commended for that."

But he shook his head. "If she was struggling with anything, then she needed to talk to me about it."

"But you wouldn't talk to her, Jamie! She tried and you refused to do it!"

"Wait...whose side are you on? Because it sounds to me like you're on her side and I don't understand why!" And yeah, he was pissed.

"This isn't about taking sides! This is about playing devil's advocate and making sure you're looking at this from all sides and not just making a rash decision based on emotions!"

"It should be based on emotion! We're talking about my son! An innocent baby! This isn't something sterile or clinical. He's my flesh and blood! There's no way to leave emotion out of it!"

This wasn't getting them anywhere...

"Jamie, I didn't say you had to take emotions out of it. I'm saying you need to be well-informed before making a decision. Punishing Jenn might seem very satisfying right now, but is it the right thing for Asher? Somewhere down the road, he's going to want to know about her and he may be upset with you if you're the reason she's not in his life."

He looked ready to argue, but didn't.

Instead, he cursed.

Loudly.

"Great! So now I'm supposed to potentially put my son in danger so that somewhere down the line he may or may not hate me? Because that sounds like bullshit. I'm sure in your big university classes that talked about this kind of stuff, they teach you to trust even when it's not warranted."

"Hey!" she snapped. "There's no reason for you to get all pissy with me and insult my education. No one's saying you have to listen to me, but I thought we were having a conversation and that involves each of us sharing our opinions. I'm just putting stuff out there for you to consider. If you don't want to listen to me, then fine. But you should talk to other people—like your siblings—and see what they have to say!"

"That's a great idea," he said snidely, and before she knew it, he was typing with lightning speed on his phone. Five minutes later, when he put his phone down, his smile was smug. "They'll all be here for dinner. Liam and Tessa are picking up pizza." Then he stood and walked out of the room, leaving her feeling more than a little bewildered.

"What the hell just happened here?" she mumbled.

It was pointless to go after him, so she got up and put her laptop away and wondered—not for the first time today—just what she was supposed to do with herself. Asher was going to be down for at least another hour, and it would be three hours before the Donovans arrived.

Walking to the sliding glass doors, Fallon slid them

open and stepped out onto the deck. Maybe she could go for a drive or could go and do a little retail therapy, but she didn't think an hour would be enough.

Why an hour? Jamie's home and can take care of his son for a couple of hours.

Decision made, she turned to go back into the house but found Jamie standing in the doorway. Again, she couldn't quite read his expression, but right now, she didn't really care.

"I'm going to go out for a little while. I've got some errands to run. Asher should be up in an hour," she told him before trying to get into the house.

But he blocked her.

"Jamie, I need to get inside to get my stuff." When he still didn't move, she huffed loudly. "Seriously? You're going to revert to acting like a child?"

Instead of responding right away, he stepped onto the deck and just completely embraced her. "I'm sorry," he whispered gruffly against her neck. "I'm so sorry."

He held her tighter than he ever had before, and Fallon could feel all the anger and frustration radiating off of him.

But she also felt the vulnerability and couldn't help but wrap her arms around him and simply hold him for as long as he needed.

Several minutes passed, and when he lifted his head, he looked completely remorseful. "I never should have lost it like that. I know you're only trying to help. This entire situation is..."

"I know," she interrupted as she caressed his jaw, soothing him. "I know."

"You've been nothing but good to me and you didn't deserve that." Taking her hands in his, he slowly backed into the house. "I need you, Fallon. So much."

While she knew sex wouldn't solve anything, she felt like maybe right now they both needed to feel close to each other—to have that connection and know that they were alright.

So she let him lead her to the bedroom.

And she let him slowly strip her down, kissing all the skin he exposed.

And when he guided them both down onto the bed, she let him love her as only he could.

Chapter Eleven

The next few days were filled with a lot of anxiety and speculation, and Jamie swore he didn't know if he was coming or going. Fallon was suspiciously quiet on the subject of Jenn and what was going to happen, and he really couldn't blame her. After his siblings had all come for dinner that night, her opinion was definitely in the minority. Ryleigh was the only one on the fence, and mostly everyone agreed that he needed to take every step to make sure that Jenn didn't get access to Asher and to have her parental rights removed.

It made things more than a little tense at home, but this morning he had called his uncle to say he'd be in late because he felt like he and Fallon needed to hash this out once and for all.

Only...they didn't.

Asher was fussy and then Fallon had gotten a request for a phone interview on some position she'd applied for. He knew that one was coming, but he still wished she didn't have to do it. What he wanted was for her to stay and take care of his son, but when he brought that up, she told him how much it was bothering her that they were sleeping together and he was paying her to watch Asher. And no matter how much he explained that the two had nothing to do with each other, she still wasn't comfortable with it.

So basically, they weren't on great terms because of this situation with Jenn, she was going to find a job elsewhere which meant he was going to have to find someone else to care for his son, and even though she was still living with him and sharing his bed every night, they hadn't made love since that afternoon before everyone came over.

Basically, his life was turning into a shit show once again.

When he arrived at the pub, the lunch crowd was dying down, and Jamie looked up to find his uncle staring at him intently.

"What? What's the matter?" He glanced at his watch. "I appreciate you covering for me this morning. I thought I would have gotten in sooner, so...sorry."

"Nothing to apologize for. We had plenty of coverage."

"Oh. Okay, good." Stepping behind the bar, he put his phone and keys down and started straightening things up.

"Everything okay at home?"

"Um...yeah. Sure."

"How are things going for you?" Ronan asked casually. "Everything good with you and Fallon?"

That was...not what he was expecting.

Smiling nervously, he wiped down a small section of the bar. "Yeah, we're uh...we're good. How come?"

"And Asher? Is he doing well?"

"He's fine." Then he smiled. "He was lifting his head this morning while Fallon was doing that tummy time thing with him, and I swear he did it for a solid minute and was looking proud of himself!"

173

"That's good. That's good," his uncle said before fussing with some of the bar glasses.

"Is everything okay? You seem a little out of sorts."

Straightening, Ronan looked over at him. "Jenn was here this morning," he said solemnly. "She was waiting outside when I got in and she was looking for you. I told her you would be here this afternoon." He paused and looked a little remorseful. "I was going to call you, Jamie. I really was. But as soon as she left, we had two deliveries show up at the same time and I had to help Bobby check them in and...I'm sorry. I hate that I'm practically ambushing you like this."

He let out a mirthless laugh. "You wouldn't be the first. That seems to be the way things happen lately."

"Jamie, honest to goodness, I'm sorry."

"Hey," he said, forcing a smile. "We're good, Uncle Ronan. I should have been here. None of this is on you, okay?"

"I just hate that you didn't have any time to prepare and..."

"It would have been the same if I'd shown up for work on time," he reasoned. Letting out a long breath, he wondered what he was supposed to do. "Do you think I need to call the attorney? Or Patrick and Liam?"

"Honestly? Call your lawyer and just let him know what's going on. As for your brothers, I don't think that's a good idea. It might put Jenn on the defensive."

It made sense, but he really didn't care too much about how she felt. She didn't care about his feelings all this time, so why should he be concerned for hers?

Still...he needed to hear her out before telling her his plans. It was time for her to get a taste of her own medicine and see how it felt to have her world turned upside down.

At least...that was what he planned on doing. Of course, there was the off chance that she was coming to give him exactly what he wanted and asking him to have papers drawn up terminating her rights to Asher.

Please be that...

For all his tough talk, he genuinely hated being the bad guy and wished more than anything that it didn't have to come to this. But where his son was concerned, when pushed, he sure as hell was going to push back. Asher's well-being was the only thing that mattered here. No matter what Fallon said about emotions and explanations, to him, it didn't matter. He was going to do what was best for his son, and that meant keeping people who didn't have his best interest out of his life.

Even if she was his mother.

Well, not Jamie's mother, but...

Just thinking about how his mother was going to react to coming home and finding out she was a grandmother made him smile. She was going to lose her mind in the best possible way. So many times he wanted to call and tell her, but he knew she'd cut her trip short and from everything Fallon had been hearing from her own mother, they were all having a fantastic time. It was the right decision to wait to tell her.

"You need to wipe that scowl off your face," Ronan murmured as he stepped in closer.

"Why?"

"Because Jenn just walked through the door."

Turning his head, he spotted her, and all he could think was...shit.

Ronan put a reassuring hand on his shoulder and squeezed. "Hear her out and don't do or say anything rash."

He nodded. The lawyer had essentially told him the

same thing the day they had talked in his office, but... keeping his mouth shut wasn't exactly Jamie's strong suit.

"You got this, kiddo," was the last thing his uncle said before stepping away.

Letting out a long breath, the first thing that went through his mind was how he wished Fallon were here, or that he at least had time to call her and hear her voice to calm him down. They might disagree on what was happening, but just the sound of her voice was usually enough to soothe him when he was feeling anxious.

Like right now.

"Hey, Jamie," Jenn said quietly as she approached the bar. He had to fight to stay calm and not lash out, but his hand kept clenching and unclenching into fists while he mentally counted to ten.

"Jenn," he said gruffly.

"I stopped by earlier and you weren't here," she began nervously. "Your uncle wasn't sure what time you'd be in; he just said this afternoon, so..."

"Welp, you found me," he said with a little more heat than he intended.

She looked thoroughly chastised. "Look, is there...um... can we talk in private?"

He didn't trust himself to talk at the moment, so he simply nodded and came out from behind the bar and led her back to the office. It would probably be smarter to just stay out in the dining room so there were witnesses, but he opted to leave the door open so Bobby could hear them if need be.

Jamie took the seat behind the desk and motioned for her to sit in the chair facing him. It wasn't an intentional power move, but he was glad it worked out that way.

They stared at each other and as much as he wanted to make her squirm, he was too eager to get this over with.

"So? Talk," he prompted.

"You're mad."

"Of course, I'm mad!" he snapped. "What did you think, Jenn? You dropped a baby on my doorstep with a fucking note! Then you disappeared so I couldn't talk to you!"

"You didn't talk to me for months!" she countered just as hotly. "I tried, Jamie! Many, many times! But you thought you could charm your way out of it and text me some sort of nonsense to get me to just go away!"

"If you had mentioned *why* you wanted to talk, then I wouldn't have done that! I mean...there's a big difference between saying, 'Hey, can we meet up for drinks because I kind of think we need to talk,' and 'Hey, I'm pregnant and we need to figure this out.' I'm no genius, but even I can tell the difference!"

"Okay, okay...you're right. I...I was scared and freaking out and my emotions were all over the place. I should have handled things differently," she said, sounding a little calmer. "But every time you blew me off, I took the bait and backed away. I kept telling myself it was the right thing to do and that you didn't need to know that I was pregnant." She sighed. "Then my therapist would tell me how I needed to make you talk."

"So even some random therapist knew you were having a baby before I did. Awesome."

"Jamie..." she sighed. "I can't go back and change the way things happened. We were both at fault, but I know I was the one who was more...well...just more."

"At least we agree on something," he muttered.

She squirmed in her seat and then reached into her purse and pulled out a folded piece of paper.

"What's that?"

"This," she said with a huff, "is something I learned about in counseling. And in order to make sure that I tell you everything, I needed to write it down."

The urge to roll his eyes was strong, but he refrained.

"Just...bear with me."

The nod was his only response.

"When I was fifteen, I tried to kill myself," she began.

Wait...what?

"I didn't really know what I was doing and I took like...five sleeping pills. I wrote a note to my parents telling them I was unhappy and how the world would be a better place without me." She looked up at him briefly before returning her attention to the letter. "I got my stomach pumped and was put on a psych hold in the hospital and then began going to therapy. I wasn't a great student, I didn't have a lot of friends, and I was just sad all the time."

If this was a ploy for sympathy and a bunch of lies, he'd make sure she never saw Asher again.

"I was clinically depressed and had a chemical imbalance," she went on. "That's what we eventually came to find out. People with clinical depression often have increased levels of monoamine oxidase A, an enzyme that breaks down key neurotransmitters, resulting in very low levels of serotonin, dopamine and norepinephrine." With a nervous laugh, she said, "Don't worry, I had to look it up too in order to understand it."

Another nod.

"I spent a lot of years on different meds and by the time I was twenty, I felt like a completely different person. I was happy and taking classes at the community college and had more friends than I ever had in my life."

Holding up a hand to stop her, Jamie leaned forward. "Jenn, I get that maybe this is part of some 12-step program, but what the hell does this have to do with me and Asher?"

She frowned. "I'm getting to that."

Leaning back, he motioned for her to continue.

Clearing her throat, she shot him a hard glare before continuing. "The thing is, when you start to feel good, you think it means you're cured. And every once in a while, I'd go off my meds and then spiral hard all over again and find myself struggling just to get out of bed or to even talk to anyone. I'd skip therapy and just shut my phone off until someone would pretty much bang the door down and force me to get up and make things right." With a long sigh, she added, "It's a vicious cycle."

"If you say so..." He knew he sounded flippant, but he refused to feel sympathetic about her past. Everyone had baggage, but most of them didn't abandon their newborns.

"When you and I were dating, I was in a good place. Even my therapist said that she couldn't remember ever seeing me have such a long stretch of being positive and staying on track with my treatments. I told her I had met a great guy and was genuinely happy."

Oh God...here it comes. She's going to tell me I'm to blame.

"I'm not going to lie to you, Jamie. I was devastated when we broke up, even though you were so nice about it."

"You knew I wasn't looking to get serious," he argued. "I never lied. I told you from the very beginning that what we had wasn't going anywhere."

She nodded. "I know, I know... I guess I just thought that maybe...I'd be the one who'd change your mind." Then she looked away. "And I might have...lied about being on birth control."

"*What?!*" Jumping up, he almost dove over the desk in pure rage. "So you were trying to get pregnant? We weren't together that long! Why would you do something like that?"

Her eyes went wide. "I...I thought it would bring us closer together! I mean...a baby! You come from a big family and I just figured you'd be excited about it!"

"Jenn? Do you even hear yourself?"

She nodded. "I do, Jamie." And then she held up the letter again. "I know now what I did was wrong. I tried to manipulate you and then I hid it from you and..." Her shoulders sagged. "I'm so sorry."

Slowly, he sank back down into his seat, but he was beyond shocked.

She'd done this on purpose.

His head was spinning.

"When I found out I was pregnant, I talked to my doctors and my therapist, and we discussed how taking my antidepressants would affect the baby. Overall, the risk of birth defects and other problems for babies of mothers who take antidepressants during pregnancy is very low, but...I didn't want to take that chance."

"So you went off your meds..."

Nodding, she went on. "I struggled so much, and it didn't seem to matter how many therapy appointments or what I did; it was like being on a never-ending emotional rollercoaster. But I was determined to make sure our baby had the best chance of being healthy."

"Even at your own expense," he said flatly.

"Exactly. By the time Asher was born, I knew I was in bad shape. My OBGYN was prepared to induce me so I could get back on my meds. That was the day I texted and said you'd be sorry."

"Yeah, what was that about?"

"That was me spiraling," she admitted lowly. "I thought maybe that would finally make you talk to me." Her laugh was sad. "Obviously I can't take a hint, right?"

And right then and there, he felt...bad. So much of this could have been avoided if he'd just manned up and agreed to meet her. It didn't excuse the way she manipulated him, but...he definitely shared the blame in everything else that happened.

"So what happens now?" he asked. "What is it you think is going to happen from here?"

Slowly, Jenn folded the letter and put it back in her purse. "I wanted us to have this time to talk and then...I wanted you to have some time to think. I'm not pushing you for anything today." Then she paused. "Although I'd really like to know how Asher is."

It was on the tip of his tongue to be spiteful, but...he couldn't.

"He's doing great," he told her. "I took him to the pediatrician and he's gaining weight and meeting all the milestones he's supposed to. He sleeps about four hours at a shot, but I'm hoping that starts to get better so I can get a full night's sleep."

She nodded. "I'm sure." Hesitating, she bit her bottom lip. "I don't suppose you have a picture of him I can see?"

"Just on my phone, but it's up at the bar and..."

"Oh. Oh, it's okay. Maybe on the way out?"

"Uh, sure." Leaning back further in his chair, Jamie raked his hand through his hair. "You said you wanted me to have time to think. What is it you want me to think about? Because if it's about you and me..."

"No," she said quickly, and then laughed softly. "No, definitely not that. I'm not ready to be in any kind of relationship and I can see now that you and I aren't right for each other. But I wanted you to think about what I shared with you and then let you decide what kind of role I can have in Asher's life."

He looked at her in disbelief. "Wait...you want *me* to decide? You can't be serious!"

"But I am," she said simply. "And I'm prepared to accept whatever it is that you want to do. Considering the way things have gone so far, it seems only fair."

"Well, then..."

"But you need to seriously think about it," she cut him off. Glancing at her phone, she sighed. "I need to go. I have an appointment with my therapist in an hour. Can we maybe get together this weekend? Maybe on Sunday and I can see Asher?"

"Jenn...I don't know..."

"Okay, okay...I get it." Her voice was low and a little trembly. "How about this, I'll call you on Friday and...you tell me where you're at with all of this and we'll take it from there."

All he could do was nod.

Jenn got to her feet and offered him a weak smile. "I really am sorry, Jamie. For everything." And then she walked out of the office and presumably out of the pub without waiting to see a picture of their son.

And he stayed in his chair and lost all track of time and wondered just what the hell he was supposed to do.

* * *

Fallon knew something was wrong the moment Jamie walked through the door.

He walked right over to Asher and picked him up and held him tight and there was an intensity there she had never seen before.

She warred with herself between asking him what happened and simply waiting him out.

Ultimately, she waited him out.

Going into the kitchen, she put the finishing touches on their dinner and warmed up a bottle for Asher. Normally they fed him first, so as soon as it was at the right temperature, she simply walked into the living room and handed it to him.

He didn't even look at her.

Okay, now I'm worried...

It took almost twenty minutes for him to join her in the kitchen. Placing Asher in his infant seat, Jamie secured him and then walked to the refrigerator and got drinks for both of them and sat down. Wordlessly, Fallon made their plates and took her seat.

"I saw Jenn today," he said, his voice void of emotion.

Swallowing the ball of dread lodged in her throat, she nodded.

Then he told her everything that happened and...while a bit unethical, Fallon felt like this was all actually kind of positive. Jenn took responsibility for her actions, was getting the help she clearly needs, and was willing to work with Jamie moving forward.

"Okay," she said when he was done. "How do you feel about all of this?"

He looked at her like she'd suddenly grown a second head. "How do I *feel?*" He snorted with disbelief. "I feel sick, Fallon! She lied to me and manipulated me and pretty much screwed me! Both literally and figuratively! There's no way I can ever trust her, and now I have to worry about Asher!"

"In what way?"

The look was even worse this time, but she didn't comment on it.

"Is Asher going to be prone to depression? Do I have to worry about him needing meds? Did she tell me the truth about her going off her meds or was that a lie and now I have to worry about whether that stuff is in his system? Should I be on the phone with the pediatrician right now? Do I have her arrested for abandoning him and endangering him? I mean...and then, according to you, I need to be worried about him growing up and hating me because I refused to let his lying, scheming mother influence his life. So, um...take your pick! It's safe to say I have a lot to worry about!"

Yeah...clearly she'd underestimated how she was viewing the situation.

"First, did you call your lawyer and tell him about what happened?"

He nodded.

"And?"

"And...he has the papers drawn up and ready to go."

"What papers?"

"The ones ending her rights. Asher can hate me all he wants later on, but once he's old enough to understand, everything will be fine. Trust me."

"Wait...so Jenn came to you and took responsibility, explained to you how she struggles with depression, and your solution is to just disregard that like it's not even a valid explanation and push her aside?"

184

"Um...yeah. I don't know why you're surprised. I told you I was planning on this all along."

It was his tone.

That smug, condescending tone.

It had been a long time since he'd used it on her, but it pushed all her buttons.

"Jamie," she said with more calmness than she actually felt. "Maybe take the time she's asked for and really think about this. You don't have to decide right this instant. Be reasonable."

"Reasonable?" he repeated with a bark of laughter. "Why do I have to be the one to be reasonable? Seems to me like she didn't even consider that while she was pregnant!"

"Jamie..."

"Tell me, Fallon, has anyone ever done something to you that irrevocably changed your life?"

"Well, no. But..."

"Has anyone ever manipulated you to try to get you to go against everything you ever wanted?"

"No, but..."

His wording, however, stopped her.

"Wait...try to get you to go against everything you ever wanted?" she repeated. "What exactly does that mean?"

"I didn't want to have kids yet, Fallon! I didn't want to settle down!" Pushing his dinner plate away, he growled with frustration. "Somewhere down the road, sure, maybe. But it wasn't something I wanted right *now* and it certainly wasn't something that should have been forced on me! And now...here I am! Forced to be a father and have everyone tell me how I have to change pretty much every aspect of my life and how I'm supposed to settle down and get married! My life isn't my own anymore!"

Everything in her went cold.

"Is that why I'm still here?" she asked numbly. "Because people are telling you to settle down and...I'm here, so I'm convenient?"

His laugh bordered on maniacal. "Oh, that's just great," he commented sarcastically. "Heap a little more on me, Fallon. Why would you even *think* of something like that? You know me better than that!"

"You know, I thought I did. But listening to you right now has me second-guessing if I ever knew you at all."

Jamie got to his feet and started to pace. "Really? Now this I've got to hear."

"Right now, you sound like you resent Asher and that worries me because for the last several weeks, you've been this fantastic father to him. I've watched you bond with him and I could tell how much you love him. But listening to you talk right now is like listening to a stranger. And on top of that, after listening to your little comment about all this pressure everyone's putting on you, I can't help but notice how the timing of our relationship falls into that timeline. Putting all of that together, the man I've been living with—sleeping with —and the man standing before me are two very different men. And I don't particularly care for this one."

His eyes went wide. "Are you shitting me right now? I'm telling you how messed up today was and how everyone is pressuring me, and you choose now to talk about our relationship? Do you really think *now* is the right time to throw that into the mix?" he demanded. "What's next? You tell me you're pregnant? Or...or...how you're in love with me and want to marry me, or how we should get married for Asher's sake?" He laughed again and mumbled several colorful curses under his breath. "Or maybe my sister orchestrated this whole thing by choosing you of all people to come and help me!"

"Me of all people? I..." Stopping herself, she simply shook her head. It would have been easy to continue to fight with him—he was definitely primed for that, and they were more than halfway there—but she refused to give in to it. Asher was sitting right there and even though he was far too little to understand what was going on, she didn't believe in exposing him to this much negative energy.

"Laurel Bay's not that big, and yet out of all the people living here, Ryleigh called you."

"I'm not doing this with you. You're angry and honestly, you're being a jerk. I'm not going to upset Asher by continuing with this conversation."

"He's a baby, Fallon! He has no idea what we're even saying!" His voice raised with every word and, sure enough, it startled Asher, who began to cry.

She gave him a smug look before picking the baby up and carrying him out of the room.

That's when she heard something crash to the floor in the kitchen.

In Asher's room, she carefully put him in his crib with shaking hands and then prayed her phone was close by. It was, and she quickly typed out a text to Ryleigh.

Fallon: Hey, I know it's short notice, but we've got a bad situation here

Fallon: Jamie saw Jenn today and he's freaking out and scaring me

Fallon: Can you please get everyone over here?

Ryleigh: Holy crap!

Ryleigh: Scaring you? Are you okay?

Fallon: For now, but I don't want to be here alone with him

Fallon: He's really upset and everything I say is making it worse

Ryleigh: Ryker and I are on our way!

Ryleigh: And I'm texting everyone else

Ryleigh: Be there soon!

Fallon: Thanks

And while she knew the only people in the world to help in this situation were Jamie's siblings, she also knew that she couldn't stay and see how this played out. She needed to step away from the situation because she was upset too. Maybe some time alone would help her put things into perspective.

Everything he shared with her was definitely a bombshell, but it all didn't only affect him.

She was a part of this and hearing him talk about being forced to settle down just hit a little too close to home. And if she stayed, she'd tell him in front of his entire family that just like he didn't believe Jenn was fit to be a mother, his words and his behavior didn't make him fit to be a father either. Honestly, Asher would be better off if they let him be adopted by two rational and loving people.

Tears streamed down her face as she packed up her things and when she heard car doors slamming in the driveway, she knew that was her cue to leave.

Walking over to the crib, she picked up Asher and kissed him. "Be sweet, little boy. Aunt Ryleigh and Aunt Arianna will be here to take care of you. I love you." Slowly, she put him back down and turned on his mobile.

Grabbing her bag, she looked around the room with a sad smile. Maybe she'd be back, maybe she wouldn't, but if she did, it would only be as a nanny—a temporary one. And not one who spent the night. There were too many things tainted by this situation, and Jamie's attitude was too much for her to deal with.

But God, did she hate that she was so wrong about him...

Quietly, she walked out of the room and then out the front door. She met Ryleigh and Ryker in the driveway walking toward her. Ryleigh took one look at her and her expression fell.

"Don't go, Fallon. Please. Let's go inside and talk this out."

Shaking her head, she said, "I can't."

"Obviously I have no idea what specifically happened, but you have to know he's upset and out of sorts," Ryleigh pled. "And you know he's a total jackass who speaks first and thinks later. You know how he can be."

"That's just it, Ry. He's had a lot of time to think and he still said a lot of hateful stuff. I get that he's worried and freaking out, but...he's just not in a good place right now and I'm making it worse."

"No. It's not like that. He just needs some time to cool down. Just...please!"

"Babe," Ryker said, touching Ryleigh's arm. "She's got a right to leave. You don't know what went on or what was said, and if Fallon's standing here with her suitcase in her hand, you can be damn sure there's a good reason for it."

Now Ryleigh was crying with her. "I hate this. I hate that this is happening."

"Don't let him be alone tonight," Fallon whispered. "I worry about Asher. Jamie's not thinking clearly and..."

"Can I call you later?" Ryleigh asked. "After the smoke clears, so to speak, can we please talk so I can get your take on it?"

All she did was nod before Ryleigh grabbed her in a fierce hug. "It's all going to be okay. It has to be."

But as Fallon walked to her car, she wasn't so sure.

Chapter Twelve

Fallon was gone.

He saw her walk out the door with her bag and he didn't do a damn thing to stop her.

Not that it would have mattered. Jamie knew he'd screwed up, but...didn't she realize just how much he was freaking out? Wasn't he allowed to express his own emotions without her walking away? What did it say about her if she was willing to throw everything they had away at the first sign of conflict?

Conflict? Pfft...this was some seriously messed up shit and he deserved a little sympathy and understanding! He deserved...

"Give me one reason I shouldn't walk over there and smack your stupid face?" Ryleigh asked as she came storming through the door with Ryker hot on her heels.

What the...?

Frowning, he looked at the two of them in confusion. "What are you doing here?"

"Fallon texted and begged us to come over," his sister

replied. "Apparently you were freaking out and you scared her! What the hell did you do, Jamie?"

"*Me?* This isn't all on me, Ry! I had all kinds of crazy shit dropped on me today and I was freaking out! And rightfully so! Then, while I'm in the middle of explaining how I feel, Fallon starts talking all crazy about how I'm using her because you're all pressuring me to settle down!"

"Why would she think that?"

He shrugged. "How the hell should I know? I told her what you were saying about me settling down and that was the conclusion she came to!"

"Ugh...why are men so clueless?" she murmured before walking into Asher's room and picking him up. As soon as she walked back out to the living room, Jamie was ready with a comeback.

"Why are women so dramatic?" he countered. "You know what? It doesn't matter. So if you're here to yell at me, save your breath. I've got enough on my plate, and Fallon will have to wait her turn."

Ryleigh's eyes went wide. "First of all, wow. That was a crappy thing to say."

He was about to argue, but the next thing he knew, Liam, Tessa, Will, and Arianna were walking in.

Great.

"Where's Pat?" Ryleigh asked.

"He called me while we were on the way here and said he's about ten minutes out," Liam replied. "Now what's going on?"

Rolling his eyes, he told everyone about his meeting with Jenn and his decision to serve her with papers ending her parental rights. "And she's going to be okay with it," he said confidently. "She said it right to my face, so I don't see what the big deal is."

Everyone stared back at him in utter silence.

"What?"

After they all exchanged looks, Liam was the one who spoke. "Okay, so if you're okay with all of this and your plan and don't think it's a big deal, then...why are you so angry and freaking out?"

"Weren't you listening? The lying? The manipulating? Wouldn't you be pissed?"

"Okay, yeah, but...she also explained herself and apologized," Liam responded.

"And...you have to admit, it was kind of brave of her to do that," Arianna commented as she took Asher out of Ryleigh's arms.

"*Brave?* Ari, are you crazy?" he demanded. "After what she did, she *needed* to tell the truth!"

"And telling the truth—especially about something so private and with such a negative stigma attached to it—is brave, Jamie," his sister argued. "And yes, she should have told you the truth sooner, but it sounds like she tried. You're not blameless here, you know."

"Yeah, I got that. But the only thing that would have changed is that I would have been pissed off sooner! She *wanted* to get pregnant! Why is everyone willing to let that fact go?"

"We're not letting it go—and you have a right to be upset," Ryleigh said. "But the fact is, you can't go back and change any of this. And if you're this resentful and angry, then...maybe Jenn isn't the one parent whose rights should be terminated."

So many emotions threatened to overwhelm him, and yet all he could do was stand there and sputter.

"Just...hear me out," she went on. "You were upset when you found Asher on your doorstep, but then you calmed down and settled in to life as a dad. Now you've talked to Jenn, and it sounds like you're using him to punish her. That's not a good thing, Jamie. And that baby has the right to be raised by people who genuinely love him and are willing to put his needs first."

"I have to agree," Liam said quietly. "It's better that you figured this out now. Asher doesn't deserve to be a pawn in all of this." He gave Jamie a solemn look. "You're entitled to be upset, but don't use your own child like this."

"I'm not doing that," he countered wearily. "It's like everyone's taking everything I'm saying and twisting it and then getting pissed at me." Raking both hands through his hair, he sighed loudly. "Why can't I just be mad? We all know I'll get over it."

"Actually, we don't," Arianna said sadly. "Jamie, you're the most easygoing out of all of us. I don't think I've ever seen you this mad. And for Fallon to reach out to us to come over because you upset her..."

"So...why was Fallon mad at you?" Liam asked.

"You heard her the night you were all here—she doesn't agree with me cutting Jenn out of Asher's life. She thinks I should cut her some slack and that Asher's gonna be pissed at me at some point down the road. Maybe. And..." he went on, "she's sympathetic to Jenn's story! I mean...how do we know that story is even true?"

"You could ask to meet with her therapist," Ryleigh suggested. "Granted, she might not share confidential stuff, but it couldn't hurt to ask. This way it could help you understand what Jenn's dealing with and what that means for the future. You owe it to Asher to know all the facts before making such a rash decision."

The front door opened and in walked Patrick.

"Sorry. I got here as fast as I could. What did I miss?"

There was no way Jamie could repeat the story again, so he motioned to Liam, who got Patrick all caught up on his conversation with Jenn. Then Ryleigh explained where they were all at in the discussion.

"Wait...so knowing what you know now, you're still just gonna serve her papers?" Patrick asked. "Dude, that's cold."

"You know, the other night you were all on my side," he reminded them. "What the hell happened?"

"We were all on your side when we didn't have all the facts," Liam said.

"I get that Jenn's almost giving you a free pass," Patrick chimed in, "but...come on. Do you really want to be the guy who kicks her when she's down? Ultimately, she realized she screwed up and tried to make things right. She could have ended the pregnancy or she could have had Asher and never told you. Think about what would have happened if she tried to take care of him while postpartum depression was wreaking havoc on her. Instead, she brought him to you because she knew you would do the right thing. And you have." He paused. "Until now."

This so wasn't going the way he expected.

"You know what? None of you understand because you've never been in this position."

They all exchanged looks again before Patrick responded. "Yeah, we haven't, but that doesn't mean we don't know what we're talking about. I think I can speak for myself, Liam, Will, and Ryker and say that we'd definitely be pissed if this happened to us. But I'd like to think that we wouldn't have a knee-jerk reaction and that we'd take some time to think things through."

"A buddy of mine in the service came home from leave a few years ago and found out a woman he had an on-again, off-again relationship with had his baby," Will said. "He completely freaked out. She told him she knew he wasn't looking to be tied down and thought it was for the best that he didn't know. They argued about it for..." He looked over at Liam. "How long was that? Remember Donny Finley?"

"Oh, yeah...it took them something like six months to get custody worked out."

Will nodded. "Now they co-parent. Donny retired last year when Liam and I did, and he seems pretty happy. He's engaged to someone else and so is the ex." He paused. "No one's saying you have to be Jenn's best friend or even share custody 50/50 with her. I'm sure you can even put a temporary custody arrangement in place to see how things go. You're a smart guy, Jamie. Don't do something stupid in the heat of the moment."

He wanted to tell Will to butt out since he wasn't family, but...he kind of was.

"Okay, fine," he said begrudgingly. "What am I supposed to do?"

"That depends," Arianna replied.

"On?"

"You need to decide if you genuinely want to be a full-time father to Asher," she told him. "All this time you were waiting to hear Jenn's story, and now that you have and you know you have options, are you all in? Because if you're not, then you need to give him the chance to be raised in a loving household." She snuggled the baby close and Jamie swore he saw tears in her eyes.

"I would never give him up," he said fiercely. "Never. I'm having a bad night and if we're all honest, everyone has a time when they feel overwhelmed."

"It was more than that, Jamie," Ryleigh said quietly. "You chased Fallon off. She's been dealing with your bullshit for years and this is the first time she ever ran away."

Yeah...now that he was feeling slightly more like himself, he could admit how he took things out on her that he shouldn't have. But he wasn't the only one who behaved badly. She could have stayed and talked to him like she usually did. They never had a problem pushing each other's buttons and then talking things out.

Until they started sleeping together.

Then it changed everything.

Duh...am I really surprised?

Collapsing back down in his chair, Jamie felt all the fight go out of him. Closing his eyes, he wished he could go back to this morning and just start the entire day over.

"I'll talk to Fallon in the morning and we'll work this out," he murmured.

"I don't think she's coming back, Jamie," Ryleigh told him soberly. "She was crying and...you should probably wait a few days before talking to her. And make sure you're calmer when you do."

"Any chance any of you are free to watch Asher tomorrow, then?" he asked wearily. "I don't want to dump more responsibility on Uncle Ronan. He already covered for me because I took the morning off."

Ryleigh volunteered. "My schedule is light for the next couple of days. I'll bring my laptop with me and get some work done while Asher naps. You'll just have to give me his schedule."

He nodded and suddenly was too exhausted to speak. It felt like the weight of the world was on him and he had no idea what to do next. The thought of Fallon walking out of his life was too much to think about. In his mind, this was one of their fights and they should be fine in a day or two. He knew how much she loved Asher and couldn't imagine her simply walking away.

Why not? Jenn did and she's his biological mother...

He couldn't afford to think like that and did his best to push that thought aside.

For several minutes everyone seemed to be talking, but Jamie couldn't focus on any of it. He knew he could be a hothead, and now that he had time to talk to his siblings, he realized everyone was right. He needed time to think this all through. And while he did, his focus had to be his son. Asher meant the world to him and he couldn't let his frustration with this situation influence how he cared for the baby.

No matter what, Asher was his top priority.

Hopefully Ryleigh could help him out for a couple of days and then...maybe...Fallon would talk to him. He knew she'd make him beg and grovel, and even though he was opposed to it right now, he'd cave and do it.

And just prayed it wouldn't be too late.

* * *

Her childhood bed felt small and lumpy and ridiculously uncomfortable.

And lonely.

Yeah, as upset as she was, she desperately missed sleeping next to Jamie.

The rat bastard.

It had only been three hours since she walked out of his house, and she physically ached with missing him and Asher. She'd forced herself to get undressed and put pajamas on and crawl into bed to keep her from getting in her car and going back over there. Fallon knew Ryleigh and the rest of the Donovans would make sure Asher was okay and well taken care of, but she hated that she'd taken the coward's way out by leaving.

"Self-preservation," she reminded herself. "It was for my own well-being."

Still, she really wished Ryleigh would call her and let her know what was going on. The fact that she hadn't called probably meant they were still working things out, but...it seemed to be taking a long time.

Staring at her phone where it sat on her bedside table, she willed it to ring.

But she ended up having to wait almost another hour before it finally did. Sagging with relief, she swiped the screen.

"Hey, Ry," she said softly. "How'd everything go? How's Asher?"

"He's fine and currently sound asleep. I'm staying here tonight to make sure everyone's okay."

"Oh. That's great. Thanks."

"How are you doing? Are you okay?"

"I think so. I'm mad at myself for letting Jamie run me off like that, but in the moment, I knew I couldn't stay. I hate that I let him get to me because I really thought we were over that part of our relationship."

"Well, to be fair, he was really not himself tonight. I think we all had a moment or two when we wanted to either shake him, slap him, or strangle him," Ryleigh said with a small laugh. "I couldn't believe how long it took to talk things through."

Fallon desperately wanted to ask what they talked about and if they got him to change his mind, but she was almost afraid of the answer.

"Was Ryker okay with you staying there tonight?" she asked instead.

"Of course. I mean...he's not thrilled, but he knew there was no way I'd be able to go home and relax. He offered to stay with me, but after seeing how small the bed was in Asher's room, we both realized he wouldn't even fit in it."

The image made Fallon laugh. "Yeah, it's not bad for one person, but it's definitely not made for two. No matter how much you like to snuggle."

"Exactly." She sighed. "So...what happens now? Do you want to come back tomorrow? Do you need a few days? Or are you just done?"

"Honestly, Ryleigh, I'm not sure. I'm so in love with Asher and want to be there with him, but with things being over with Jamie, I'm not sure it's such a good idea."

"Fallon, come on. The two of you had a fight. All couples fight. And the two of you have been fighting with each other for over twenty years. Take a few days to relax and regroup, and then the two of you should sit down and talk."

It all sounded completely logical, but...

"Can I ask you something?"

"Absolutely," Ryleigh said confidently.

"Did you purposely reach out to me to help Jamie because I was the only one available, or did you have ulterior motives?"

"I'm not sure what you're implying."

Ugh...she hated that Jamie got in her head. And what was worse was how she was now doubting Ryleigh—who she always considered to be a good friend.

So who am I supposed to believe?

At her hesitation, Ryleigh tried to bring the subject back a few paces. "Would you consider just going back as Asher's nanny? Like if Jamie knew to just let the personal aspect of your relationship go until you were ready to talk about it, would you do it?"

"It's hard to say right now what I'm going to do, but the practical side of me is saying that we originally agreed to me helping him out for three weeks and...we went a little over that. He knew he was going to have to find someone to take over at that point."

"Okay, I get that, but...have you found another job?"

"I had a phone interview earlier today, but it wasn't something I was too excited about. And I'm not going to find something to get excited about if I stay on taking care of Asher. I adore that boy and the longer I stay, the less I'm going to want to leave."

"Yeah, I get that. He's so freaking adorable, and just holding him makes me want to have one of my own." She paused. "But...you and Jamie? I hate to think of this being over between the two of you."

"Which brings me back to my question: What was your motivation for asking me to be the one to come and help Jamie out?"

Ryleigh sighed. "At first, it was legit just about you being available and having the background in early child-hood stuff and I remembered how much you used to babysit, so I knew you could handle the position. It wasn't until I was around the two of you that I got hopeful. I'd been noticing Jamie's reaction to you for a while, but that didn't play into why I thought of you. Believe me, there was nothing nefarious about my reaching out. And, if anything, Jamie was the one who brought up the two of you getting together for Asher's sake."

Shit.

That's what she was afraid of.

"Oh."

Muttering a curse, Ryleigh tried to backpedal a bit.

"What I mean is...we were talking the day of the barbecue and I mentioned how he was going to need to settle down a bit and maybe think about having someone here full time. You know, not like a nanny, but a partner. A wife. And he thought I was hinting at the two of you, and..."

"It's okay, Ryleigh. It just proves my point on what I was asking him earlier and he got super defensive. This just confirms that I wasn't crazy."

"Look, my brother is a lot of things, but he's not manipulative and he's not a schemer. If he was with you, it was because he wanted to be and not because of some stupid idea I put in his head."

If only she were right...

"You're wrong, Ry. While Jamie's not your typical manipulator and he doesn't do it to be harmful, he knows how to use his charm to get what he wants." Closing her eyes, Fallon willed herself not to cry. "And after years of making fun of the girls who fell for that charm, I ended up falling victim to it too. So..."

"Fine, he's a flirt and a charmer, and he just can't seem to help himself, but you have to know it was different with you. The two of you have a history. This whole thing had to catch you both off guard and, if you're brutally honest with yourself, you know my brother would never marry you or anyone else if he didn't want to. I may have told him he needed to settle down, but he wouldn't do that just because I told him to. Besides being charming, he's stubborn."

That was true...

"You know what? I'll tell you exactly what I told Jamie earlier. I can't help but notice how the timing of our relationship falls into that timeline. Putting all of that together, the man I've been living with—sleeping with—and the man standing before me are two very different men. And I don't particularly care for this one." She let out a long breath. "I understand that there were extenuating circumstances today. I really do. But...I just need some time to let it all sink in."

"But..."

Fallon couldn't help but chuckle. "Yup. There's always a but."

"I have a feeling this one isn't a good but."

"Would you want to be in a relationship where you felt like you were the convenient choice?" she asked sadly. "Would you settle for second place?"

"It wouldn't be like that..."

"But I'll never know, will I? I'll always be wondering if Jamie and I would even be a thing if we hadn't been forced together the way we were. If there were no Asher, would he ever have even tried to look at me as a woman rather than the pain in the ass he grew up with?"

"Damn."

"Believe me, I know."

"This sucks."

"I know that too."

"Fallon, I just...I wish..."

"Yeah," she said wearily. "Me too."

They were both silent for several long moments. "So what happens now?"

"Now...I'm going to probably cry myself to sleep, spend all day tomorrow feeling sorry for myself while eating all the junk food I can get my hands on, and then...I'll put some serious time into looking for a new job that maybe isn't so close to Laurel Bay." The nervous laugh was out before she could stop it. "I guess I got a little too ahead of myself on that one."

"No," Ryleigh said quietly. "You didn't. You were in love and trying to plan for your future."

"It wasn't love," she argued, her tone equally quiet. "It was too soon for that."

"If Jamie had been someone you just met, then yes. But you've known each other for practically your entire lives. It was love."

"Joke's on me then, because obviously I was wrong. About all of it. I'm never someone to daydream or give in to whimsy and...he made me believe in all of it."

"Or maybe you believed because it was true."

Yawning, Fallon got a little more comfortable—or as comfortable as she could get—in the bed. "It's all too much to wrap my head around tonight."

"I understand."

"And Asher's okay? You're good with staying with him?"

"Absolutely."

"He sometimes will sleep until three, so you'll only have to get up once," she explained. "And be sure to keep the lights dim in the room while you go and heat up his bottle and change his diaper. Speak in soft tones so he knows it's not time to get up and play or anything."

"Jamie told me that."

"Oh." She paused. "Did you read him a book before he went to sleep? It's something that we've been doing and..."

"Actually, Jamie read to him."

"Oh." Another pause. "In the morning, after Jamie leaves for work, we've been going for walks and Asher really loves to spend time in the swing. I usually put him in it while I make lunch. And it helps when he's fussy too."

"Fallon?"

"Hmm?"

"It's all going to be okay. If anything happens that I can't handle, I promise to call you."

"Thanks, and...sorry. I'm sounding like a nervous parent, which is weird, since I'm definitely...you know...*not* his parent." And then tears stung her eyes and she knew she didn't want to still be on the phone when she began to cry.

"You're the best kind of parent," Ryleigh told her. "You took care of him and loved him and nurtured him because you genuinely wanted to. So if you ask me, Asher got lucky when you came into his life."

"Dammit, Ryleigh," she said, her voice shaking. "I need to go."

"I'm sorry! Don't cry! I just meant..."

"I really need to go. I'll talk to you tomorrow, okay?"

"It's all going to be alright. Get some sleep and we'll definitely talk tomorrow."

All Fallon could do was nod before hanging up.

Then she rolled over, buried her face in her pillow, and cried as if her heart were breaking.

She had no idea if it would ever heal or if she even wanted it to. This was the most emotion she had felt in her life and, sadly, it was possibly a good thing. After getting fired twice, she was beginning to fear that she was too detached emotionally to connect with people. But these last few weeks with Jamie and Asher proved that she could feel and connect.

She just wished it hadn't led to her feeling like she'd never be happy again.

Chapter Thirteen

Three days.

Three of the longest days of his life.

How many women had he watched walk away without really feeling a thing?

Not this time.

Having Fallon walk away hurt more than he ever thought possible. And it had nothing to do with her working for him and caring for Asher, it was on a deeply emotional level.

One that he didn't even realize he had.

It was a hell of a way to find out.

Now, he was trying to navigate...life. He knew Fallon had pretty much saved him the day she first showed up at his house, and he knew that—thanks to her—he knew how to care properly for his son. Now he had to figure out how to work full-time and make sure Asher had the best care.

Ryleigh was a total lifesaver these last few days. She was there for him and Asher and made sure his son's life wasn't disrupted in any way. He knew this too was temporary, but he was beyond grateful for her. But he also knew that she had a life of her own and a job and something was going to have to give soon. Their parents were due home in another ten days and at that point, he knew things would get easier, but he still had to get through those ten days.

When he got home from the pub, he found Ryker's truck in the driveway along with his sister's car. Not that he was surprised, but he was tired and not feeling particularly hospitable.

"Hey," Ryleigh said as he walked in the door. "How was business today?"

"Good. We had a killer lunch crowd and the weekly order thing for that office group. Bobby's got it all down to a science, but I think when Mom and Dad get back, we still should look into hiring someone else part-time to help in the kitchen."

"That makes sense. I'd like to cut back on doing it, personally. But I didn't want to do anything until after they got back from their trip." She was sitting on the sofa feeding Asher.

"Hey, Ryker," Jamie said as he grabbed himself something to drink. "How are things going over at your shop?"

"Can't complain. I'm heading out to a convention next week in L.A. so my schedule's a little light right now. Whenever there's a trip coming up, I need time to focus on all the travel arrangements and getting everything to where it needs to be."

Nodding, he sat down in the big, oversized chair that he favored.

Ryleigh gently cleared her throat. "Which means we need to have a talk," she said hesitantly.

Holding up a hand, Jamie stopped her. "You don't need to say anything. You've already helped out more than I ever expected and I'm guessing you're going to L.A. with Ryker."

"Exactly. I'm fine doing my work here—it's not nearly as hard as I thought it would be—but...I'm going to need time before we go to pack up and wrap up some projects, so..."

"Ry, I get it. I appreciate everything you've been doing, so just tell me when you need to not be here, and I'll figure something out."

She and Ryker exchanged looks and Jamie almost dreaded what was coming next.

"I'm going home tonight," she told him. "I'll be back in the morning, but...I miss sleeping in my own bed and being with Ryker."

"Ew...TMI, Ryleigh," he joked.

"Don't be such a baby," she teased right back. "I think things have calmed down and you're perfectly capable of handling the nights on your own."

Like he had a choice...

"I know I am," he told her, but even he didn't believe it.

"Have you thought about calling Fallon?" she asked.

"No," he said gruffly. "I screwed up. I know I screwed up, but...so did she."

Ryker groaned loudly, and Ryleigh's eyes nearly bugged right out of her head. "How on earth did you come to that conclusion?"

"All couples fight, Ry. You know it, I know it, and I'm sure Ryker knows it too."

"Oh, I do," Ryker said with a smirk.

"Yeah, okay, I get it," Ryleigh went on. "But what did Fallon do that you can possibly call a screw up?"

"We've been fighting our entire lives," he said, but there was no real heat or malice in his words. "And the first time we fought as a couple, she packed up and left. The old Fallon would have stayed and given me hell for being such an ass, but instead, she went inside and called in the cavalry and then snuck out without a word."

His sister was quiet for a minute before she responded. "It was a bad night and I think she just felt like everything she said to you was making you even angrier than you already were. And for all the so-called fighting the two of you did, it was never that personal, Jamie. She had a right to be upset and I think she took the high road by leaving."

He eyed her suspiciously.

"You've talked to her," he said. It wasn't a question; he simply knew.

She nodded. "Of course I did. We're friends."

It would be childish to remind her that he was her brother, but...

"Wouldn't you like to work things out with her?" she asked.

More than anything...

"My life is far too complicated right now," he said solemnly. "I'm obviously not great at multitasking because look at what a mess I've made of everything."

"You didn't make a mess, Jamie. You became a father with zero notice and you're doing a great job, you're running the pub and business is doing great, and you had one bad day." She paused. "I hate to bring up a sore subject, but...have you thought anymore about what you're going to do about Jenn?"

"Ryleigh..." Ryker said with a groan. "You promised you weren't going to bring that up."

"I know, I know, and I'm sorry, but...I'm curious!"

The thing was, he had been thinking about it a lot and nothing was clear anymore. The biggest issue was that he seriously didn't feel like he could trust her. It would be fine if it were just him involved, but there was no way he was going to gamble with his son's well-being. And after the way everyone came down on him the other night, Jamie felt it was probably for the best to take their advice and simply...think.

His brain was actually starting to hurt from all of it.

Had he come to any conclusions?

Not really.

From the moment he read Jenn's letter, he was fairly confident that he knew exactly what he was going to do if she ever came back. And once she did and he heard her story? It confirmed that he was doing the right thing.

But now—thanks to his family's lectures and Fallon's words—he was second-guessing himself. He really wished he could talk to Fallon about it, but he had a feeling that both of their emotions were raw and too close to the surface for them to have an unbiased discussion.

God, I hate how I'm growing...

"Uh...Jamie?"

Oh, right. His sister was curious.

"I'm taking everyone's advice and thinking about the situation from every angle. I've been in touch with my attorney, and...I might ask Jenn if I can talk to her therapist. I'm not sure if that sort of thing is allowed, but it can't hurt to ask."

Ryleigh started smiling from ear to ear.

"What? What are you smiling about?"

"Because I'm proud of you! A few days ago, I wanted to strangle you, but I knew you just needed a little time to redeem yourself!"

"Redeem myself? Seriously?"

"Dude, you were such a major jerk that night! We all wanted to punch you. Actually, Liam had to pay Patrick not to punch you, so...yeah. Jerk."

It shouldn't have been funny, and yet it was.

"Like I said that night, no one can really understand unless it's specifically happening to you. As bystanders, it's easy to pass judgement and say what I should or shouldn't be doing. But I can guarantee you, if you were the one going through it, it wouldn't be so easy."

"No one thought it was easy," she countered. "We just knew you were smarter than you were behaving."

"Let's just say I'm working on it," he said vaguely. "But...I need to know that whatever it is that I decide, you'll all support me."

"Jamie..."

"Fine. That you'll at least keep your opinions to yourselves if you don't agree with me."

"I don't like the sound of that."

He shrugged. "It's the best I can do."

Fortunately, the topic finally changed and Ryker talked about the tattoo convention they were going to. It still seemed wild that his fairly straightlaced sister was engaged to a tattoo artist. They were polar opposites in almost every way, but anyone could see how they were crazy in love.

Just like Liam and Tessa.

Sweet little Tessa was the cheeriest woman on the planet and an elementary school music teacher. Meanwhile, Liam was mild-mannered—or grumpy—and most of the time, he seemed a little too serious. And yet...they worked.

And that led him to thinking about Arianna and Will and how the two of them really shouldn't work. His baby sister was loud and impulsive and overly opinionated, while Will was quieter and more reserved and liked to fly under the radar. Plus, the ten-year age gap should have been a bit of a deterrent, but it wasn't. No one saw this relationship coming—and when they did, they were against it—but...

they're engaged and planning their lives and also sickeningly in love.

He and Fallon were total opposites.

They'd spent years being enemies.

And in a million years, he never imagined himself ever falling in love with her.

But...he had.

Awesome. He was the only Donovan who fell for someone that didn't make any sense and couldn't make it work.

How many years had he fought for his place—for the chance to be seen as a peer rather than the lesser brother? And in the end, his siblings all still had him beat.

Something to worry about at another time.

Right now, his plate was already overflowing with shit he needed to deal with.

* * *

"Oh my goodness! I think he's grown! Don't you think he's grown?"

Beside her, Ryleigh chuckled. "In three days? Um...no."

Fallon smiled down at Asher and couldn't stop smiling. She knew he was too young to really be smiling at her or even recognizing her, but in her mind, he was excited to see her. She cuddled him against her chest and almost sighed at how good it felt to hold him.

"I'm so glad you called," she said to Ryleigh.

"Well, I knew you had to be missing him and you mentioned walking in the park, so I thought you might like this."

"I really do. You have no idea how much I needed this."

They sat in companionable silence for several minutes,

which was fine with her because she just wanted to soak up every minute with this sweet baby boy.

"So, how are things going?" Ryleigh asked. "Any interviews lined up?"

Inwardly, she groaned.

"I had one this morning for a daycare center coordinator."

"And?"

"The pay was awful, and I'm fairly certain the place has multiple violations. When I got home, I actually reported some of them myself."

"No!" Ryleigh laughed. "You didn't!"

Nodding, she grinned. "I really did. It was terrible and it just made me sad. The place had so much potential, but it was like nobody cared about it anymore. It needed a complete overhaul. The location was great—near the south side of Magnolia Sound—but it would need a lot of time, money, and TLC to make it a place I'd feel comfortable being in." She sighed. "I seriously wish there was a nice place here in town for kids like Asher, you know? A place that Jamie could bring him to that was clean and updated and had a low teacher-to-child ratio."

"I'm just throwing this out there, but...have you thought about opening one?"

"What?!" she cried. "Are you crazy? Do you have any idea how much something like that would cost?"

"Nope. But what I do know is that there is a lot of space available in downtown that could easily be converted. Patrick could totally help you with that and find you the perfect space in a heartbeat. And I think it's something that Laurel Bay really needs. Even if you did it as a part-time place—something parents can use while they run errands or where they can drop their kids off for a couple of hours rather than making it a forty-hour-a-week gig."

"Maybe..."

"Plus, you already have the degree, Fallon. It would just be a matter of getting the license and the funding in the form of a small business loan," Ryleigh went on. "The way I see it, you keep looking for jobs and none of them sound inspiring or even mildly interesting to you. Maybe that's because you need to do something on your own."

It sounded like a great idea, but then she remembered the comments from her previous employers and felt a little sick to her stomach. She'd never shared with Ryleigh what went wrong, but...perhaps she could help.

"Um...can I tell you something?"

Nodding, Ryleigh said, "Of course."

"I got fired from my last two jobs. My only jobs since I graduated," she added for emphasis. "They both said I wasn't connecting with my co-workers. I'm...I'm unlikable and...how am I supposed to hire a team and lead them—or how am I supposed to instill confidence in parents who might want to register with me—if no one likes me?"

And dammit, she didn't want to cry!

But she did.

"Oh, sweetie, I had no idea!" Taking Asher from her arms, Ryleigh placed him in the stroller before facing Fallon again. "I'm so sorry that happened, but...maybe it's a blessing in disguise."

Glancing over, she fought the urge to roll her eyes. "How?"

"It brought you here. Maybe those jobs didn't work out because you weren't comfortable with them because they weren't where you were supposed to be. Just...think about it. I'm not saying you have to do this, but...it's an option, right?"

She nodded and knew she'd be researching the hell out of it when she got home.

"Listen, I'm...I'm going away with Ryker next week. To California. We're going to be gone for a week and I was curious if...you know...maybe you'd consider helping with Asher."

It was beyond tempting, but she knew she wasn't ready to be around Jamie like that again. Not yet. Although...

"I don't think so. I'm not ready," she admitted quietly. "Do you know what he's going to do?"

Ryleigh shook her head. "He said he'll work it out, but I'm not sure how. I know Tessa said she could help maybe for a day or two, and Ari volunteered to take a day off, but I didn't get into it too much with him. I feel like I'm the last person he's going to take childcare advice from."

"Because of me?"

"I want to say no, but..."

"Then it's because of me," Fallon said flatly. "I'm sorry."

With a hearty laugh, Ryleigh looked at her like she was crazy. "What are you sorry for?" But before she could answer, her friend added, "You know what? We're not going to go there again."

"Whew!" she said with amusement. "Thank God!"

Reaching out, she touched Asher's little feet and then his hands and just absorbed every minute she had with him.

"When do you leave?"

"Next week."

"Any chance we can do this again tomorrow?"

"You're on!"

* * *

For the next three days, Fallon met Ryleigh at the park and got in an hour of snuggle time with Asher. It was the perfect distraction for her days and the best encouragement to keep looking into maybe starting up a daycare center of her own.

That's how she found herself having lunch with Patrick at the pub.

Jamie had taken the day off—something she confirmed before agreeing to meet him there—and as she slid into the booth, she still couldn't help but look around anxiously.

"Trust me," Patrick said with an easy grin. "Jamie's home. My uncle confirmed it, and so did Ryleigh. You're not going to run into him, okay?"

She let out a long breath and nodded. "Okay. Sorry."

"Nothing to apologize for. I'm sure things are still a little...you know...weird."

"That's one way to describe it," she said with a nervous laugh.

"Okay, no more talk about my brother. Ryleigh said you're looking to open a business and needed to find some space, but she wouldn't elaborate. So...talk to me."

She always liked Patrick. He was fairly easy to talk to, always polite and friendly—although not as laid-back as Jamie—and from everything she'd heard, he was a real estate whiz.

"This wasn't something that was on my radar until I met up with Ryleigh the other day," she began. "But I'm exploring the possibility of opening a daycare center here in Laurel Bay."

His eyes went a little wide, but his smile was genuine. "I think that's a fantastic idea. We don't have one and you know there's always a need for one." Pulling out his tablet from his satchel, he began taking notes. "Tell me what kind of space you're looking for, residential or commercial?"

"I'm thinking commercial. I don't want to live there."

He nodded. "Storefront or a standalone building with property?"

"I know the rent would probably be cheaper with a storefront, but it would be nice to have some property to fence in for a playground, and we'd definitely need parking."

He nodded again. "I'll have to do some research on zoning and licensing, but in the meantime, I have a couple of properties we can look at today. Just remember that it's possible none of them might work, but we should walk through and get ideas for what you realistically think you'll need and what modifications would have to be considered."

She let out a shaky breath. "It all seems a bit over-whelming. Maybe this isn't the best idea. I don't have any money, I'd have to get financing for all of it, and considering I don't have a job, and..."

Reaching across the table, he took her hand in his and gave it a reassuring squeeze. "Fallon, breathe. Yes, there are going to be a lot of hurdles, but I think once you put together your business plan, things could fall into place faster than you think. That's why it's important that we do our homework and gather as much information as we can."

"Um..."

"My assistant Marissa is fantastic with research. After we check out some properties today, come back to the office with me and we'll sit down with her and let her know what you're planning. She'll do everything she can to gather the data we need to put in with the bank." He winked. "Don't worry. You've got this."

With a weak smile, she said, "It sounds more like you've got this. I feel like I'm in over my head."

He squeezed her hand again. "It's always a little

daunting starting something new—especially a business. But I promise you're not going to have to go through it alone. You'll have a ton of people on your side helping you navigate everything if you decide this is what you want to do."

When Ryleigh first mentioned it, the idea intrigued her. The more she thought about it, the more excited she got.

And then terrified, and then excited again.

It was an absolute roller coaster ride and she still hadn't decided if she wanted to stay on or jump off.

Turning her hand in his, she gave it a little squeeze too. "You have no idea how much that means to me. Just know you'll probably have to remind me of that like a hundred times a day."

"You got it," he told her.

Someone cleared their throat to get their attention, and Fallon felt like the floor had dropped out beneath her when she turned and saw Jamie standing beside their table. She slowly pulled her hand from Patrick's and noticed how Jamie's eyes followed that movement.

"Hey," Patrick said with an easy grin. "I thought you had the day off today."

"I do, but I needed to come in and do some payroll stuff. I've got Asher with me, but Uncle Ronan's got him at the moment."

Fallon glanced toward the bar and couldn't help but smile at how Ronan was cradling the baby and showing him around behind the bar.

"So? You two look cozy," Jamie said with a hint of disdain. "What's going on?"

Patrick looked at her and she hoped the panicked look in her eye conveyed that she didn't want anyone knowing about but she was working on.

"I have a client who is thinking of opening a daycare center here in town," Patrick said smoothly. "They didn't seem to know a lot about the process and I'm trying to help as much as I can, so I thought I'd talk to Fallon. With her degree, I knew she'd be able to answer a lot of my questions."

She almost sagged with relief and knew she'd have to thank him profusely when they were alone again.

"Plus, I knew it was pot roast day here and you know it's my favorite," he went on, "and it just made sense to meet here. We were just..." His words were cut off by the sound of his phone ringing. Frowning at the screen, he slid out of the booth. "Um...excuse me for a moment. Sorry, Fallon." And then he was gone.

Dammit.

Unable to look up at him, Fallon studied her hands as she clasped them on the table.

"So, um...how've you been?" Jamie asked as he took his brother's seat.

With no other choice, she glanced up and her heart kicked hard in her chest. "Good," she said, hating how shaky and breathless she sounded. "How's Asher doing?"

Not that she had to ask. She'd seen him every day for the last several days.

"He's good. He had some colic issues last night, so neither of us got much sleep, but...other than that, he's awesome."

Nodding, she said, "That's good."

It was an awkward silence and she prayed Patrick would come back soon, but as she looked around, she didn't see him anywhere.

"Yeah, um...when he gets a call, he tends to walk outside," Jamie explained. "No one knows why, but it happens like that all the time." He paused. "Have you ordered lunch yet?"

"No. We were just talking and no one came over to take our orders yet."

"Let me get you something to drink at least, and then I'll send Sadie over to..."

"Jamie," she interrupted. "It's okay. I can wait for Patrick."

"You might be waiting a while."

She really hoped not.

"I'll be fine. I'm sure you need to get to that payroll stuff," she prompted, hoping he'd take the hint. "And your uncle won't be able to amuse Asher for long, so..."

He nodded, and Fallon watched as he started to slide out of the booth. She held her breath and prayed he'd keep going, but...he stopped.

"I miss you," he said gruffly.

Everything in her stilled. The words secretly thrilled her, but...this was what Jamie did best. He'd schmooze and charm, and she couldn't allow herself to be taken in again. That's why she held her tongue and said nothing.

"I...I just wanted you to know," he said after a moment. "I know I messed everything up, but...I'd really like the chance for us to sit down and talk sometime. Maybe you can come over for dinner, and..."

"I don't think that's a good idea."

"Okay, we can go out someplace...that restaurant we went to in Beaufort..."

She shook her head.

"Or the coffeehouse..."

Again, she shook her head. "Jamie, I just don't feel like there's anything to say that won't cause an argument. And honestly, I'm tired of fighting with you." Her shoulders sagged. "I *can't* keep fighting with you," she corrected. "I have to focus on my own life right now and...and I'm sorry if you're struggling to find childcare, but I can't help you again. I'm sorry."

His expression was bleak. "It had nothing to do with childcare and everything to do with the fact that I miss you, Fallon. I miss seeing you and talking with you...I miss laughing with you and sleeping beside you." He swallowed hard. "You left a giant hole in my life and even if you can't forgive me, I'd hate to think that we lost everything—even the tentative friendship we finally achieved."

She laughed softly. "I miss you too," she admitted. "But the only way I'm going to move on and feel good about myself is if I stop looking back. You and I will never see eye to eye on things and while I respect that and know that no two people can agree on everything, some of those things aren't ones I can live with on a daily basis."

He nodded. "Yeah, I know." Sliding a little more out of the booth, he paused one more time. "If you ever want to come by and see Asher, I promise I can arrange for Ryleigh or Ari to do it if you don't want to see me. I hope it doesn't come to that, but I'll accept it if it does."

All she could do was nod and whisper, "Thanks."

"Let me go and get you a drink." He glanced toward the door. "Here comes Patrick. I'll make sure Sadie comes over to get your orders."

"Thanks, Jamie," she said and their gazes held for a long moment. It felt like a lifetime since they'd looked at each other like that, and it felt like they were the only ones in the room.

"Wow, sorry about that!" Patrick said as he walked back over. He clapped Jamie on the back. "Can you send someone over to take our orders? I've got some showings in an hour that I need to get to."

With a curt nod, Jamie walked away and it felt like a little piece of her heart walked away with him.

"You okay?" Patrick asked.

No.

Offering him a weak smile, she nodded. "Yeah. Sure."

"Excellent! Let me tell you what I have planned for this afternoon..."

Chapter Fourteen

"And you're sure about this?"

Jamie nodded. "I think it's a good start, don't you?"

"I do, but...this will be the fourth revision. I want you to be aware that you're paying me by the hour, and these revisions take a lot of time."

Arthur McDermott was a local attorney and one who his family worked with on everything. He was pretty much the only one outside of Jamie, his siblings, Ronan, and Fallon, who knew everything that was going on. His time didn't come cheap, but Jamie knew it was important to have someone who knew the law inside and out to help him with this issue.

Chuckling, he shook his head. "I know, but...it needs to be handled the right way so no one gets hurt ever again."

Nodding, Arthur made a few more notes on the document. "Can I offer you a little advice?"

"Sure."

"Take another day to think on this and...do your research. I understand what you're saying and what you're trying to do, but considering how many times you've asked for me to make changes and tweak things, it tells me you're still not settled." He paused and gave Jamie a stern yet concerned look. "You know what you need to do."

It was pointless to argue because it wasn't like he was the only person giving him that same advice, and as much as he hated it and wanted to tell everyone to mind their own business, maybe they were all right.

And Lord knows how much he hated being wrong.

With a curt nod, he rose. "Okay. I'll be in touch."

Arthur stood and shook his hand. "Take your time on this one, Jamie. Some things are hard to undo."

"Thanks, Arthur."

Walking out of the office that was only down the block from the pub, Jamie considered whether he was ready to go to work or if he wanted to go home for a little while and spend some time with his son while he did some serious thinking.

"Home," he murmured. They had plenty of coverage at the pub and today was Ryleigh's last day with Asher before she left for L.A. with Ryker. Tomorrow, Arianna volunteered to take a personal day, and then the two days after that, Tessa was stepping in to help. He knew he needed to sit down and start looking at daycare options, but his heart wasn't in it. Asher was too little for that and Jamie liked the idea of him being cared for at home.

He just had no idea how to make that happen.

Although part of him was trying to juggle it all until his parents got back. Then things would be a little easier. He could take some time off and he knew his mother would help. It wasn't ideal and it wasn't like he wasn't willing to pay someone to watch the baby, but...he wanted it to be someone he knew and someone who would love and protect him.

Groaning, he muttered, "I have issues."

Driving through town, his mind wandered to his own childhood in Laurel Bay and all the things he wanted Asher to experience here—the baseball field at the elementary school where he played Little League, the giant hill behind the middle school that was great for sledding the few times they got snow, riding his bike to go to a friend's house, and playing on the playground at the park. The house he was currently renting was only a block away from that park and while Jamie knew he wasn't in any rush to move, he liked the idea of staying in that area so it was something Asher could go to whenever he wanted.

As he got closer to the house, he spotted Ryleigh pushing his son's stroller, and it looked like she was heading to the park now. Smiling, he slowed down and watched as she walked into the park. He was about to get out and join her when he spotted Fallon walking toward her. They hugged, and then Fallon picked Asher up out of his stroller and held him close. Her smile was radiant and his gut twisted.

Seeing her the other day with his brother left him feeling angry and hurt. It bothered him that Patrick had the right to be with her and talk with her and make her laugh when he no longer could. It wasn't fair, and he just wanted things to go back to the way they were before. And not just because of the way she took care of his son, but because of the way she made him feel. He missed her.

He loved her.

And it was a hell of a time to figure that out.

Rather than staying in his truck like a creeper, Jamie pulled away and went home. He had a lot to think about and maybe having the time in the house with no one around would help. And when he walked inside, it hit him how it had been over a month since he'd been alone with no one there. It felt quiet and empty and...wrong.

He used to love to come home and have the place to himself—like his own little fortress of solitude after a day at the pub or a night out with friends or a woman—but now he'd give anything to come home and play with Asher and then have dinner with Fallon and end the day making love to her in their bed.

Raking a hand through his hair, he collapsed on the sofa and closed his eyes. He could have all of that again, but it would take a lot of work. Normally, Jamie did his best to skate his way around doing things the hard way and tended to find a loophole so others would have to do the grunt work for him.

But this would be completely on him.

And he knew the end result would be worth it.

His mind raced with all the things he'd need to do and knew it would require him to leave his comfort zone, but with a little help from his siblings—because this is what they did for one another—it could work.

An hour later, Ryleigh came walking through the door with Asher. "Hey! What are you doing here? Did everything go alright with the attorney?"

Sitting up, he took his son from her when she got closer. "Yeah, everything went fine. I just needed a little time to let everything sink in."

She nodded, but the last they had spoken, his sister still wasn't on the same page as him.

No one was.

"How often do you meet Fallon at the park?" he casually asked.

Her eyes went a little wide. "Um...what?"

"Was today the first time?"

"How do you know I saw Fallon at the park?"

"Because I was driving home and saw you," he said with a laugh. "And before you get all defensive and pissy, I'm not mad about it. I think it's great."

"Really?" she asked suspiciously.

"You know I miss her and I'm sure she misses Asher." He shrugged. "I know I'm the reason she won't come here to the house to see him, so if the two of you worked something out, then I'm glad."

"Oh...then...okay. We've pretty much been meeting up for almost a week. We hang out in the park for an hour and talk and...that's it. She knows I'm leaving for L.A. so..."

"Did you tell Ari to meet up with her?"

She nodded.

"And Tessa?"

She nodded again.

"You didn't have to keep it a secret, Ry. I'm not an ogre."

"That's debatable. You weren't particularly rational for a little while."

"Yeah, well...I'm working on it." Smiling at Asher, he talked nonsense to him for a few minutes before looking at his sister again. "Can I run something by you?"

"Of course!"

"And do you swear not to blab it to everyone?"

"Um..."

"How about you can blab it to Ari, Liam, Patrick, Will, Tessa, and Ryker, but no one else?"

"So...not to Fallon, is that what you're getting at?"

He nodded.

"Today was the last time I was going to see her before I left, so I think I can refrain from calling her. But this better be good."

"Are you seriously trying to debate this with me? Because I can just as easily call Patrick or Liam or..."

"Okay, okay, okay!" she said quickly. "I promise that I won't call her and I'm sure whatever it is you're about to say is the greatest thing ever. There. Satisfied?"

The snarky tone and impish grin were so perfectly Ryleigh that he couldn't help but laugh.

"As a matter of fact, I am," he joked, and then took a moment to compose himself. "Just keep in mind that most of this literally just came to me in the last hour so I don't have it all worked out yet."

"Gotcha. Okay, so...lay it on me."

And he did.

For a solid ten minutes, Jamie spoke out loud about all the things that he had thought about and how he'd like to implement them in order to make things work the way he wanted them to. The entire time he spoke, she sat quietly and listened.

"So? What do you think?"

"Wait...so...you're going to do all of this while I'm gone?" she asked incredulously.

"Yup."

"And I thought you had your mind set on..."

He knew where she was going. "I can't help being wary, Ry. That's not something that's going to go away overnight. I'm working on it, though."

"I can tell, but...damn, Jamie. I hate that you're doing it all next week and I'm going to miss it!"

With a grin, he said, "I'm sure you'll hear all about it when you get home."

"I know, but...I'm the one who's helped out the most! Can't you wait a week?"

"Absolutely not. This has all dragged on long enough.

The sooner everything is finalized, the better. I'm ready to move on with my life. Plus, I think it's best for Asher to have some stability too."

"You haven't exactly gotten a guarantee on that one."

"I know, but hopefully Mom will be willing to lend a hand while I work out the rest."

Laughing softly, she shook her head. "You know she is going to freak out when she gets home and finds out she's a grandmother."

"I'm already expecting the lecture and the smack upside the head."

"Well, at least you've got it all planned out. I'm just bummed that I won't be here to see it."

"Knowing our family, Ry, someone's going to be filming it."

Her smile grew. "They'd better!

* * *

Fallon looked at her watch and wondered if she had maybe gotten the time wrong. She and Tessa had texted back and forth a few times and had met here in the park yesterday, but...she was late. Was something wrong with Asher? Should she call and check?

"Ugh...don't be naggy," she quietly warned herself. It was possible that something came up and Tessa didn't think to text to let her know.

Sitting on the park bench by the big oak tree, Fallon looked around and sighed. It was a gorgeous day out and she was thankful for the chance to be outside and away from the stress of sitting at her parents' dining room table trying to figure out a business plan for a daycare center.

Yeah. It wasn't going well.

Patrick's assistant had been amazing at doing the research to help them narrow down all the parameters for a location, but so far, there wasn't anything available that would work.

Or...there was one that would work, but it required a lot of renovations to get it up to code.

Which meant it would cost a fortune.

In the meantime, she'd applied for more positions and even received two job offers that she was currently considering, but...

"Nothing feels right," she murmured.

Now that she got the idea in her head about opening a place of her own, she was excited about it. It would be hard to find a position working for someone else that might make her feel the same way.

Glancing toward the park entrance, she perked up. Tessa was walking toward her, and Fallon instantly got to her feet and went to meet her halfway.

"Hey! I was worried that maybe something had happened and you weren't coming," she said when she reached Tessa's side.

"Sorry about that. We were walking out the door when he needed a diaper change—of the urgent kind, if you know what I mean," Tessa said with amusement. "How does one tiny person make such a big mess?"

Unable to help herself, Fallon reached into the stroller and picked Asher up. "Hey, sweet boy. Did you give Aunt Tessa a hard time with a stinky diaper? Huh? Did you?" she said sweetly to him as she nuzzled in close. "He smells wonderful now, so...thank you."

Laughing, Tessa walked toward their bench. "No need to thank me. Consider it my gift to the entire outdoors."

They sat and she got comfortable with the baby in her

lap and smiled down and talked gibberish to him like she usually did.

"So..." Tessa began after a few minutes. "How's your day going?"

She shrugged. "Okay, I guess. Still job hunting and still uninspired." Then she looked over at her. "Maybe I should apply with the school district. What do you think?"

"I thought you were looking into opening your own daycare center. What happened to that?"

"It's going to be a lot more money than I feel comfortable with. All the properties Patrick's shown me need a lot of work." She sighed. "Like...the place in Magnolia that I had the job interview at a week ago would be perfect if I could...you know...take it over and do the renovations to get it up to par. But that's not what they're looking for."

"How do you know? What if you approached the owners and presented a plan to them? It might not lead to anything, but...it also might? It can't hurt, Fallon. Then you'd be in a position of running the place without it being the money out of your pocket."

"I don't know. Maybe." With another sigh, she put her attention back on Asher. "I swear he just gets bigger every day. He's changing so much. It's crazy!"

"That's a good thing, right?"

"Oh, definitely. It's just so amazing to see." She marveled at his hands and how much more controlled his movements seemed. She'd studied early childhood development, but it was so much more incredible to see it happen rather than read about it. "I could just watch him all day and never get bored."

"This is definitely a good age," Tessa agreed. "I'm with kids from kindergarten through fifth grade and they are exhausting!" Then she laughed. "I love them to death and I love singing with them, but some days it's a struggle to keep everything in order."

"It felt like that those first few days when I started taking care of him. I had no idea what his schedule was like or how he would react to certain things. It was a lot of trial and error, you know? I imagine that even though your students are older, it still must feel that way."

Nodding, Tessa let out a soft sigh. "Every child learns differently and reacts to certain social situations differently. You have to pay attention to their personalities if you really want to make a difference. Sometimes kids don't have the best home life, so it's important to do what you can while they're in your care."

"That's what I hope to do if I ever find a job." The nervous laugh was out before she could stop it and she was about to comment on it, but when she looked up, she spotted Jamie walking toward them.

With a woman.

It felt like someone had kicked her in the gut.

Part of her knew she shouldn't be surprised—after all, he was a consummate flirt. Nevertheless, did he have to show up with his new girlfriend here? Was nothing sacred anymore? Couldn't he keep his romantic relationships someplace private rather than a public park with his son?

Swallowing hard, she willed herself not to do something stupid like cry or get sick. Instead, she forced herself to keep her expression neutral. Asher was holding both her thumbs and she swore it was that little touch that was keeping her grounded.

"Hey, Tessa," Jamie said casually before looking over at Fallon. "Hey, Fallon."

With a small nod, she forced herself to acknowledge him. "Jamie."

"I'm sorry we made Tessa late," he said, looking directly at her. "Besides Asher needing an emergency diaper change, I'm afraid we were all talking and lost track of time. I know you usually meet up here at the park at one, so I'm sorry about that."

He knew about these secret meetings? Why would his sisters rat her out?

"It's not a big deal," she told him and began to hand Asher back to Tessa. "Um…I should go."

"No," he said quickly. "Please don't. We came here to see you."

Ugh…he is seriously the worst. Now he wants to introduce me to his new girlfriend? What a jackass!

Tessa gently guided Asher back into Fallon's arms with a serene smile and she wanted to scream at the unfairness. She had thought these people were her friends, but apparently they were all getting a good laugh at her expense.

Yeah, I'm definitely not opening any kind of business here. Maybe I should start looking up in the Northeast somewhere.

"Fallon Murphy, this is Jenn Randall. Asher's mom," Jamie said, his voice sounded calm, even a little peaceful. "Jenn, this is Fallon. She was the one responsible for making sure Asher was completely taken care of."

Jenn smiled, but Fallon could tell she was nervous. Holding out her hand, she said, "It's a pleasure to meet you, Fallon. Jamie's been singing your praises and I can't thank you enough for all you've done for Asher."

Fallon shook her hand, but now she was more confused than ever.

"Um…it was my pleasure," she said slowly before focusing on Jamie. "I don't understand what's happening right now. Are the two of you back together or something?"

They both laughed before Jamie reached and carefully took Asher from her arms. "No. Jenn and I are not back together," he told her. "We've reached a custody agreement and today is the first day of it."

Gasping softly, she looked at Jamie, then Jenn, then Tessa, and then back at Jamie. "Oh, um...I didn't realize..."

He smiled down at her. "It was important for me to introduce Jenn to you so she could meet the woman I hope will continue to help me raise Asher."

She froze.

There was no other way to describe it.

Everything in her just...stilled at his words.

Jamie handed Asher to Tessa before reaching out a hand to Fallon and gently tugging her to her feet. "We'll be back in a few minutes," he said to Jenn and Tessa before leading her away from them.

"But...my...my purse, and..."

"Tessa and Jenn will watch it," he said softly as they casually strolled away, her hand still in his.

She wanted to be indignant and pull her hand away, but she really missed his touch.

Plus, she was wildly curious about what was going on.

When they were a fair distance away, she couldn't wait for him to explain. "Jamie, what is going on?"

He laughed—it was low and rumbly and so masculine that she almost sighed dreamily.

Don't feed his ego...

"The night I came home after talking to Jenn, I was so damn certain that I was doing the right thing," he began, all traces of his lighthearted mood gone. "I was mad at everyone because I couldn't believe no one was backing me up." Then he looked at her. "Including you."

"Yeah, I got that," she murmured and was surprised when he stopped walking and stepped in front of her.

"Looking back, I wish you had stayed and fought with me the way we used to. I know I wouldn't have handled it well, but I genuinely want to believe that you would have snapped me out of my delusional rage."

The snort of disbelief was her only response.

"I get it, Fallon," he said in earnest. "I was a total jerk to you and you didn't deserve that. Not only because of the way I feel about you, but because you were right."

She honestly wasn't sure which of those statements she wanted to focus on first.

"I...I was right?"

Ugh...I'm so vain...

"Yeah. I was being mean and spiteful and totally having an emotional reaction instead of thinking it through. I think I knew you were right, but...in typical Jamie fashion, I had to keep pushing because I didn't want to be wrong."

"Well, to be fair, no one enjoys being wrong."

"Sending my siblings over was playing a little dirty, though," he said with that boyish grin that used to irritate her so much.

"It wasn't meant to be like that," she told him. "I knew you were spiraling and I know how close you are with your family and how you're all always there to support one another. You needed people around you who would help you calm down." She shrugged. "I thought I was doing a good thing."

"It was, Fallon. I'll admit that I didn't take anyone's advice that night and was pretty aggressive toward all of them." He let out a small, mirthless laugh. "Hell, I didn't take anyone's advice until a few days ago."

"What changed your mind?"

With her hand still in his, she felt him gently caressing her wrist. "Seeing you with Patrick started it," he admitted. "I know there was nothing romantic going on, but I hated how he could sit and talk with you and I couldn't. I wanted our life back—the one we were building before... well...before."

Her heart was beating erratically at his words, but she was still afraid to get her hopes up.

"Then I went to try to finalize some paperwork with my attorney and even he seemed disappointed in me and asked me to please go home and think things through. Well, he just asked me to think things through, but I decided to go home instead of going back to the pub."

"And that made a difference?"

He nodded. "I was driving through town and thinking about all the things I couldn't wait for Asher to experience— the things I grew up doing—and then I saw Ryleigh walking into the park. I saw you walking over to greet her and I knew that I needed to make things right."

"Jamie..."

"But the biggest thing was...I got home and I was alone. I used to love that feeling—you know, coming home at the end of the day and just being able to enjoy the quiet and relax. There was nothing relaxing about it that time, though. I wanted to come home to you and Asher, Fallon. I wanted to come home to our family." He paused, reaching up to caress her cheek. "I love you. I miss you and I need you, and I love you."

There were still so many questions racing through her mind, but she felt like that declaration needed to be dealt with first.

"Jamie, I..."

One strong finger gently pressed against her lips. "I

need to tell you the rest."

She wanted to argue that he really didn't—at least not right now—but he was already speaking again.

"I can't help how I feel about Jenn," he explained. "I don't trust her and I'm not willing to take a risk with my son. However, she messed up and she took responsibility for it and is repentant about it. So, we're taking things slow. For the next year, Jenn will have supervised visitation with Asher twice a week. Honestly, she's not sure she can handle more than that. I met with her and her therapist and we all agreed that the slow and low-pressure approach is what's best for her."

Lowering his finger, Fallon was finally able to respond. "Wow. That's...that's a wonderful solution, Jamie. I'm proud of you."

"I want you to know that you're the reason I'm willing to try. You made me think. It just took me a while to actually do it." He smiled slowly. "You know how stubborn I can be."

Laughing softly, she nodded. "Yes, I do." Looking up into his eyes, Fallon knew how sincere he was being. He was genuinely trying. "I don't want to be the reason you're doing something you're so against. If anything were to happen, you'd blame me and..."

"No," he said adamantly. "Believe me, you weren't the only one telling me I need to give Jenn a chance. Everyone felt the same way after they heard her story. But it wasn't until I sat with her and her therapist that I felt convinced that it was the right thing to do. The last thing I want is for anything to happen to Asher."

"I know," she said, stepping in a bit closer to him. Then she realized how this might look and glanced over her shoulder. "Um..."

As if reading her mind, Jamie tucked a finger under her chin and guided her to look back at him. "Jenn and I are over. We never really...it was never serious. I know that sounds callous and makes me seem like a douche, but...there it is. Neither of us is interested in anything more than co-parenting our son." Now it was his turn to step in closer. "She knows about you—about us—and that's why I brought her here to the park today. I wanted her to meet you so we can all move forward to take care of Asher in the best way possible."

This was such a complete one-eighty from the man she argued with more than a week ago, and if she were being honest with herself, she was a little dazzled by the change. She knew he was capable of it—had seen other changes in him just after Asher came into his life—but this version of Jamie was possibly the best she had ever witnessed.

But...was it enough for her to get over her own insecurities? Could she simply forget the more personal aspect of their argument that night? Was she still just a convenience? Someone to make his life easier?

I love you. I miss you and I need you, and I love you.

Sure, he said that he loved her, but...was he just confused? Or was she?

I love you. I miss you and I need you, and I love you.

He was watching her intently, and she knew she was going to have to say something soon—not only because it was getting awkward, but because they couldn't stand here in the middle of the park all day.

Letting out a long breath, she decided that honesty was always the best way to go.

"You're not the only one with trust issues, Jamie," she quietly explained. "I have them too and...I'm not sure where we go from here."

Chapter Fifteen

It felt like Fallon had kicked him in the gut.

Actually, that would have hurt less.

"Oh."

She glanced over her shoulder again toward Jenn, Tessa, and Asher, and he knew she was distracted.

Which meant he needed to think fast.

"Are you busy this afternoon?" he asked.

When she turned and looked at him, he almost smiled at the pure confusion on her face.

"I was thinking we could all walk back to the house. Tessa has a faculty meeting in an hour, Jenn has an appointment, and Asher and I are just going to hang out at home. Maybe you can come and hang out with us and we can talk." Swallowing hard, he added, "And we seriously need to talk, Fallon."

With a small nod, she whispered, "I know."

So, in the most awkward moment of his life, the two of them walked back to the park bench. He saw the hopeful look on Tessa's face and he discreetly shook his head so she wouldn't say anything. She looked at him quizzically, but all he did was whisper, "We're going back to the house to talk."

Jenn pushed the stroller while the rest of them casually followed behind. He was holding Fallon's hand and he took it as a good sign, and Tessa—bless her heart—talked the entire time so there weren't any lulls in the conversation.

"You guys should totally come to the school next Friday night," she was saying. "We're having our end of the year concert—the kids are singing a bunch of classic songs about the summer, including a Beach Boys medley! I'm telling you, it's going to be amazing!"

"I used to love to sing in the chorus," Jenn said with a smile. "I had the solo in the sixth-grade winter concert. I sang 'Winter Wonderland.' We had fake snow and everything!"

Tessa shared the story about how Liam crashed the school's holiday concert last year to sing for her, and beside him, Fallon laughed.

"I don't remember hearing about this," she said as they continued to walk.

"There's even a video," Jamie told her. "Remind me to show it to you. It was hysterical."

"It wasn't hysterical," Tessa interrupted. "It was incredibly sweet and it was the reason I knew for sure that I was in love with him." Holding up her hand, she waggled her fingers to show her engagement ring. "And for the record, he sings a lot more now because he knows how much I love it and how it always leads to a little..."

"No!" Jamie said loudly with a bark of laughter. "Just... no. We don't need to know what it leads to, so...we're good."

With a devious grin, she looked over at Fallon. "Great sex," she said proudly. "It usually leads to great sex."

Groaning, Jamie was thrilled to see they were turning into his driveway.

Fortunately, Tessa said her goodbyes in the driveway and he made a mental note to ask his brother to maybe encourage her to share a little less.

Jenn came into the house and got Asher settled in his swing before turning to face him and Fallon.

"I want to thank you, Fallon, for having a little faith in me when no one else did," she said solemnly. "You didn't even know me and yet..." She paused. "I just want you to know how much I appreciate it. I'm sorry for all the grief and inconvenience I caused you and Jamie and I hope moving forward, that maybe we could be friends."

He turned his head and saw Fallon was smiling. "I'd like that very much, Jenn."

"I should go." She looked over at Asher one more time before turning her attention to Jamie. "And I guess I'll see you on Sunday, right?"

"Yeah. My folks will be back and I want to bring Asher over to meet them, so if the morning works for you?"

She nodded. "I'll make sure it does. Thanks." And with a small wave, she let herself out, leaving him alone—finally —with Fallon.

He waited until the door was firmly closed before he took an easy breath. "So..."

"So..."

His throat felt dry, and he was suddenly nervous. "I'm just gonna grab a bottle of water. Can I get you one?"

"That would be great. Thanks."

Grabbing the waters, he took a moment to think about what he was going to say.

You're not the only one with trust issues. I have them too and...I'm not sure where we go from here.

There was no quick response he could make, no simple explanation to put her mind at ease, and definitely no flirty words or promises he could use to win her over.

And it left him feeling somewhat terrified.

He'd risked everything by leaving his comfort zone and hoped she'd see that and it would be enough to make her want to come back to him.

Clearly, I was wrong...

When he walked back into the living room, Fallon was sitting on the sofa at the end closest to Asher. She had a serene smile on her face as she watched him swing back and forth, and he'd never seen her look more beautiful.

"Hey," he said quietly, so as not to startle her. Handing her the water, he smiled and couldn't decide if he should sit beside her or over in the chair.

Ultimately, he decided to be bold and take the spot beside her, but...not too close.

"I was telling Tessa how much he seems to change every day, but I don't think she believed me."

"I see it too," he told her. "Sometimes it's just something small—a reaction to something or an expression he makes—but it's kind of fascinating to watch this little person experiencing the world like this."

Turning her head, she smiled. "Exactly."

Jamie held her gaze for a moment and knew he could easily keep staring at her, but they needed to get things settled between them. So, with no other option, he dove right in.

"I need you to tell me what I can do to prove you can trust me," he began cautiously. "I thought I was doing the right thing by taking your suggestion about Jenn, so...I don't know what I did wrong."

And man, did he hate admitting that.

"It's not that easy, Jamie," she replied, and he could tell she was nervous. "We've known each other for so long and while most of that time we never got along, you were never so openly hostile. I didn't appreciate being on the receiving end of that."

All he could do was nod.

"This last month, you've opened my eyes to the kind of man you really are. I have to admit, there was a part of me that couldn't wait to see you try to handle a baby." She laughed softly. "I mean...you normally don't have any problem winning most people over, but..."

"There was no way I could charm a baby," he finished for her with his own small chuckle. "But if I could, Asher would be the most well-adjusted and loved baby in the world."

"I think he already is." Her gaze locked with his. "I'm serious. Watching you adjust to being a father was incredible to see. Every day you became more at ease and once you stopped fighting me on everything..."

"Yeah, I know that too. Like we've already established, I'm stubborn." Reaching out, he took her hand in his. "I can't totally change that, but I'd be willing to try. There isn't anything I won't do to prove that you can trust me. I just...I miss you so much and we were in a really good place until... we weren't."

"It's just that..."

"There are no guarantees, Fallon," he blurted out, feeling more than a little desperate. "And you need to realize that by running away that night, you aren't completely blameless."

"Excuse me?"

There's my uppity girl...

Nodding, he went on. "Since when have you ever

243

walked away from a disagreement with me? When have you ever let me have the last word?"

"Jamie..."

"I'm serious. That night, you just walked out. You didn't give me any time to just cool off and you didn't push back. You left."

"I didn't want to fight with you," she countered. "And I certainly didn't want to fight with you in front of Asher."

"And while I respect that and love how you want to protect him, the fact is there may be times when we're going to argue in front of him or we're going to raise our voices! I'm not saying it's something I want to do, but it can't always be avoided. And it shouldn't be avoided when something so important is on the line!"

She let out a long breath and nodded. "You were never that mean before and I just...it was all too much. I couldn't handle it."

"And now?"

"And now what?"

"I am so sorry for the things I said. I swear I never meant to hurt you. I was...I was completely overwhelmed and behaved horribly. But I promise you right here, right now, that it was all me and it will never happen again."

"You can't know that, Jamie..."

"And neither can you." His voice was quiet and almost pleading. "I want another chance. Please let me prove to you that what we have is worth fighting for." Caressing her hand, he gave her his most endearing smile—one that had gotten him out of tenser situations than this.

"Oh my God..." she groaned before laughing. "How is it possible that you can bat those big brown eyes at me and make me believe everything you're saying?"

He grinned. "Told you, part of my charm."

"Jamie..."

"This isn't about charming you, Fallon," he said with a little more intensity. "This is me telling you the truth. I'm in love with you and I want another chance. I don't know how else to say it!"

"Here's the thing, though—if things don't work out between us, it's not just you and me, Jamie. There's Asher! And it's not fair to him if something happens and I leave! Right now, he has no idea what's going on, but what happens when he's older?"

"I have the solution for this," he said with a straight face.

"Really?"

He nodded.

"What is it?"

Moving in close, he rested his forehead against hers. "Don't leave me," he whispered. "Ever. Stay with me. Love me. Raise Asher with me, and any kids we have together."

Her soft gasp had them both pulling apart.

"Jamie...I...any kids we have together? What...it's so soon, and..."

Placing a finger over her lips, he guided them back to their earlier position. "I know it's soon, but...that's where I see us going eventually. I'm not going to rush you and I'm not proposing, I'm just...I'm hopeful."

And then he held his breath and waited for her response. He wasn't above begging, but she really wasn't giving him any clues about how she was feeling or if anything he was saying was making a difference.

Did he push her for a response?

Demand one?

Beg?

She sighed as her eyes met his and...she looked defeated. And everything in him felt like he'd lost her.

There were no more words, no flirty quips, no cheesy lines, or boyish grins.

Just a sense of emptiness that he knew was going to be with him for a long time.

Possibly forever.

* * *

I'm stronger than this...

That had been Fallon's thought when she agreed to come home with Jamie. She'd listen to him, accept the apology she knew he'd offer, but then tell him they were better off as friends.

But...she was lying to herself.

She loved him.

Dammit.

For all his goofy antics over the years, and snarky comments and teasing, she still ended up falling in love with him. And no amount of logic or thinking about things he's done to annoy her could change her mind.

She was about to say something when he raised his head and pulled back.

What the...?

"You want to know something funny?" he murmured. "I honestly thought I could convince you—that I could make the smartest woman I've ever known, fall in love with a dope like me." Lifting her hand, he kissed it. "I'm sorry for manipulating the situation today and...and I'm not going to pressure you anymore."

"Wait...what? What are you talking about?" she demanded.

"It's obvious that nothing I'm saying to you is making a

difference and I was prepared to beg, but...that's not fair to either of us. If you really had feelings for me or wanted any of the things I've been yammering on about, you would have said so by now. So...it's okay if you don't feel the same way that I do. And I won't stop you from seeing Asher." He moved a little further away before standing up. His smile was downright pitiful. "I'm sure you have things to do, so..." Motioning toward the front door, he added, "I guess I'll see you around."

When he turned to walk away, it took her a moment to gather her thoughts.

Then...she got to her feet.

"Are you kidding me right now, Jamie Donovan?" she demanded as she went after him. "You go on and on and on and then because I don't jump into your arms right away you just give up? How do you say I love you to someone and then be willing to let them leave? Do you even know what love is?"

Slowly he turned and looked at her.

And that stupid grin was on his face.

It should have infuriated her, but it was so typically Jamie that she had no choice but to walk over, wrap her arms around him, and kiss him soundly. As soon as his arms banded around her, Fallon felt like everything in her world righted itself.

The feel of his warm body, the touch of his tongue gently sweeping against hers...it was everything she wanted and had been missing. She thought they'd be a little more frantic with each other, but this was so much better. It was like coming home—all comfort and joy and knowing that this was exactly where she was supposed to be and that Jamie was the man she was meant to be with.

Breathlessly, they broke apart a few minutes later.

"I need to hear the words, Fallon," he gruffly admitted. "I need to know how you feel and that I'm not in this alone."

"You're not alone," she said and kissed him again just because she could. "I love you. You make me crazy and I still say you're too handsome for your own good, but I love you. And I want all those same things that you want. I've missed you."

"I thought you were mad at me."

Unable to help it, she rolled her eyes. "It's possible to miss someone even when you're mad at them."

"Seems weird, but okay…"

"So what was all that about? The whole motioning to the door like you wanted me to leave?"

His smile grew. "A challenge." Then he kissed her— long and slow and deep and wet. When he raised his head, he added, "Because that's who we are, beautiful. That's what we do and it's one of the things I love most about us. I love it when you do the same to me. I don't want that to change."

"It's going to change. The way we were toward each other before was just…it was annoying!"

"Okay, yeah. Sometimes it was, but I think it's kind of hot when you argue with me a little and make me think about things I wouldn't normally even consider. I love watching you get that little wrinkle on your forehead when you look at me like I'm crazy. It's sexy as hell, just like everything about you."

"Jamie…"

"Shh…look." He pointed to Asher who was sound asleep in his swing.

"Should we move him to his crib?"

"Definitely. Because then I'm going to move you to my bedroom and keep you there for a long time. Clearly my son is the perfect wingman because he knew exactly what to do so I could do exactly what I wanted to do." He winked lecherously, and it was impossible not to laugh.

Together, they took Asher to his room and carefully lay him down in his crib. Fallon was so happy to be there, and couldn't help but stand and watch him for a few minutes. Jamie stepped in close behind her, wrapping his arms around her waist.

"I really could just look at him all day," she whispered. "I must sound like a broken record, but...it's true."

He began kissing her neck, her shoulder...gently nipping at her earlobe and she let out a shaky breath.

"You can look at him all you want later. Right now, I really want to look at you sprawled out in our bed."

She smiled as her head fell back against his shoulder. "Our bed?"

"Yeah. It's been very lonely there without you," he murmured against her throat. "Please, Fallon. Please come inside."

Humming with pleasure, she nodded.

The small voice inside of her wanted to argue that she was being weak, but to her, she was actually being strong because she stood her ground with him and didn't cave that very first night.

Therefore, I deserve all the pleasure I'm about to get.

Suck it, small voice...

In the bedroom, Jamie led her next to the bed before turning and kissing her like his life depended on it. This was the kind of passion and frantic need she expected only minutes ago, and it was thrilling to experience it now.

Wrapping her arms around him, she kissed him back in the same way—it was wet and messy, but she kind of liked how dirty and sexy it felt.

"More, Jamie," she panted against his lips. "I want more."

"Anything you want," he murmured as his hands slid under her shirt to cup her breasts. "Tell me what you want and it's yours."

It was a heady feeling knowing how much he wanted her.

"Don't go slow," she told him as she pulled her top up and over her head. Kicking off her shoes, she added, "I want it all right now."

Pulling back slightly, he gave her a heated look. "That's my girl."

After that, Fallon wasn't sure who was in control or who moved faster; all she knew was that it was perfect. It was everything. And she was finally home.

* * *

"You know this isn't part of the schedule."

"I know."

"And you realize that without a schedule, things can get chaotic and difficult."

"I'm aware."

"Then how come you're allowed to do it, but whenever I did, you got mad?"

With a huff of annoyance, Fallon turned and looked at him. "We just had mind-blowing sex and we're lying here in bed while I feed Asher, and you're complaining?"

He shrugged with a boyish pout. "I'm just saying...he normally doesn't get his bottle for another hour."

"And he also took an unplanned nap. It's okay to go with the flow once in a while." Besides, this felt so good and she was so happy that she'd gladly let the schedule go for one afternoon. "Now get back under the blankets with me," she cooed. "I already miss having you next to me."

Wearing only his boxer briefs, he did as she asked. Asher's cries had come not long after they finished making love, and while Jamie had gotten up to get him, Fallon slid his shirt on to cover herself. No need to be naked while feeding the baby.

"This is good," he said gruffly, kissing her shoulder. "Moments like these are what I missed the most. Just the three of us." He kissed her again. "Thank you."

Meeting his gaze, she asked, "What are you thanking me for?"

"For not giving up on me."

Her heart melted a little because that one sentence spoke volumes. No matter how confident he tried to appear to the rest of the world, he was still vulnerable. And she had a feeling she was possibly the only person who ever saw that part of him. She doubted he even showed his siblings.

"Then I should thank you for the same thing. We have such a negative history with each other to overcome, but I'm glad we overcame that and realized what we could have is so much better."

They snuggled closer while Asher finished his bottle. "What do you think the chances are that he'll immediately go back down for a nap?"

Laughing softly, she shook her head. "Not even a tiny one."

"Maybe I can convince him." Reaching for his son, Jamie cradled him in his arms. "Hey, buddy. I know you're just as happy as I am that Fallon's home, so maybe you can find it in your heart to take another nap so we can have a little more private time. What do you say?"

"Jamie..."

He shushed her and went back to talking to Asher. "If you do this for me, I promise to get you a pony and an ATV and a puppy and a…"

"Oh my goodness, stop!" she laughed. "Just accept the fact that you cannot charm a baby!"

"Sure I can," he countered easily. "I can buy him all these things and…"

Shaking her head, she tried to sound firm. "There is no way you are giving this baby a pony or an ATV. And besides, it's not like he understands what you're even saying right now."

"Which was my point to you not that long ago."

Groaning, Fallon knew that life with Jamie would never be boring and—more than likely—more than a little frustrating.

"Jamie," she whined.

"Okay, okay. The pony and ATV aren't practical. But what about the puppy?"

She'd always wanted a dog, but was now the right time?

"How about this," she carefully began. "Let's get some other aspects of our lives settled first."

"Like what?"

"Like daycare for Asher, me finding a job and a place to live because I do not want to keep living with my parents, and you dealing with your folks when they come home and find out you have a son!"

He was quiet for several long moments. "I hear what you're saying, and I already have some solutions."

"Already? Okay, lay them on me."

"For starters, you move in here. I know it's small and not totally ideal, but I think we can make it work for a while. Maybe next year we can think about moving, but for now we can handle being…cozy, can't we?"

It wasn't the worst idea and it would be the place she'd be happiest, so...

"Done," she said. "What's next?"

"Really? Wow, I thought I was going to have to do and say a lot more to convince you."

"Is that your way of trying to back out?"

"What? No! Definitely not! I loved it when you were staying here. And now knowing it will be permanent? I'm freaking thrilled!"

She sighed happily. "Okay then. What's next?"

"My folks are going to be a no-brainer. My mom is going to be so freaking excited and I think she can help a lot with taking care of Asher. Between the three of us, I think we can get through the next several weeks until we find a reputable daycare for him."

She nodded. "Agreed. So that just leaves me and my nightmare of a job search." Then she told him about all the things she'd applied to and interviewed for lately and her possible plans for opening a place of her own.

"That sounds like so much work, Fallon. Are you sure you're ready to take on such a big project?"

"I thought I was, but it feels like every day there's something else to consider and there really isn't anything available that I can go in and retrofit, you know? Maybe Patrick just hasn't found the right place yet."

"Believe me, if the place exists, my brother is aware of it. It's insane how much he knows about real estate in this area and how much of it he is either buying, selling, renting, or managing. I mean...it's still only Laurel Bay, so it's not like he's a big-time real estate tycoon, but he's certainly doing more than his share to improve the town."

"Oh, I know he's good at what he does, but I just don't think what I'm looking for exists right now."

"It's possible. But then...where does that leave you?"

"There was a place I interviewed at down in Magnolia. It was for a daycare center coordinator."

"And?"

"I told Ryleigh about it. It was really disappointing. I ended up reporting some violations I noticed when I got home from the interview. Plus, the pay wasn't great."

"Damn. Okay, so...that was a big no."

"I thought so. I mean, the place had so much potential, but it was like nobody cared about it anymore. It needed a complete overhaul. The location was great—near the south side of Magnolia Sound—but it'd need so much done to it for me to be comfortable there."

"Why do I feel like there's more to it than you just reporting them and moving on?"

"The thing is, Jamie, I feel like I can go in there and fix it—make it right. I'm just not sure I'm brave enough to go in and propose such a thing." She let out a low laugh. "Your sister put both those ideas in my head—opening my own place and overhauling the Magnolia one."

"Which do you want more?"

"Honestly? I'd love to do the overhaul and then see how I do with the coordinator position."

"Then that's what you should do," he told her. "I believe in you and I think there isn't anything you can't do."

"I don't know. I've never overhauled anything in my life. What if I get in over my head?"

Putting his arm around her, he hugged her close. "Sweetheart, you came in here and completely overhauled my life and it's so much better and satisfying than anything I could have imagined. If you could take a mess like me and fall in with me, then believe me, there isn't anything you can't do."

Ryleigh gave her hope.

But Jamie made her believe.

"I love you, Jamie Donovan. So much."

And there was that killer smile. "I love you too, Fallon. And I think the best is yet to come."

Chapter Sixteen

Having Fallon move into his house was exciting and it made him incredibly happy.

Sharing that news with his siblings was awesome and they celebrated by everyone coming over for a barbecue.

But getting ready to head to his parents' house for Sunday dinner with Asher for the first time was stressing him out so much, he was practically breaking out in hives.

"What's wrong with your face?" Fallon asked when she spotted him at the kitchen table Sunday morning. Jenn had just left after her scheduled visit with Asher, and Fallon had just walked her out.

"What are you talking about?"

"Are you seriously still freaking out? This is just dinner with your family! Don't you do this sort of thing every Sunday?"

"We do, but...I told my mother that I was bringing two extra people and she sort of made a disapproving sound."

"Why?"

"If I said I was bringing someone—as in singular—she would have been thrilled and figured I was bringing a girl home with me. But I think it's the two that's throwing her off. I don't know." He let out a long breath. "I know it's going to be fine once we walk in the door and she sees you, but...I'm a little scared about how she's going to be disappointed in me about Asher."

"Oh my God! Are you serious right now? She is going to be so in love with him that she's not going to focus on anything else!"

"I know you think you know my mother, but I'm telling you, she's going to put two and two together and remember Jenn and how I blew her off and..." Groaning, she sank down lower in his seat.

"Aww..." Leaning down, she kissed him on the cheek. "I'm sure all you have to do is bat those big brown eyes at her and tell her how much you love her and she'll forgive you. After all, you're her baby boy."

He couldn't help but grin. "Yeah, that sounds like something I'd do."

"But now you have me worried about me."

"Why?"

"What if she gets upset that you're with me instead of Jenn? I know how traditional your mom can be and...maybe she'll feel that as Asher's parents, the two of you are the ones who should be together. And then she'll resent me for being the reason you're not!" She collapsed in the chair beside him.

And that was honestly the kick in the ass he needed to snap out of his pity party and do what needed to be done.

Standing, he kissed the top of her head. "I'll be back in an hour."

Her expression was one of mild panic and confusion. "What? Why? Where are you going?"

"I'm going to talk to my folks before everyone gets there.

This way, if there's any disapproval or any other nonsense, it can happen without an audience."

"Jamie..."

But he headed for the door, grabbed his keys, and walked out.

So many times in his life he relied on the security of having his siblings close by to either back him up or form a distraction, but this was something that he needed to handle on his own.

The drive to his parents' house was short and he only had to knock twice before letting himself in.

"Jamie!" his father called out as he greeted him. "It's early! What are you doing here already?"

"Hey, Dad." Giving him a hug, he smiled. "I wanted a chance to talk to you and Mom before everyone got here."

"Kate! Jamie's here!"

"What? It's early! I don't have food ready yet!" she yelled back.

"I'm not here for food..."

"Do you want to talk about the pub?" his father asked. "It sounds like everything went great while we were gone. And honestly, I'm not sure I'm ready to dive back into work mode. I'm very relaxed."

"It's not about the pub."

"Oh." And with a serious look, Shane Donovan turned and walked to the kitchen. Jamie heard his parents talking in hushed tones and his palms started to sweat.

Swallowing hard, he walked into the living room and sat and waited for them.

And waited.

And waited.

When they finally joined him, neither looked overly friendly. It felt like he was fifteen again and they were coming in to tell him how disappointed they were and how they were grounding him for sneaking out after curfew.

Before either spoke, Jamie got up and hugged his mother and kissed her on the cheek. "How was your trip?"

"We'll talk about it when everyone's here," she said stiffly. "Now, why don't you tell us why you're here early and looking as guilty as the devil himself?"

Oh, good grief...

"For starters, I'm not looking guilty. I have something important to share with you. Actually, two important things, and I felt like I should do it before everyone got here."

His parents exchanged looks before simply nodding at him.

He took a moment to compose his thoughts and calm his nerves before he began. "Mom, Dad...I have a son."

"What?!" Kate cried. "When did this happen? How old is he?" Then she groaned. "Oh, I knew this would happen! You with your Casanova ways! Who was it? Are you marrying her? Please tell me you're marrying her!"

Okay, so Fallon was right on the nose with that one.

"Do you remember Jenn Randall? We dated briefly..."

"Of course we remember her," his mother snapped. "She was completely gaga over you and didn't take the breakup well." Then she gasped. "You got her pregnant? And you refused to take responsibility for all this time?"

That's when the tears started.

"How am I supposed to show my face around town now?" she wailed. "Shane, how did we raise someone so heartless?"

"Um..."

"Mom," Jamie interjected. "If I could please... uh...explain?"

"Explain what? That you tossed the girl aside in her time of need?"

"It wasn't like that!" he snapped.

The good news was that his mother instantly stopped crying.

The bad news was that she looked thoroughly pissed.

That's when he explained everything to them about Jenn and how Asher came into his life.

"Oh my goodness," she said quietly.

"Jamie," his father chimed in. "What did you do? How did you handle running the pub during all of this?"

"Well, Ryleigh called Fallon Murphy and she stepped in to help," he explained.

Kate laughed. "Oh, I would have paid good money to see your reaction to that! Did you try to run that sweet girl off?"

"I think I was still too much in shock and I was desperate for the help." He paused. "She was amazing. Honestly, I don't think Asher and I would have survived without her."

"Fallon's good people," Shane said. "Her parents are worried about her right now, but it's good to know that she wasn't alone while they were away."

His mother nodded. "I agree. We'll have to have her over some time to thank her." Looking calmer, she gave him a small smile. "So I'm guessing you'll be bringing Jenn and Asher to dinner later?"

"Just Asher," he replied.

"But...you said you were bringing two people."

It was his turn to nod. "I did. And I'll be bringing Asher and...Fallon."

"Oh, well...that's nice of you! Now we'll get to thank her in person," Kate said, not fully understanding what he was implying. "You know we always love seeing her. I'm glad the two of you are friends now."

"Yeah, um...sort of?"

When he glanced over at his father, he knew he understood what Jamie was saying.

"Jamie, you need to stop this rivalry with Fallon," his mother said. "After all she's done for you, how could you not be friends with her?"

"I *am* friends with her, Mom, but I'm also...I'm in love with her," he said and then braced himself for her response.

Which was more over-the-top than he expected.

"Oh! Oh my goodness! Oh! *Oh!* I need to call Caroline! We need to invite them over too!" She jumped up and ran over and nearly smothered him to death with the ferocity of her hug. Then she pulled back and cupped his face. "This is like a dream come true! Where's the phone? I should call them right now, and..."

"Mom!" he said, cutting her off. "Fallon hasn't talked to them yet, so...please don't call Caroline, okay? We were going to go over there last night, but you guys all got in late, so..."

She looked flustered and she was smiling like a loon, but at least she wasn't mad at him.

"So you're telling me I'm a grandmother and you and Fallon are together like a couple? Do I have that right?"

He nodded.

Glancing over at Shane, Kate's smile grew. "And just when we thought life was looking good, Shane! It just got even better!"

Fortunately, his father looked equally excited.

"Why didn't you bring them both with you?" his mother asked. "Why would you come alone?"

"Um..."

"Oh, call them! Call them now and tell Fallon to come over with Asher! Please! Please, Jamie!"

He already knew Fallon had the car seat base in her car, and it wouldn't be an issue, but he wasn't sure she was ready for this.

"I'll text her and make sure Asher's awake," he said as he pulled out his phone.

Jamie: Hey! Is Asher awake?

Fallon: Yup! Just got up a few minutes ago

Fallon: How's it going there?

Jamie: Better than expected

Jamie: They want you to bring Asher over now. Are you okay with that?

Fallon: Um…I guess? His bag is already packed.

Fallon: Should I feed him first or let your mom do it?

Jamie: OMG. Definitely let her if you think he can wait

Jamie: You'll earn brownie points for that

Fallon: Do I need them? Lol

Jamie: No. But she wants to call your mom so bad

Fallon: Crap. I didn't think of that

Jamie: Should I let her and then we'll get that out of the way too?

Fallon: Sure. Why not?

Jamie: Okay. Good.

Jamie: How soon till you can get here?

Fallon: I'm putting him in his seat now, so...ten minutes?

Jamie: See you then

Jamie: Love you!

Fallon: Love you too!

His parents were staring at him expectantly. "Um... they'll be here in ten minutes."

His mother immediately started bustling around fluffing pillows and then running to change her clothes.

"She realizes that Asher's a baby, right? He's not going to notice if she's wearing something new," he asked his father.

"Let her do it. She's excited." Leaning forward in his seat, his father held his hand out to him. "Congratulations,

Jamie. I know this wasn't planned or done in a traditional way, but...I know you're going to be a great dad."

"I learned from the best," he replied.

Before either could say anything, his mother was back. "Shane, we're grandparents with the Murphys! Oh, how I wish we could call them! This is just so exciting!"

While she wasn't completely correct, he understood her excitement. Someday, they really would be grandparents with the Murphys for sure, though. He just really needed him and Fallon to settle into their lives first.

"I mentioned it to Fallon, and she said she wouldn't mind you calling them, but if it's okay with you, we'd prefer to tell them our news."

Kate's expression fell. "So...I can't even tell Caroline that the two of you are dating?"

"Mom..."

"Okay, okay...fine. I'll just invite them to dinner and mention that Fallon is coming? Will that be okay?"

He nodded. "That sounds fine. Thanks."

Next, she was on the phone and then fluttering around the kitchen, and before he knew it, Fallon was at the door.

"Brace yourself," he murmured as he kissed her hello. "They're just a little excited about all of this."

"As long as they're not mad, they can be as excited as they want," she whispered as she walked in.

"They're here! Oh, they're here!" his mother said before she came running toward them and Jamie wrapped his arm around Fallon's waist and felt more at peace than he ever had in his life.

* * *

Spending the day and sharing a meal with the entire Donovan family was nothing new to Fallon.

Spending it and feeling like she was part of the family was.

And it was awesome.

The entire day had been like one big party and everyone was so damn happy for them that she couldn't stop smiling. There was so much joy and laughter that it felt like it should be a holiday or someone's birthday rather than just an ordinary Sunday. Everyone was there—Will and Arianna, Liam and Tessa, Ryleigh and Ryker, her parents, and Patrick. She kind of felt bad for him because he was the odd man out, but it didn't seem to bother him.

Although...he seemed more than a little distracted.

"So what happens from here?" Fallon's mother asked. "What can we do to help?"

"In what way, Mom?"

"Well, you're still job hunting, Jamie's working full-time, Patrick's looking for a building for you but neither of you seem to be impressed with anything you've found...I'm just wondering if you could use an extra hand or two with Asher?"

Fallon looked over at Jamie who seemed just as surprised by the offer.

"You'd want to babysit?" Fallon asked.

"Are you kidding me? I would love it!" Caroline said.

"Now wait a minute," Kate interrupted. "If Caroline gets to babysit, I should too. I can cut back my hours at the pub to help out!"

Ryleigh snickered loudly.

"And what's so funny about that, young lady?" Kate asked.

She shrugged. "I'm thinking that would be awesome for

Asher." Then she grinned. "And I'm sure the serving staff wouldn't mind you hovering less..."

Kate waved her off. "I'll be hovering a *lot* less now. I've got a grandson who needs me!" She smiled at Fallon and Jamie. "You just let me know when you need me, and I'll be there!"

"Me too!" Caroline added.

Then the two of them started trying to coordinate their schedules between them.

"If you play your cards right, you might never have to pay for daycare," Fallon said quietly.

"I'm not sure that's a good thing," he teased. "Can you imagine how spoiled Asher's going to get?"

She nodded.

"And think of how much worse it will be when the next one is ours?" he whispered for her ears only.

Turning her head, she kissed him lightly on the lips. "You keep saying that."

"Because I mean it. You tell me when you're ready and there will be a ring on your finger and we can start making plans."

When he said things like that, she couldn't help but let out a very girly sigh. "I kind of love this side of you," she told him. "I can see why the masses of women in Laurel Bay were falling at your feet for so long."

"Sweetheart, the only woman I want for now and for always is you. I'm all yours."

"I love the sound of that." And she kissed him again.

Heck, right now, she'd love to keep kissing him, but there was a roomful of Donovans talking around them.

Later.

They could do all the kissing they wanted when they got home.

And then every day after that—hopefully for the rest of their lives.

When she settled back in her chair with Jamie's arm around her, she tried to pick which conversation she was going to join. But as it turned out, Patrick leaned over and asked if he could talk to her in private.

Jamie frowned, but they promised they'd be right back.

They stepped out onto the back deck, and she looked at him quizzically. "What's going on?"

"I hope you're not offended, but Marissa reached out to the place in Magnolia that you interviewed with," he said.

"What? Why? And about what?"

"After you shared your experience there with her, she got to thinking and reached out to the owners."

"O-kay..."

"Let me just be clear—I didn't ask her to do this, but Marissa is freaking amazing at what she does. She sees a potential problem and fixes it. It's almost scary."

"What did she say to them?"

"She mentioned how the facility seems to be falling into disrepair and is aware of some of the potential violations and asked what they were going to do about it."

"Oh God..."

"The thing is, they're looking to sell—either just the building or the business along with the building," he explained. "It's a little out of your price range, but if you're interested, I'd like to invest in it with you."

Her eyes went wide. "What? Really?"

Nodding, he replied, "We've known each other since forever, Fallon. I know you and I trust you. I've gone over your business plan with you and I think this is a fantastic opportunity and I'd hate for you to miss out on it."

"So...we'd be partners in it?"

"Only if you want to. I'm sure you could reach out to any number of people to partner with—your parents, your siblings, hell, even my parents or siblings—but I wanted to talk to you about this alone and let you know what your options are."

"Holy crap, Patrick. This is...completely unexpected!"

"I was going to call you tomorrow, but with the way the conversation was going, I figured I could mention it now."

"Can I talk to Jamie about it?"

"Of course! There's no pressure. I swear."

"Would you and Marissa consider coming for dinner one night this week so we can talk about it?"

"Um...me and Marissa?" he asked hesitantly.

"Well, yeah. She talked to them, so I just figured it would be easier if she was part of the overall discussion."

"I...I can't speak for her, but I'll certainly ask."

She smiled before leaning in and hugging him. "Thanks, Patrick! This is very exciting news!"

He hugged her back before they went back inside.

"What was that all about?" Jamie asked as she sat back down.

"I think your brother may have found a business opportunity for me."

His smile was dazzling. "Really? That's awesome! What is it?"

"Let's talk about it when we get home. Right now, I'm enjoying basking in all the Donovan love we're getting here."

Moving in close, he murmured, "And tonight, you'll be basking in this particular Donovan's love. Repeatedly."

And suddenly, she couldn't wait to get home.

Epilogue

Three months later...

"It's a lot messier than I thought it would be."

"Yeah, but it will be worth it."

"And louder."

"Mmm...but we're in the home stretch. Another week and the cleaning crew will be here to get it all neat and tidy and ready for inspections."

Fallon looked around the daycare center that was officially hers—and Patrick's—and smiled. The sale had been swift, and the construction and renovation work had begun almost immediately. Thanks to all of his connections, Patrick had things lined up even before they got started.

She was on site almost every day to see how things were going and to make sure everything was going according to plan. She trusted all the contractors and knew Patrick was checking in frequently as well, but this was going to be her baby and she didn't want to simply wait to see it all once it was done.

"You did something amazing here, Fallon. I'm so proud of you."

Smiling, she looked up at him. "I'm kind of proud of me

269

too. Six months ago, I was so lost and had no idea what I was going to do with my life, and in a million years, I never thought that this was where I'd be."

"Is that a good thing?"

Wrapping her arms around him, she said, "It's a great thing."

"I'm glad. Because I feel the same way. I still can't believe how much our lives have changed in these last months."

"And they're still changing. Are you sure you're okay with it all?"

He shrugged. "I had a feeling my folks were looking to cut back their hours at the pub, so I wasn't surprised. And I have a feeling they'll be around more than they think."

"It was only a partial retirement," she reminded him.

"And I think we're in a good place with the pub. We've got a solid staff and things are running smoothly. With your mom and mine helping with Asher, I feel like you and I aren't nearly as stressed as we were in the beginning."

"Babe, I was never stressed. I was always in control," she reminded him.

"Yeah, well, in the beginning, all you had to worry about was Asher. Once the business stuff started happening…"

"Okay, then I was stressed."

"This time next month, this place will be open. Are you ready for it?"

Nodding, she glanced around. "Oh, yeah. I'm going to be very hands on, and I've hired some great people. I think it's going to be everything I imagined."

They stepped apart so Fallon could walk around one last time and check on everything.

"Are you ready to go?" he asked a few minutes later.

"I just need to lock up and then I want to show you how

the playground is coming along. I can't believe how perfect it all looks."

When they stepped outside a few minutes later, Jamie stood in shock. "How did this all get done so fast? None of this was here last week."

"I know, right?" Taking him by the hand, she showed him all the new playground equipment, landscaping, and fencing. "We were able to use the existing trees and incorporate them into all of this. It's like a little oasis back here. I'm totally in love with it."

That was the cue he was waiting for.

Actually, his brother had been keeping him updated on the work and had mentioned more than once how much Fallon was gushing over the playground area and how it seemed to be her favorite part of the entire renovation. He didn't quite believe it, but hearing her talk about it now, he knew his brother hadn't lied.

"Show me your favorite spot," he prompted.

"It's back here," she told him. "They built this pirate ship that the kids are going to absolutely adore, and behind it is a little garden area. There are a couple of benches and a tiny bridge leading to a gazebo. I plan on doing story time back here in the warmer months." Letting go of his hand, Fallon walked over the little bridge and into the gazebo. Turning back to him, she asked, "Isn't it great?"

Then she gasped when she saw him down on one knee.

"Fallon Murphy," he began, smiling up at her. "You've been making me crazy since we were five years old. You have challenged me, bested me, infuriated me, and always managed to put me in my place. But lately, even when you're still doing all those things, it's done with love. I look forward to spending a lifetime continuing with our banter and challenges, but more than anything, I look forward to the building a future with you and adding to all the incredible blessings we already have."

Pausing, he pulled a ring out of his pocket and held it up to her.

"I'm more than likely always going to do or say something to make you roll your eyes or make you question why you even love me, but I promise you that no one will love you more than I do. You complete me, Fallon, and I would be honored if you would be my wife."

Tears slowly streamed down her face as she dropped to her knees in front of him, nodding the entire time. "Yes," she whispered. "Yes."

Slipping the ring on her finger, he breathed a sigh of relief that it fit. Then, reaching up and cupping her face, he kissed her—long and slow and sweet.

Just like the road they took to get to this very place.

Who will be the next Donovan to
fall in love?

Find out in

Kiss Me

Chapter 1

"This cannot be my life."

What was supposed to be a quick stop at home for lunch had turned into a nightmare. She needed to get back to work but there was no way that was going to happen right now.

Or possibly today at all.

Looking around, Marissa Barrett let out a loud sigh. The house was trashed; every drawer was open, every closet had stuff pulled out of it, and most of the valuables were gone. Heck, even the non-valuables were gone—or...smashed into a million pieces on the floor. All the Precious Moments figurines her mother collected along with her worthless collection of commemorative plates were shattered all over the dining room.

She'd known something was up the moment she pulled into the driveway and saw the front door was ajar. Right now she was the only one living in the house and knew without a doubt that she'd not only closed the door this morning when she left for work, but locked it as well.

And for the first time in five years, she forgot all about

getting back to the office on time and focused on the mess in front of her. It would be easy to text her boss and let him know what was going on, but he had gone out of town and wasn't due back for two more days.

"So technically...he won't know I'm late." Feeling better that she'd come to grips with that, she let out a loud breath.

There were several cops walking around the inside of the house and several more outside. Everyone was talking and asking questions and taking pictures, but all Marissa could think about was how on earth she was going to get everything cleaned up. Somehow she was going to have to go back to work, clean this mess up, get a security system installed, and not have a total breakdown.

"Easy, right?" she murmured.

For several minutes, she didn't move. Rage simmered inside of her and she wanted to shake her fist at the universe and demand to know why she'd been dealt such a shitty hand in life. She was hardworking, friendly, an overall decent human being who did volunteer work and was nice to animals. So why was she surrounded by all this negativity?

"Because you can pick your friends, but you can't pick your family."

Yeah.

Her father had walked out years ago, her mother was an alcoholic who was currently in the hospital after suffering a stroke, and her brother was a damn criminal.

And prime suspect in this burglary.

She knew what he was looking for, but she was smart enough not to keep anything of real value here at the house. Besides that, there was never any cash around and all the important documents on insurance policies were kept at her office—along with her laptop, tablet, and anything else with personal information on it. No one knew she kept it there—not even her boss. Although Patrick Donovan didn't care about anything but buying, selling, and managing real estate. There wasn't a doubt in her mind that she could bring in a six-foot tall file cabinet and tell him it was her own personal thing and he'd simply shrug and go back to scrolling through local property listings.

She wished she could simply shrug and ignore what was going on in front of her right now.

The urge to take the day off to handle the mess was strong, but the right thing to do was to go and try to put in at least a couple of hours, call Patrick and let him know she had some personal business to attend to, and then find someone to come back here with her to clean up. Besides needing the help, she didn't want to take a chance on her brother showing up and finding her here alone.

And man did it suck that she had to think like that.

What she wanted to do was simply pack her things and leave and say the hell with the house and this entire situation. Unfortunately, that wasn't an option. Three months ago–during one of her mother's more lucid moments—she had signed the house over to Marissa along with making her the sole beneficiary on her life insurance. They both knew her brother was growing more and more out of control and he wasn't even being coy about how he deserved to have control over all their mother's things.

And if she had to take a guess as to why everything in the house was literally upside down, she'd have to say that Daren was searching for not only money or anything he could sell but also any paperwork he could take and manipulate to try to get the control he was being denied.

"Oh, Mama...why didn't you set him straight years

ago?" she whispered. "Why do I need to keep cleaning up his mess?"

Again, all she wanted was to grab her things and go, but...while her mother might not have been the greatest mom in the world, she was battling an addiction and recovering from a stroke. Did she really want to heap more stress on her by leaving her to clean up this ransacked house when she got out of rehab?

If she got out of rehab...

Rubbing her temple, Marissa sighed loudly and knew she was only going to make herself crazy if she continued to stand here and obsess about all the ways her life was out of control. Walking around, she picked up the overturned kitchen chairs and then fixed the sofa cushions in the living room. Next, she straightened the blinds. Turning around, she faced the space again and shook her head.

"Baby steps," she said wearily. As much as she wanted to dive in and start cleaning everything up, it was probably best for her to wait until the police officers were done looking around and making their report.

Sighing because she hated standing around feeling useless, she contemplated calling Patrick. In the last few months their relationship had gone from strictly business to a little more personal. He'd become a friend when she needed on the most. Marissa hated showing any kind of weakness, but when Patrick had found her crying one night at the office—and she was definitely there hiding out from her brother—he had been her refuge. He'd sat and listened to her and then took her home, fed her dinner, and let her crash in his guest room. And it had been exactly what she needed.

It still boggled her mind that her serious and broody and sometimes a total pain in the ass boss was the one who essentially pulled her out of a really dark situation. Although, she really shouldn't be surprised. They worked well together and essentially Patrick was a problem solver. So naturally he took one look at her that fateful night and figured out how to help her.

Which was to get her to stop crying under her desk and get her someplace where she was safe and could relax.

For that one act alone, she'd be forever grateful.

Maybe I should call him...

No. It was far too chaotic in her house right now and as much as she would love a little reassurance that everything would be okay, he was undoubtedly busy and had more important things to do. He was a master at real estate negotiations and was on a mission to totally revamp the little town of Laurel Bay. She loved watching him work and had learned so much from him and her job had basically become a haven for her. They argued, they yelled at one another, and she knew there were times when she challenged his decisions when she shouldn't, but for those glorious eight to ten hours a day, she was a different person.

A happy person.

An intelligent person.

A successful person.

But more than anything, an appreciated person.

Yeah, the hours she spent at work took her away from living with two addicts who only cared about the money she brought home.

And she learned early on to only bring home a fraction of it.

She'd been saving and saving and saving hoping to move out and having a life of her own. But that dream kept moving further and further out of her grasp.

But that didn't stop her from dreaming.

The sound of her phone ringing had her heart jumping into her throat as she instantly panicked that it was her brother calling her. But when she glanced down and saw Patrick's name, she forced herself to relax.

"Hey," she said, making sure her voice was steady and confident. "How are things going up in Richmond?"

"Boring as hell," he replied. "This conference is about as exciting as watching paint dry."

"Then why are you still there?"

"Because I paid for it and I know if I leave, those last workshops will have information that I need."

"Ah. FOMO."

"Um...what?"

"FOMO—fear of missing out. I get it."

"It's not a fear..."

"Oh, please. It's totally a fear," she countered. "You've been at this conference for four days already. I'm pretty sure you could gage what the rest of the workshops are going to be like."

"Well, I can't," he admitted grumpily. "And besides, I've got several meetings set up for tonight and tomorrow so even if I wanted to leave, I couldn't."

"You could always move those meetings to Zoom calls," she suggested as she logged into her computer. "I'm sure we could get them all scheduled in no time."

Silence.

This was the game they played—he complained, she offered a solution, he goes quiet as he thinks about it, and then he would tell her she was right and to set everything up.

"Maybe. I don't know," he said, but didn't sound happy about it.

Normally he was the most decisive person she knew, so this was completely out of character for him.

"To be honest, I need this time away."

And that was even more surprising.

"How come?"

"It's nothing."

With a quiet chuckle, Marissa fixed the sofa cushion and sat down. Patrick might say that it was nothing, but she knew him well enough to know it was definitely something.

"You know you'll feel better if you talk about it..."

He sighed loudly.

"Of course, if you're too embarrassed to talk about it," she goaded. "I mean...if it's female troubles or something like that..."

"It's not that," he snapped. "Not really. It's just..." Pausing again, he groaned. "Okay, you know my family, right?"

"Yes, Patrick. I know your family." He was one of five kids, and they were all pretty awesome. His family owned the local pub and, as far as Marissa could tell, they were everything she wished her own family could be.

"Yeah, well...I just need a bit of a break from them. Between Arianna and Will's wedding coming up, and Liam and Tessa's not far behind..."

"Have Ryleigh and Ryker set a date?" she asked.

"Yup. And so did Jamie and Fallon."

"Already?" she asked excitedly. "Oh, wow! That's amazing!"

"Are you done?" he asked flatly.

Oh, right. None of this was probably exciting to him.

"I am. Sorry. Go on."

"I'm very happy for all my siblings, but...they're all a bit exhausting to be around right now. Plus...now that all four of her children are getting married, you know who my mother has set her sights on, right?"

"Already?" The small laugh was out before she could stop it. "I would have thought all the wedding hoopla would have bought you some time."

"You and me both. So obviously, this conference is really helping my sanity."

"Then you should definitely stay," she told him. "And don't worry, things are quiet here so you have nothing to rush back for."

"Captain!" one of the officers from outside called out. "We've got a situation out here!"

Marissa gasped as she got to her feet.

"Marissa?" Patrick asked, concern lacing his voice. "What's going on? Is everything okay?"

"Um…" Following the officers outside, she listened in horror as they discussed how gasoline had been poured all along the perimeter of the house.

"It's too dangerous for us to handle," Officer Sloane stated. "We'll need to get the fire department here."

"I'll call it in," someone said.

"Marissa!" Patrick said, louder.

Honestly, she had no idea who to focus on first. "Um… hang on," she told him before turning back to Officer Sloane. "What's going on?"

"Whoever was here was definitely looking to do some damage."

It annoyed the hell out of her that no one seemed to want to call her brother out on all of this, no matter how much proof she presented.

"But…" Honestly, Marissa had no idea what to even ask or say. Why pour gas all along the ground and then leave? And what good would burning the house do?

Daren's name wasn't on anything; it had all been signed over to her.

"Ms. Barrett, does your mother have homeowners' insurance?" he asked.

She nodded. "Actually, she recently signed everything over to me, so it's all in my name."

"Is your brother listed on the policy?"

Finally! Someone was seeing what she'd been trying to tell them all along!

"No," she murmured. "But he used to be on her life insurance policy. She recently took him off, but he doesn't know that." Her heart kicked hard in her chest. "You don't think he'd go to the hospital and..."

She felt dizzy and a little nauseous as everything started to spin. Officer Sloane gently guided her over to the front steps and helped her sit down. It was all too much and she swore someone was calling her name from somewhere. Looking around frantically it took several moments to realize she still had her phone in her hand and Patrick was calling out to her.

"Hey," she said a little breathlessly. "Sorry."

"What the hell is going on?" he demanded.

"Um...gas leak," she lied. If she told him what was really going on, he'd leave the conference early and she'd hate to be the cause of that. "Yeah, so..."

"At the office? Are they evacuating the block?"

"Actually, no. I came home for lunch and this all just happened, so...I should go and deal with it." She paused. "But...I might not make it back to the office today. I hope you don't mind."

"Marissa, you don't have to ask. I completely trust you."

And she knew he did.

"I appreciate you saying that, but I wouldn't have felt right not going back without letting you know."

"Are you sure this is just about the gas leak? Is everything else okay?"

Ugh...not even a little, but there was no way she would share that with him.

"Everything is fine," she lied. "But I really should go and see what's going on with all of this."

He didn't say anything right away.

"Was there anything you needed me to take care of today?" she asked. "Because I can go back to the office once everything calms down here."

"Dan Miller is supposed to drop off a set of keys for a place I'm going to be selling for him. It's a fishing cabin that's been in his family for something like forty years. He's not using it anymore because he's moving to Maryland and asked to handle the sale."

Marissa quickly looked around for a notepad or something to take notes on, but there was too much debris everywhere. "Okay, and would you like me to go and look at the place and take pictures?" It was something she usually did and figured this would be no different.

"Yeah, but...don't worry about that today. I'll call Dan and ask him to come in tomorrow instead."

"Patrick..."

"Marissa..." he mimicked.

The sound of sirens rang out in the distance, and she knew she needed to get off the phone. "I really need to go. Thanks for being so understanding and I'll talk to you tomorrow."

"I'll call you later and check in."

"That's not necessary," she countered and was saved

from saying anything else because the sirens grew louder. "I'll just talk to you tomorrow! Bye!"

When they hung up, she slid her phone into her pocket and braced herself for whatever was coming next.

* * *

"Donovan's Pub! This is Ronan!"

"Hey, Uncle Ro. It's Patrick."

"Patty! Where've you been? We haven't seen you here all week!"

"Oh, I'm up at a conference in Richmond, but I'm calling to make sure everyone's okay." Marissa's house wasn't that far from the pub, so if there was a gas leak, there was a good chance it was affecting downtown too.

"Sure we are! Why wouldn't we be?" Ronan asked.

"I just got off the phone with Marissa and she said there's a gas leak at her place," he explained. "So I just thought…"

"This is the first I'm hearing of it. Here, talk to Jamie and let me see what I can find out. We've got a couple of off-duty guys from the fire squad here for lunch. I'll go ask them what's going on."

"Thanks," he murmured before his brother got on the line.

"What's going on?"

Patrick repeated what Marissa had just shared with him. "So basically I was just calling to make sure you guys were alright."

"I thought I saw one of the firetrucks go by a few minutes ago, but other than that no one's said anything," Jamie said casually. "Where are you at that you can't just walk down here and ask?"

"Richmond, but I'm on my way home."

"Oh, that's right. Now I remember you mentioning that. I thought you were going to be there until Friday."

So did he. After hearing Marissa's voice, however, he knew something else was going on. They'd gotten closer in the last several months and between that and the fact that they'd known one another for five years, he was fairly confident that he could read her moods. She hadn't mentioned anything crazy involving her mother or brother lately, but he knew that wouldn't last long.

Leaving the conference really wasn't an issue. If anything, he was looking for an excuse to leave. He just hoped he would get back to Laurel Bay and find out he had panicked for nothing.

"Hang on, Pat. Uncle Ronan looks like he's got news. See ya when you get back!"

His uncle was on the line a moment later. "Okay, Patty, here's the deal. There was a break-in at a house over on Dover and apparently whoever broke in doused the outside lawn with gasoline. Now...I can't say who my sources are..."

His uncle was a legendary gossip and right now, Patrick was beyond thankful for it.

"Thanks, Uncle Ro," he said solemnly. "I appreciate the info."

"Marissa lives on Dover, doesn't she?"

"She does," he murmured.

"So do you think...?"

"I do. I definitely do."

"Then I hope you're on your way home!" his uncle stated firmly. "That poor girl has no one to help her except you! And with her mother in the hospital..."

"Wait. *What?* Her mother is in the hospital? When did this happen?"

"Sunday. Irene had a stroke. Last I heard, she was in stable condition, but not great."

Unable to help himself, Patrick chuckled. "Is there anything in this town that you don't know?"

"Well, now...you know people love to come in and talk over a few drinks," Ronan said with amusement. "Being a bartender is the best job in the world!"

"Um..."

"Now you listen to me, Patrick Michael Donovan. You need to get your tail back here and help Marissa out. We all know you're sweet on her and now's your chance to do something about it!"

"Do something...? Sweet on...? What the hell are you talking about?" he demanded.

Rather than answer right away, his uncle laughed. "Fine. Be that way. Be clueless. Just get back here and make sure Marissa is safe. Although...I'm sure if I let your mother know, she'll find some nice local guys to go over and help."

He hated that he was taking the bait. "I'm on my way! I can only drive so fast, you know."

"Good boy. If I hear anything more, I'll let you know."

"Yeah. Thanks." Once he hung up, Patrick seriously considered calling Marissa back and getting an update, but he needed some time to think.

We all know you're sweet on her...

That was possibly the last thing he expected anyone to say to him. Marissa was his employee. His assistant. They worked together and only recently had they started to become friends. There wasn't anything inappropriate about his behavior toward her and he certainly didn't think he did anything to make anyone suspect that he had a thing for her.

Which he didn't.

Or…maybe he did, but knew nothing was going to come of it.

We all know you're sweet on her…

"Uncle Ro has just been hanging out with mom too much," he grumbled. "Damn match-making nonsense. I'm not sweet on anyone. And who even says that anymore?"

With a growl of frustration, he drove along I-95 and cursed the fact that it would be three hours before he was back in Laurel Bay. With the radio playing softly, Patrick managed to wait a full hour before calling Marissa for an update.

But she didn't answer.

He tried to reason that she was busy and couldn't talk and decided to wait fifteen minutes before calling her again.

And she didn't answer.

Muttering a curse, Patrick glanced at the clock and knew if traffic was on his side, he could be home in ninety minutes. A little sooner if all the traffic lights were on his side once he got off the interstate. Another fifteen minutes passed before he called again and he swore if Marissa didn't answer this time, he was going to call the pub and send either Jamie, Ronan, or his mother over to her house to check on her.

"Hey, Patrick," she said distractedly when she answered. "What's up?"

"I was really just checking to make sure everything was okay. Did the gas leak get taken care of?"

"Um…yeah. It's all fine." She paused. "Can you just… hang on for a moment?"

"Sure."

It sounded like she put her hand over the phone because everything she was saying was muffled and she clearly wasn't alone.

"Patrick, listen, I need to go. The gas company is finishing up and I need to deal with that. Can we just touch base tomorrow?"

Something was definitely up, and he was glad he would be home soon.

"Sure. We'll talk then. Bye."

Unfortunately, traffic had other plans.

It was almost three hours later that he finally hit the Laurel Bay town limits.

By that time. All he wanted was to sleep in his own bed and stay under the radar for a few more days before he had to deal with his family.

Not like that was going to happen. Sunday dinners were mandatory at the Donovan home, and anyone who didn't show up would have to deal with their mother's wrath.

And he definitely wasn't in the mood for anyone's wrath.

But...he needed to stop by Marissa's and talk to her. It bugged the crap out of him that she was being so evasive and wouldn't even tell him about her mother. He thought they had grown closer and that she knew she could talk to him about this kind of thing.

"Pfft...clearly I was wrong," he murmured, determined to get to her house and talk this out. But as he drove down Main Street—and past his office—Patrick noticed the lights were on. "What the hell?"

Pulling up to the front, he parked and was out of the car in the blink of an eye. The front door was locked, but he could see Marissa staring wide-eyed at him as he unlocked it and let himself in.

Her expression went from shock to politeness in the blink of an eye. "Oh, hey! I thought you were going to stay for the rest of the conference?"

He knew a diversion when he heard one.

"My heart wasn't in it and besides, I was worried about you."

"Oh, um...there's no reason to." Shrugging, she immediately began collecting her things and pulling her purse from her desk drawer. "Everything's fine. I just decided to come in and take care of some stuff since I had to take the afternoon off." She gave him a smile, but he could tell it was forced.

He nodded and watched as she was inching her way toward the door.

"Have you eaten dinner yet?"

She stopped in her tracks. "What?"

"Dinner. You know, the evening meal," he said with a grin. "Traffic was a bitch, so I didn't have time to stop and get something to eat. I was just curious if you maybe wanted to grab a bite with me. You can get me caught up on anything I missed this week."

Patrick already knew there wasn't anything they needed to get caught up on and Marissa could run his business for him for an entire month and everything would be done to perfection. She was an incredible assistant who understood every aspect of his job. He knew the only reason he'd achieved the level of success he had was because of her.

But just because they were in sync where business was concerned, didn't necessarily mean the same thing once they were off the clock. She knew everything about his personal life and only recently did he start to learn about hers.

And it was purely by accident.

On a night that was almost identical to this one, he'd shown up at the office late and found her here crying. At first, he thought she was hurt, but after a few minutes, she admitted that her home life was an absolute disaster—alcoholic mother and a low-life brother who basically was trying to steal everything he could from the both of them. It had taken him hours to get most of that out of her and it was only after he'd taken her home with him and ordered dinner for the two of them that she'd relaxed enough to share the details.

To say that he was shocked would be an understatement. He never would have guessed she was struggling with so much because she never let it show. After that night, he started watching her a little more closely.

Liar.

Okay, maybe his uncle was on to something. If he were brutally honest with himself—which he normally prided himself on doing—he'd admit that he'd been watching Marissa closely for a long time. It wasn't appropriate and he would never act on it, but...she was a beautiful woman. Stunning, actually, and everything about her called to him; her intelligence, her work ethic, her humor...in a perfect world, he would have met her in another way and asked her out. Unfortunately, he couldn't change it, so he had to deal with the fact that she worked for him and was a friend and nothing more.

No matter how much he wanted it to be different.

"Patrick?"

"Hmm?"

"You sort of zoned out," she said with a hint of amusement. "I think maybe you've had a long week and it sounds like a long drive. You should go home. There isn't anything pressing we need to deal with. We'll be fine to hit the ground running in the morning."

Raking a hand through his dark hair, he wondered if maybe she was right.

Then he noticed her inching toward the door again and remembered why he needed to get her to stay a little longer.

With a small laugh, he shook his head. "Honestly, the thought of getting back in the car right now is beyond unappealing. I think I'm going to order something to be delivered here and..." Pausing, he yawned for dramatic effect. "I'll just hang here for a couple of hours and then head home."

Her shoulders relaxed a bit. "You only live ten minutes away. Just call in something to be delivered to your house."

He shook his head and yawned again. "I guess it didn't hit me how tired I was until I got out of the car." Slowly, he walked over to the sofa that took up their waiting area and sat down on it with a loud sigh. "Yeah...no. I'm just gonna hang out here. You can go and..." Yet another yawn. "Have a good night."

You could have heard a pin drop in the room and he took a moment to peek out of one eye to see if she was even considering staying.

And by the way she was biting her lower lip, he guessed that she was.

Good.

Getting a little more comfortable, he let out a low hum as if to say he was getting sleepy.

Did he feel ridiculous? Yes.

Did he know he needed to be this ridiculous so she would relax and wouldn't take off? Definitely.

When he heard Marissa let out a low huff, he knew he had her.

"You clearly can't drive like this," she said. "Come on. I'll drive you home and you can pick your car up tomorrow."

Damn. He hadn't thought about that.

"Or..." he countered as he sat up and stretched. "You can follow me back to my house where we'll talk over dinner about how your mother is doing and why you didn't tell me about her being in the hospital. What do you say?"

"A minute ago you said you were too tired to drive."

Oh, yeah...

"With someone following me, I'll feel better about it."

Lamest. Excuse. Ever.

"Patrick..." she whined wearily.

"Marissa..." he mimicked as he stood.

Her lips were pursed and he knew she was annoyed, but also knew she wasn't going to argue.

Much.

"Fine."

Doing his best to hide a triumphant smile, he ushered her toward the door. "I'll order food on the way. What are you in the mood for? Pizza? Chinese?"

"How about burgers from the pub?" she asked, and once he met her gaze, he knew she was teasing.

"Ha, ha. You're hilarious," he murmured. Once they were outside, he pulled his phone out. "What did we decide?"

"Pizza. Pepperoni and mushrooms, please."

He nodded. "And we'll eat at my place. Will that work?"

"That's fine, but I need to stop by my house first. My cat hasn't been back since everything with the gas leak and I'm a little worried. I'm hoping he'll be there now that it's been quiet for a little while," she went on. "How about I meet you in say...thirty minutes?"

"You have a cat?"

With a small eye roll, she nodded. "Yes, Patrick. I have a cat."

"You never mentioned that before. And you have to go and let him in?"

Another nod. "I'm really hoping he came back. He's not an outdoor cat, but he obviously must have gotten out when everything was going on, so..."

It was his turn to nod. "Well...then you go and let him in and I'll meet you at my place in thirty."

"I thought you were too tired to drive without someone following you."

Crap.

"I'm sure I'll be fine, but I'd still like it if you could join me for dinner."

Rather than argue like he expected her to, she simply nodded. "Thanks," she said quietly before getting into her car. Patrick watched her drive away and knew she wouldn't be able to relax if the cat wasn't home yet. So he placed their dinner order and then drove to her place. They could eat there and talk just as easily as they could at his house.

Feeling good about his decision, he pulled away from the office and made a quick stop at the grocery store for some ice cream. He knew Marissa was partial to chocolate chip cookie dough ice cream and figured having it on hand for dessert might make her feel better after the stress of her mom's stroke, the gas leak, and her missing cat.

"Well...hopefully the cat's not missing and will be waiting for her when she gets home."

Fortunately, he didn't run into anyone he knew at the store and fifteen minutes later he was pulling up to Marissa's. Her car was still there and he could see her walking around inside through the big front window. Even from a distance he could tell she was frowning and that told him that maybe the cat hadn't returned yet.

"Maybe ice cream won't be enough..."

Walking up the front steps, he noticed the front door

was open and quickly knocked on the screen door before letting himself in.

"Hey! I thought we'd..." He instantly stopped in his tracks when he finally focused on what he was seeing. "Holy shit, Marissa! What the hell happened here?"

Get your copy of KISS ME here:
https://www.chasing-romance.com/kiss-me

And check out the entire DONOVANS series here:
https://www.chasing-romance.com/the-donovans-series

Also by Samantha Chase

The Donovans Series:

Call Me

Dare Me

Tempt Me

Save Me

Charm Me

Kiss Me

The Magnolia Sound Series:

Sunkissed Days

Remind Me

A Girl Like You

In Case You Didn't Know

All the Befores

And Then One Day

Can't Help Falling in Love

Last Beautiful Girl

The Way the Story Goes

Since You've Been Gone

Nobody Does It Better

Wedding Wonderland

Always on my Mind

Kiss the Girl

Meet Me at the Altar:

The Engagement Embargo

With this Cake

You May Kiss the Groomsman

The Proposal Playbook

Groomed to Perfection

The I Do Over

The Enchanted Bridal Series:

The Wedding Season

Friday Night Brides

The Bridal Squad

Glam Squad & Groomsmen

Bride & Seek

The RoadTripping Series:

Drive Me Crazy

Wrong Turn

Test Drive

Head Over Wheels

The Montgomery Brothers Series:

Wait for Me

Trust in Me

Stay with Me

More of Me

Return to You

Meant for You

I'll Be There

Until There Was Us

Suddenly Mine

A Dash of Christmas

The Shaughnessy Brothers Series:

Made for Us

Love Walks In

Always My Girl

This is Our Song

Sky Full of Stars

Holiday Spice

Tangled Up in You

Band on the Run Series:

One More Kiss

One More Promise

One More Moment

One More Chance

The Christmas Cottage Series:

The Christmas Cottage

Ever After

Silver Bell Falls Series:

Christmas in Silver Bell Falls

Christmas On Pointe

A Very Married Christmas

A Christmas Rescue

Christmas Inn Love

The Christmas Plan

Life, Love & Babies Series:

The Baby Arrangement

Baby, Be Mine

Baby, I'm Yours

Preston's Mill Series:

Roommating

Speed Dating

Complicating

The Protectors Series:

Protecting His Best Friend's Sister

Protecting the Enemy

Protecting the Girl Next Door

Protecting the Movie Star

7 Brides for 7 Soldiers:

Ford

7 Brides for 7 Blackthornes:

Logan

Standalone Novels:

Jordan's Return

Catering to the CEO

In the Eye of the Storm

A Touch of Heaven

Moonlight in Winter Park

Waiting for Midnight

Mistletoe Between Friends

Snowflake Inn

His for the Holidays

Wildest Dreams (currently unavailable)

Going My Way (currently unavailable)

Going to Be Yours (currently unavailable)

About Samantha Chase

Samantha Chase is a New York Times and USA Today bestseller of contemporary romance that's hotter than sweet, sweeter than hot. She released her debut novel in 2011 and currently has more than eighty titles under her belt – including THE CHRISTMAS COTTAGE which was a Hallmark Christmas movie in 2017! She's a Disney enthusiast who still happily listens to 80's rock. When she's not working on a new story, she spends her time reading romances, playing way too many games of Solitaire on Facebook, wearing a tiara while playing with her sassy pug Maylene...oh, and spending time with her husband of 32 years and their two sons in Wake Forest, North Carolina.

Sign up for my mailing list and get exclusive content and chances to win members-only prizes!
https://www.chasing-romance.com/newsletter

Start a fun new small town romance series:
https://www.chasing-romance.com/the-donovans-series

Printed in Great Britain
by Amazon